THIS SERIES IS DEDICATED BY THE PUBLISHER TO THE MEMORY OF

JOHN CALDER AND MARION BOYARS

Mercury Books, an imprint of Michael Walmer, is set up to republish major works in translation which have been hard to procure in nice editions. The series design is an homage to the pioneering designs of the great John Sewell for Calder and Boyars.

NOSTALGIA

MERCURY BOOKS

1. Alphonse Daudet: KINGS IN EXILE
2. Selma Lagerlöf: GÖSTA BERLING'S SAGA
3. Karel Čapek: MONEY and other stories
4. Grazia Deledda: NOSTALGIA

NOSTALGIA

by

GRAZIA DELEDDA

translated, and with an introduction by
Helen Hester Colvill

Mercury Books

SANDNESS
MICHAEL WALMER
2024

Nostalgia (Nostalgie) first published 1905

This translation first published 1905

This Mercury Books edition published 2024

by

Michael Walmer
Little Pradies
13a Melby
Sandness
Shetland, ZE2 9PL

ISBN 978-0-6457519-5-6 paperback

The publisher gratefully acknowledges the assistance of Robert Heatley in the typesetting process for this volume.

INTRODUCTION

SINCE the days of Latin, to how few authors has it been given to obtain an European reputation!

We English seem exceptionally slow in making ourselves acquainted with the works of foreigners. Dante and Cervantes, Goethe and Dumas, are perhaps no worse known among us than they are in their homes; but we seldom find out a modern writer till he has been the round of all the other countries. We are opinionated in England. We think other folk barbarians, even if we don't call them so; we visit them for the making of comparisons, generally in our own favour; of trying their manners and customs, arts and morals, not by their standard but by ours. We never forget that on the map of Europe there is the big continent, and away in a corner, by themselves, extraneous, cut off, and "very superior," physically and morally isolated and self-contained, are our two not over enormous islands. We don't regret that sea-voyage, literal and metaphorical, which is necessary to transport us to the lands of the barbarians; and though we travel a great deal, I declare I think we all (and especially newspaper correspondents) go about enclosed in a little bubble of our own foggy atmosphere, seeing only the things we intend to see, hearing the things we mean to hear, and already believe. We are poor linguists moreover, and when we talk with the barbarians we only catch half they say and omit all attention to what they hint; we frighten them by our abruptness, our unintentional hortatoriness and unconscious conceit, so that they don't say to us what they mean, nor tell what they suppose to be true. We come home swollen with false report and evil surmise, and at once commit ourselves to criticism and laudation equally beside the mark. I wonder now do we really understand the errors of Abdul Hamed and Nicholas II. as thoroughly as we think we do? and in our long glibness about the Dreyfus case has it never occurred to us we may have been partly deluded? — as the barbarians were deluded when they chattered of us in the time of the Boer War!

Well, we can't help our position in the far-away corner of the map; but perhaps we should become less odd and more sympathetic if we read the barbarian's books a little oftener; books in which he is talking to his brother barbarians, and has not been questioned by an island catechist; books, superior or inferior to our own it matters little, which at least are written from another standpoint, and which by their mere perusal must extend our knowledge, and remind us that "it takes all sorts to make a world."

The best way, of course, is to read foreign books in their original language. Don Quixote was right when he said translation was a bad job at its best. But life is short and the gift of tongues is miraculous; some of us are too busy with our Dante and our Schopenhauer to waste time on a railway novel, and more are lazy and can't be bothered to look out words in a dictionary. The humble translator has his function.

If he can succeed in giving any of his author's spirit, he may interest his reader enough to send him to the original itself next time; — in which case the translator will have done a worthy deed, and the author will perhaps forgive a certain mangling of his ideas, spoiling of his best passages and general rubbing of the bloom from his peach, inevitable in a process scarce easier than changing the skin of an Ethiopian or repainting the spots of a leopard.

———

Grazia Deledda, the new writer, for not so many years have passed since the publication of her first book, has already conquered not only her fellow-countrymen but many more distant peoples. Several of her novels have been put into French for the *Revue des Deux Mondes* and have appeared in Germany in various magazines and journals. One at least has been published in America, and this particular book, *Nostalgie*, is in process of translation into German, Spanish, Russian, Dutch, Swedish, and French. In England alone — poor, isolated, ignorant England — is the author's name almost unknown.

She is a Sardinian, and most of her books have been about her native island, the simple folk, and quiet histories of a forgotten corner where the tourist has hardly penetrated. But Signora Deledda now lives in Rome, and true to her method she observes and describes the things and places about her, the people among whom her lot is cast. The scene of *Nostalgie* is therefore laid in the capital, but with constant allusion to a district in the north of Italy evidently familiar — her husband's country — which she tells us is dear to her as a second home, and from which she has dated her preface. As a writer she prides herself on her Realism — strange, ill-comprehended, often misapplied word! The realism of the highly imaginative may easily seem romance to the prosaic; and Signora Deledda will pardon us if we say that if only in her pictures of scenery, in her intimate knowledge of the influence of Nature on the heart and the mind of her votaries, there is something very superior to realism—at least in the common acceptation of the term. Grazia Deledda sees her figures set in a landscape, belonging to it, born of it. Half the tragedy of this book arises from the fact that the heroine having lived alone with Nature is suddenly transplanted to a city where she imagines herself bereaved of the mighty mother. Years have to go over before she realises that the mighty mother never really deserts her children, and that the "still sad music of Humanity" is as much a part of Nature as the sough of the wind, the rustling of the leaves in the poplar-trees, and the unending roll of the river waters.

The form of Signora Deledda's novels is almost autobiographical. There is one principal character, hero or heroine as the case may be, and the story develops from his or her point of view. In the book before us, we know all about Regina, we are, as it were, inside her; but the other personages are known to us only in so far as she knows them. We are never admitted to a scene from which she is absent, nor is anything explained to us but in so far as she understood or guessed it herself. The minor characters are little more than sketched; figures in a crowd of which Regina saw the outside and occasionally touched the soul. One *feels* the gracious influence of her mother as she felt it, but we are told little about her and practically never see her in action. The plot is slight, but it hangs together perfectly with unity and focus, never giving a feeling of strain. It is all very un-English; neither the life nor the actors are like ours, nor at all like what is described in our novels. The history and romance of Rome are sternly omitted. History and romance are already the property of the foreigners "who come down on Rome like a swarm of locusts," who wear "dress fasteners" and "impossible hats," who "resemble a nation of inquisitive children amusing themselves in the desecration of a stupendous sepulchre."

Yet even for the foreigner the supreme interest of Rome must be that it is no mere museum, but a living city still. Busy with churches and temples, statues and paintings, inscriptions and sites, we are apt to overlook the contemporary Romans whom we have not come forth to see. To themselves they must necessarily be the most important part of the Eternal City; and the greater number of them are not princes and dukes with historic names, nor even renowned churchmen, or patriots and kingdom builders, but good, simple, workaday, middle-class persons such as are the backbone of all countries and of all societies.

It is among such unnoticed folk that Grazia Deledda has taken us in *Nostalgie*; and it is not too much to say that her pages have a distinction and a force which recalls, at least in a measure, the *style qui rugit* of the author of *Madame Bovary*.

HELEN HESTER COLVILL.

AUTHOR'S PREFACE

TO MY HUSBAND—

Do you remember a young and attractive lady who called on us one day in the course of our first year's residence in Rome? Her visit was surprising; for I did not know the coronet-surmounted name on her card, and at that time few outside our small circle of intimates had discovered our nest in Via Modena, or had courage to climb a century of steps in pursuit of two useless persons unpractised in giving letters of introduction or inditing dedicatory epistles. The lady, whom I will call Regina, explained, however, that she came from your native province and was the bearer of messages from your friends. We talked a long time of that vicinity, dear to me as a second home; then she asked if I did not yearn after my native Sardinia, whose children are reputed always great sufferers from homesickness.

"Not so much," I replied. "I love Rome with all my heart; besides, I am so busy with my work that I have no time for the indulgence of idle phantasies."

"You work so hard? Happy you!" sighed the young lady; and added, "But, no! no! Homesickness is not mere phantasy; nor is it a disease, as so many call it! It is a passion; and, like other passions, can drive one mad if ungratified. During my first months in Rome I suffered from acute and morbid nostalgia; but now I have been home for a while and have come back almost cured."

"I don't know —," I said; "such nostalgia as I have felt has been quite harmless."

"Then there must be several kinds, some harmless, some dangerous," conceded the young lady with a smile; and she continued rather shyly: "but our whole existence is one long chain of nostalgia — don't you think so? The nostalgia of yesterday, the nostalgia of to-morrow; the longing for what is lost, the yearning for what can never be attained —"

After this first visit we saw Regina several times. I liked her, she was so clever and original; but to you she proved unsympathetic. "I can't see clearly into her life," you complained to me more than once.

This much we learned about her. Her husband was far from rich and she had brought him but a slender dowry, yet they rented a handsome Apartment and lived almost luxuriously. We, on the other hand, who worked hard and between us made an income the double of theirs, were content with the modest life of poor artists; gladdened indeed — like the careless existence of the birds building in the laurel below our windows — by the songs of love and the mere joy of living and struggling on in good hope of victory.

Remembering, as I minutely do, the whole simple romance of our early married life — on this day when we have attained to almost all our hopes (a little by my good-will, chiefly by your intelligence and activity, never by stooping to any transaction disapproved by our conscience) — to you, dear comrade of my work and of my life, I dedicate this tale. In it the reader will not find one of those stale themes for which my romances have been unjustly blamed. It is a simple narrative, a transcript from life, from this our modern life, so multiform, so interesting, sometimes so joyous, oftener so sad; beautiful always as an autumn tree laden with fruit — some of it rotten, — and with leaves — many of them already dead.

A simple narrative, I say; so simple that criticism deeming it a test of my literary powers, hitherto devoted only to the passions and sorrows of a primitive society, may deem that I have failed. But such judgment will not disturb me. This novel has not been written as a test; and criticism resembles the Exchequer which almost always taxes us on capital greater than what we really possess.

Alas! that we cannot contest its terrible authority nor make it understand that our patrimony, though small, is at least our own! If we forced ourselves to give all it has the audacity to demand, we should not only ruin ourselves, but to the last remain unsuccessful in appeasing our creditor.

GRAZIA.

RONCADELLO (CASALMAGGIORE). *October*, 1904.

PART I

CHAPTER I

ROME was near.

The November moon illuminated the Campagna — an immense mother-o'-pearl moon, clear and sad. The violence of the express train was met by the violence of a raging wind.

Regina dozed and was dreaming herself still at home; the rumble of the train seemed the clatter of the mill upon the Po. Suddenly Antonio's hand pressed hers and she awoke with a start.

"We are near arriving," said the young husband.

Regina sat up, leaned towards the closed window and looked out. The glass reflected the interior of the compartment — the lamp, her own figure wrapped in a long, light-coloured cloak, her face wan with weariness. She half-closed her large, short-sighted eyes, and in the misty moonlight, against the grey background caused by the reflection of her cloak, she made out the landscape — bluish undulations fleeting by, a mysterious pathway, a tree with silver leaves lashed by the wind, and in the distance a long line of aqueducts, the arches of which disappeared into the moonlight and seemed like a row of immense inhospitable doors. This of the aqueducts was no doubt optical illusion; but Regina, who had little confidence in her eyes yet was obstinate in refusing spectacles, felt none the less excited by the sublime visions she believed herself seeing in the dimness of the wind-swept window-pane. Rome! she was filled with childish joy at the mere thought that Rome was near. Rome! the long-dreamed-of wonder city, the world's metropolis, the home of all splendours, all delight — Rome, which was now to become her own! She forgot everything else; fatigue, mourning for the dear things lost, trepidation as to her future, fear of the strangers awaiting her, the embarrassments of the first days of marriage, all sadness, disappointment, delusion — all disappeared in the realisation of her long dream so ardently indulged.

Antonio got up and joined her at the window, which reflected his fine person — tall, fair, easy in attitude, dominant in manner. Regina saw — still in the glass — his long grey eyes looking at her caressingly, his well-shaped mouth smiling and suggesting a kiss, and she felt happy, happy, happy!

"Think!" said Antonio, bending over her as if to confide a secret; "think, my queen! We are at Rome!"

She did not reply. "Are you thinking of it?" he insisted.

"Of course I am!"

"Does your heart beat?"

Regina smiled, a trifle contemptuously, not choosing to let him see all her excitement and delight

Antonio looked at his watch.

"A quarter of an hour more. If there wasn't such a wind, I'd make you look out."

"I will. Put down the glass."

"I tell you there's too much wind."

"I'll look out all the same," she said, with the obstinacy of a spoilt child.

Antonio tried to open the window, but the wind was really too strong, and Regina changed her mind.

"Shut it up! Shut it up!" she cried.

He obeyed.

"But think! think!" he repeated, "you are at Rome! They will be just starting for the station," he observed gravely, and advised her to put on her hat and get herself ready. "Settle your hair," he said; "and where have you put the powder?"

"Am I very hideous?" asked Regina, passing her hand over her face.

She sat down, opened her dressing-bag, smoothed her hair, powdered her face; then again put on the grey cloak which Antonio held for her, and buttoned it up. Her little face emerged from its sable collar as from a cup. It was pale and tired, all lips and eyes, reminding one of the pretty little face of a kitten.

"That's all right!" said Antonio, surveying her adoringly.

Again she rose and leaned against the door. A long wall was fleeting past the train; then came houses, hedges, gardens, canes bending under the wind, now and then lamps flaring yellow in the great whiteness of the autumn moon.

"San Paolo! The Tiber!" said Antonio, still at Regina's side.

San Paolo! The Tiber! Regina just perceived the sheen of the river and her heart beat strongly. Yet, as often happened to her, after the first moment's wild delight, a shadow of melancholy diffidence stole over her soul.

"Yes!" she thought, "Rome! the capital, the wonder city; where there is no fog, which is full of sunshine and flowers! But what is there in store for me there? Young, happy, loved,

I have to throw myself into the arms of Rome as I have thrown myself into the arms of Antonio. What will Rome be able to give me? We are not rich, and the great city is like — like *people*, who give little to and care little for those who are not rich. But we aren't poor either!" she concluded, comforting herself.

The engine whistled, and Regina started involuntarily. Behind a wind-blown hedge, straight before her in the moonlight and the glare of the lamps which now had multiplied in number, a small house started into sight for a moment, and vanished as if by magic.

"It might be my home!" she told herself sadly, remembering the dear maternal nest, planted pleasantly on the high bank of the Po.

The train shrieked again, beginning to slacken speed.

"Here we are!" said Antonio; and Regina's recollections dissolved as the apparition of the house had dissolved a moment before.

After this, notwithstanding her resolution not to be upset, not to be surprised, but to make calm study of her own impressions, she became hopelessly bewildered and saw everything as through a veil.

Antonio was pulling the light luggage down from the rack; he overturned the bonnet-box containing the bride's beautiful white hat; she stooped to pick it up, flushed with dismay, then returned to the window and rearranged her cloak and fur collar. Lines of monstrous houses, orange against the velvety blue of the sky, fleeted by rapidly; the wind abated, the lamps became innumerable, golden, white, violet — their crude rays vanquishing the melancholy moonlight. The glare grew and grew, became magnificent, pervaded an enclosure into which the train rushed with deafening roar.

Rome!

Hundreds of intent egotistic faces, illuminated by the violet brilliance of the electric light, passed before Regina's agitated gaze. Here and there she distinguished a few figures, a lady with red hair, a man in a check suit, a pale girl with a picture hat, a bald gentleman, a raised stick, a fluttering handkerchief — but she saw nothing distinctly; she had a strange fancy that this unnamed alien crowd was a deputation sent to welcome her — not over-kindly — by the great city to which she was giving herself.

The carriage doors were thrown violently open, a babel of human voices resounded above the whistles and the throbbing of the engines; on the platform people were running about and jostling each other.

"Roma—a—a!"

"Porter—r—r!"

Antonio was collecting the hand luggage, but Regina stood gazing at the scene. Many smiling, curious, anxious persons were still standing in groups before the carriage doors; others had already escaped and were disappearing out of the station exit.

"There's no one for us, Antonio," said Regina, a little surprised; but she had no sooner spoken than she perceived a knot of persons returning along the platform, and understood that these were *they*. She jumped out and looked harder. Yes, it was they — three men, one in a light-coloured overcoat; two women, one short and stout, the other very tall, very thin, her face hidden in the shadow of her great black hat. The thin lady held a bouquet of flowers, and her strange figure, tightly compressed in a long coat of which the mother-o'-pearl buttons could be seen a mile off, struck Regina at once. This must be Arduina, her sister-in-law, editress of a Woman's Rights paper, who had written her two or three extraordinary letters.

"Mother!" cried Antonio, flinging himself from the carriage.

Regina found herself on the fat lady's panting bosom; then she felt the pressure of the buttons she had seen from afar; in one hand she was holding the bouquet, the other was clasped by a plump, soft, masculine hand.

The slightly amused voice of Antonio was introducing —

"My brother Mario, clerk in the Board of Control; my brother Gaspare, clerk at the War Office; my brother Massimo, junior clerk at the War Office —"

"That's enough," she said at last, bowing graciously. All smiled, but Antonio went on —

"And this is Arduina, the crazy one —"

"Joking as usual!" cried the latter.

"Well, here is Regina, my wife! Here she is! How are you, Gaspare?"

"Pretty fit. And you? Hungry?"

"Are you very tired, my dear?" asked the trembling voice of the old lady, her face close to Regina's.

Notwithstanding the scent of the flowers, Regina could have wished her mother-in-law's lips further off, and she shuddered involuntarily. In that strange place, at that late hour, under that metallic, unpleasantly glaring, electric splendour, all these people, pressed upon the bride, speaking in an unfamiliar accent and staring at her with ill-concealed curiosity. She conceived a dislike to them all. Even Antonio, who at that moment was more taken up with them than with his wife, seemed unlike himself, a stranger, a man of a different race from hers. She felt completely alone, lost, confused; had presently the sensation of being carried away, borne along in a wave of the crowd. Outside she saw a mountain of enormous vehicles drawn up in line on the shining wood pavement; it seemed to her made of blue tiles, and on the damp air she fancied the scent of a forest. The electric light blinded her short-sighted eyes; she thought she saw a forest in the distance, a line of trees black against the steely sky; and the violet globes of the lamps suggested in the heart of those black trees some sort of miraculous burning fruit. There was magic in the late hour, in the vastness of the enclosure bounded by the imaginary wood; the people silently lost themselves and disappeared as into a wet and shining morass.

"Let's walk — it's quite close," said Antonio, taking her arm. "Well! it's pretty big, isn't it, this station yard?"

"It *is* big!" she responded, genuinely astonished; "but it's been raining here, hasn't it? How lovely it all is!"

Regina felt happy again, at Antonio's side, squeezed up against him by the large and panting person of her mother-in-law. Yes, certainly! Rome was the dream-city, full of gardens, fountains, sublime buildings; a city great and splendid by day and by night! She felt joyous as if she had drunk wine; she chattered with feverish animation. Never afterwards did she succeed in remembering what she said in that first hour of arrival; she did remember that her pleasure was marred by the panting and sighing of her mother-in-law, by Arduina's silly laughter, by the talk of the brothers who stepped just behind her, arguing about trifles.

Antonio had requested his family not to announce his arrival to the more distant relations; however, no sooner had they got to Via Torino and the great palace in which the Venutellis lived on the fourth and fifth floors, than the panting old lady confessed —

"Clara and her girl are here. They came in to spend the evening, and we couldn't get rid of them. They guessed, you see."

"The deuce!" said Antonio; "never mind, I'll soon pack them off for you!"

The gas was lighted, and Regina was impressed by the grand entrance hall and the marble staircase, which seemed continuation of the splendours she had found in piazza and street.

"Courage, my queen!" said Antonio; "this is a veritable Jacob's ladder! Go on in front, you fellows!"

The three men and Arduina pressed forward with the nimbleness of habit; Regina herself tried to run, but she soon got tired and out of breath.

"These stairs are the death of me!" sighed the mother-in-law; "Ah! my dear child, I did not always live on a fourth floor!"

Regina was not listening. Cries, laughter, exclamations, a merry uproar, rang from the top of the stair; — then came a whirlwind, a rustle, a whiff of scent, a vision of flounces, chains, lace, yellow hair, which overwhelmed and nearly overturned the bride, the bridegroom, and the old lady.

"Mind you don't break your neck, Claretta, my dear!" cried Antonio.

The lovely being clasped Regina tight in her fragrant arms, covering her with impassioned kisses.

"Dearest! Welcome! Welcome, dearest! A thousand good wishes and congratulations! Mamma is up there waiting for you!"

"Pray reserve some kisses for me!" said Antonio, dryly.

Claretta, without ado, kissed him rapidly on the cheek; then again seized Regina's hand, and drew her up and up, shouting and laughing, tall, rustling, fragrant, elegant. Regina followed, a little envious, even jealous, but childishly bewitched by so much easy loveliness. Claretta, filling the whole stair with her cries and peals of laughter, almost carried the bride, brought her into the drawing-room, threw her on the soft bosom of fat Aunt Clara, and then herself dragged her through the whole Apartment on a tour of inspection. The rooms wore lighted by gas, and all the furniture was polished and smelly with paraffin: space everywhere was narrow and choked up with furniture, coarse draperies, jute carpets, crochet work, great cushions embroidered in wool, Japanese fans and umbrellas. In some of the rooms it was impossible to move. Regina's throat was caught by a feeling of suffocation. The remembrance of her beautiful country home, of its large rooms, so sunny and so simple, assailed her with an anguish of tenderness. To comfort herself she had to say to Claretta —

"We shall only stay here till we've found a nice Apartment for ourselves. That'll be easy, won't it?"

"Not so very easy. The foreigners come down on Rome like a swarm of locusts."

This was the discouraging reply of the cousin, who stopped before every mirror to admire herself, bending this way and that, and talking loud that the young men in the dining-room might hear her.

"Here! this is your own room, your *nid d' amour*, you birds of passage!" she said, taking Regina into a corner room, where they found Antonio, his mother, Arduina, the maid-servant, and the portmanteaux.

The room was large, but had an oppressively low ceiling, painted grey with vulgar blue arabesques; three windows, one close to the foot of the bed, were smothered in heavy draperies, and the massive bed itself was burdened with huge pillows and counterpanes. The bridal trunks and portmanteaux completed the barricade, and Regina's sense of asphyxia perceptibly increased. Silent and sad she surveyed the ugly room; she seemed lost in some painful dream, in some strange prison where everything fettered and mortally oppressed her. Oh dear! all these people! These women, who surrounded, crushed, smothered her! Tired and sleepy, her physical irritability made itself almost morbidly felt at the touch of all these unknown, inquisitive, cruel people. She was yearning for solitude and repose; at any rate she wanted to wash, dress, rearrange her hair. They did not leave her a moment alone. Claretta had no notion of forsaking the looking-glass; Arduina, on the look out for copy, catechised her about her impressions; the mother-in-law never stopped staring with lachrymose eyes.

Regina took off her hat and cloak; her little face, all eyes and lips, seemed pale and frightened under the waves of her hair, black, abundant and curly. Antonio was paying no heed to his bride; he arranged the luggage, and asked his mother news of this one and that. The old lady puffed and sighed, and answered his questions, but never took her eyes off the new daughter-in-law.

"Where shall I wash my hands?" asked Regina. Her warm brown eyes, generally velvety and sweet, were now drooping with fatigue, and in expression almost wild.

"Here!" cried Arduina, precipitating herself on the washstand, "you'll find everything here, dear! soap, powder, comb — What sort of soap do you like?"

Regina did not answer. Mechanically she washed herself, accepting the towel which her sister-in-law presented, and smoothed her hair, stooping to look in the low looking-glass.

"Sit down," said Arduina, setting a chair, "you can't see like that."

"No, I can't see sitting; I'm short-sighted," said Regina, with increasing irritation.

This piece of news plunged the ladies into consternation. Claretta actually turned her back on the glass; Signora Anna, who was examining the lining of Regina's cloak, looked up almost in tears; Arduina studied her sister-in-law's beautiful orbs with astonishment.

"Short-sighted? With such lovely eyes! and so young!" exclaimed the old lady.

"Have you eye-glasses?" asked Claretta.

"Yes, but they're no good. I hate them."

"They're very *chic* though," said Arduina. "My dear, do loosen your hair at your temples — it's too dragged. What splendid hair you have! I'll do it for you to-morrow. Wait a moment —" and she raised her hand; but the bride's little head, which seemed so small and insignificant, shook itself fiercely.

"No, no. It will do well enough," she said.

Her tone admitted of no reply; and the authoress understood that Regina was a commanding creature of a superior race. For this reason she looked at her with pitying tenderness and compassionate admiration. Struck by this look, Regina for the first time noticed her sister-in-law, whom Antonio had described as a fool. Arduina was tall, with a narrow chest and a countenance of yellowish wood. She had small, colourless, frightened eyes, thin lips with discoloured teeth, and three curls of pale hair. She was singularly plain, and now Regina perceived further that she was melancholy and enslaved. But this produced no pity in the bride, rather a sense of malicious consolation. In this odious world into which she had stepped through the door of the Apartment, there were victims like Arduina, in comparison with whom she was an empress! All this passed through her mind during the few minutes in which she was settling her hair in the presence of the three staring women. Antonio at last noticed his bride's annoyance, and sent the ladies away, pushing his cousins out familiarly.

"Be so kind as to take yourselves off. I don't require your assistance at my toilette. Go away. Make haste. We want rest."

"You can sleep all to-morrow. It's going to rain," said his mother.

"Let us hope not."

"I expect it will."

"Bother the weather prophets!" said Regina.

At last the women were gone; and in an instant Antonio was by Regina's side, kissing her, leaning his face against her troubled one, and saying in his caressing voice —

"Cheer up; don't be so depressed! You shall just eat a mouthful and then get at once to bed. To-morrow we'll escape — we'll go out by ourselves. We won't let them bore us. Cheer up!"

He put his arm round her and drew her to the dining-room, humming a merry tune —

> "Mousey doesn't care for cream,
> Mousey wants to marry the Queen;
> If the King won't let her go,
> Mousey'll break his bones, you know."

But Regina had no smiles left.

Scarcely was she seated on one of the comfortless Vienna chairs which surrounded the overburdened table than she felt her back broken and her eyelids weighed down by the whole fatigue of the journey. Again she seemed in a bad dream, looking through a veil at a picture of vulgar figures. Yes, vulgar the face of her mother-in-law — fat, red, puffy, outlined by the hard line of hair, over-shiny and over-black for nature; vulgar that of Mario, which was much like his mother's, with the same small blue eyes, the same mouth hanging half-open as he breathed slowly and noisily; vulgar, again, the face of Gaspare — rosy all over, hairless below the shining line of his bald forehead; and that of Massimo, who was dandified but decadent, something like Antonio, but with long, reddish, oily hair and bold grey eyes. Claretta herself was vulgar; the very type of a *bourgeois* beauty. Without understanding why, Regina remembered the crowds half-seen at the passing stations and on the Roman platform; the faces now surrounding her stood out from the confusion of those unnoticed ones, but themselves belonged to the crowd, and were no better than the crowd. A whole world separated her from them.

Notwithstanding the hour and Antonio's promise of dispatch, the supper lasted an immense time. It was served by a strapping, fair-haired girl in a pink blouse, who never took her astonished eyes from the bride's face, and every moment tripped and stumbled, as if determined to break something.

This figure which came and went seemed the principal one of the picture. Every one watched the girl and talked to her. Signora Anna started every time she opened the door.

Even Antonio addressed her.

"Well, Marina, and how are all the sweethearts?" he asked: and added, indicating Regina, "are you satisfied? Which is the prettier, she or Signora Arduina?"

Marina blushed, giggled, ran away, and did not return.

Presently Gaspare rose gravely, threw his napkin over his shoulder, and went in search of her. An altercation was heard in the kitchen. Then Gaspare returned, wrathful and very red.

"Mother, the mutton is burnt!" he announced tragically; "you must go and see after it."

The old lady groaned, got up, went out, came back — and did not stay quiet for another moment!

"Mother!" implored Antonio, "do sit down!"

"Mother!" urged Gaspare, still wrathful, "go and look after her!"

"Oh, these servants!" said the mother-in-law, turning to Regina, "one shouldn't mention them, I know, but they're the ruin of families. I'll tell you afterwards —"

"It's one of the gravest of social problems," said Massimo, sarcastically, looking straight before him.

"But one can't live without servants," cried Gaspare.

"Yet the servants are the death of you?"

"Oh, I'll be the death of them if they don't do their business," said Gaspare, and they all laughed.

Notwithstanding the old lady's irruptions into the kitchen the courses were a long time coming. Talk grew animated. Massimo chattered with the cousin; Signora Anna expatiated to Signora Clara on the delinquencies of the maid.

"How are you getting on with your Gigione?" Antonio asked Gaspare; and his brother replied, abusing his chief as he had abused Marina.

"Did you get my last letter?" Arduina demanded of Regina, under cover of the general noise.

"Which?"

"The one in which I asked information about the state of private benevolence in Mantua."

"Oh, pray leave her in peace," interrupted Antonio testily. Regina thought of her old home, of the beautiful picture seen through the window of the great dining-parlour, the woods, the silver river sparkling in the summer sunshine — all lost! The actual picture of the woods, and the painted picture above the chimneypiece, a river scene by Baratta, showing the green banks of the Parma, and white boats against a violet sky — all vanished — vanished for ever! Seated on this back-breaking chair, among all these people who chattered of vulgar things, dismay again invaded her soul, the dismay felt by the condemned at the thought of association with his fellow-prisoners. Antonio paid her little attention; he was sucked into the current of his brothers' talk and had become a stranger to her. Again he made some jest at Arduina's expense; the maid looked at the ladies and laughed. Indeed, they all laughed. Why did they laugh? Was happiness making Antonio cruel? His brother Mario — a man no longer young, who seldom spoke, but always reddened when he heard his thought expressed by somebody else — detested, as they all knew, his wife's scribbling mania. So Antonio persisted in questioning his sister-in-law about her newspaper, *The Future of Woman.*

"It has reached a circulation of three copies," said Massimo, "and it's clearly anxious to provoke quarrels, for it has printed a sonnet from a Calabrian paper without leave."

"My goodness! how witty you are!" cried Arduina, laughing, but her whole face expressed a vague terror.

Sor Mario, his eyes on his plate, grunted and munched like an angry bullock. There followed a perfect explosion of childish cruelty towards the poor creature, who, even to Regina, suggested a caricature.

"I've never succeeded in discovering the office of her paper," said Claretta; "one ought to be able to go there if only to find the editor."

"There are plenty of editors in the street," answered Arduina; "a girl like you could find one anywhere."

"I don't see the sense of that!" cried Gaspare.

"We never expect *you* to see the sense of anything."

"Come, show sense yourself!" interposed her husband, threatening her with his fork.

"Are you in the Woman Movement, Regina?" some one asked.

"I? No! " answered the bride, as if starting from a dream. Then, wishing to defend her sister-in-law, less out of pity for her than out of dislike to the brothers, she added, "Perhaps Arduina will convert me."

"Antonio! get out your stick!" cried Gaspare, and again they all laughed.

The topic changed. They discussed a certain Madame Makuline, a Russian princess long resident in Rome, to whom Antonio had been introduced by Arduina, and who occasionally employed him in the administration of her affairs.

"She should give a wedding present to Regina," said the authoress; "I expect her to dinner to-morrow; will you two come?"

This intelligence somewhat restored Arduina's prestige, and Regina breathed more freely. The conversation ran on countesses and duchesses; Claretta cried, turning to Massimo —

"Oh, now I remember! You were seen yesterday —"

"Wasn't I seen to-day?"

"— running after Donna Maria del Carro's carriage. It was raining, and you had no umbrella."

"That's why I ran," he said, flattered and pleased.

"No, my dear boy; you ran after the carriage."

"Why?" asked the innocent Regina.

"How sweet you are!" said the cousin. "He ran to be seen, of course! The Marchesa del Carro likes handsome young men, even when she doesn't know them."

"Thank you very much," said Massimo, making a bow.

Then they all got excited and talked of innumerable titled persons of their acquaintance, telling their "lives and miracles." Signora Clara, not to be left out, was insistent in describing the reception costume of a countess.

Regina listened. She did not confess it to herself, but she was certainly pleased that her new relations had friends among the aristocracy.

At last they arrived at the coffee, and Signora Anna turned to Regina intending to say something pleasant.

"I expect you miss your Mamma," she began; "you can't get accustomed to the idea of a second mother."

But she was interrupted by Gaspare, who came from a second inspection of the kitchen.

"My dear mother, just come and look. Come!" he insisted, flicking the corner of his napkin, "there's a flood in the kitchen. She has left the tap running."

The old lady had to get up; panting and puffing she followed her son to the kitchen. Presently Marina was heard sobbing.

"The man's unbearable!" said Arduina; "is that poor girl a slave? From the point of view of —"

"From the social point of view —" suggested Massimo.

"Pardon me," observed Aunt Clara, "she left the tap running."

"If ever I marry a man who meddles in the kitchen," said Claretta, tightening her sash at the looking-glass, "I'll give him — from the social point of view — such a hiding —"

"I too!" agreed the authoress.

Sor Mario, who was picking his teeth ferociously, uttered a grunt.

Signora Anna came back followed by Marina, her eyes red, her lips quivering.

"Pooh! don't cry!" said Massimo, "it makes a fright of you. If the pastrycook saw you now —"

"What, is it a pastrycook this time?" joked Antonio. "Yes; his name's Stanislao."

"But when I went away it was a penny-a-liner!"

"I got rid of him. For more than three months I had no one," declared Marina, all smiles again.

"*Brava!*" said Claretta, "that's the best plan. Have you had a great many?"

"Four. No — five, counting the first. He was Peppino. He was an official."

"Good gracious! Where?"

"At Campo Verano."

"Oh! Did he perhaps dig there?"

"Yes," said the girl, simply.

They all burst out laughing, and again Regina felt choked.

Were they always like this in this house? Even Antonio, her Antonio, who was always gay, but with her never had shown himself vulgar — even he appeared in a new light.

Suddenly, however, while Signora Clara was repeating her description of the countess's dress, Regina saw her husband looking at her with distressed eyes, and she knew that her brows must have been contracted in a frown. He got up, came over, and stroked her hair.

"It's time for bed now. You're tired, aren't you?" he whispered, his voice almost supplicating.

Regina rose. Arduina and Claretta thought it necessary to run after her, embracing and kissing her. When they had conducted her to the bedroom, they kissed her again.

Now she was alone with Antonio, and great was her relief. But alas! the door opened immediately, and in came the mother-in-law.

"What is it?" asked Regina, dismayed; and she threw herself on one of the immense, encumbering arm-chairs, and closed her eyes.

Signora Anna, sighing as usual, advanced to the bed.

"Oh!" she exclaimed, in accents of tragedy, "these maids, now-a-days, know nothing of their business! They have no heads. Forgive me, my dearest child —"

"What on earth has happened?" asked Antonio, half undressed.

"She hasn't turned down the bed!" cried the poor lady, attacking the pillows with her fat and trembling arms.

She fussed about, altered all the blankets, tidied the dressing-table, examined the jugs. Regina was waiting to undress; but as the old lady would not go away, she leaned back in the arm-chair, her eyes still closed, her hands folded in her lap. She listened to her mother-in-law's uncertain step and panting breath; and she thought with anguish of to-morrow.

"And the morrow of that, and the next day, and for ever and ever, I shall have to put up with these people! It's awful!"

"Where are your things?" asked Antonio, in his pyjamas.

Regina opened her eyes, got up hastily, and searched her portmanteau. Lo! behind her the heavy panting of the old lady!

"Let me, dear child! You go and undress. I'll find everything for you."

"No, no!" said Regina, vexed, "I'll do it myself."

"Leave it all to me. Go and undress."

"No!"

"There's nothing for me but to dance!" said Antonio, cutting capers; he was well made, and agile as a clown.

"My dear daughter! what are you thinking of? That's a petticoat, not a night-dress! This? Surely that's one of Antonio's flannel shirts? Ah! a flannel night-dress! Dear me! doesn't it tickle you? But I believe it's very cold in your part of the country. It's cold here, too, when the *tramontana* blows. The *tramontana* blows for three days at a time. Dear! what lovely embroidery! Did you do it yourself? Listen —"

But Regina could listen no longer. Rage possessed her, while the old lady rummaged in the portmanteau, examining everything with the greatest curiosity. Antonio was waltzing round the arm-chair; he suddenly seized Regina, and whirled her away with him.

"Oh!" she exclaimed, with a cry of suffering protest, "it's time now to leave me in peace!"

The hint was lost upon the old lady. She put everything straight in the portmanteau, then came to Regina and embraced her lengthily.

At last she did take herself off, and at last Regina was really alone with her husband, but it was too late for her to feel great comfort in the fact. She undressed and got into bed; into the huge, solid bed, hard, and wide and cold as the bed of a river! She felt shipwrecked; around her floated gaping trunks, boxes, curtains, unpleasing furniture; above beetled the grey ceiling, overwhelming as a rainy sky. Confused noises, vibrations in the silence of night, penetrated from the distance, from some unknown and mysterious place. Arduina's foolish laughter, Claretta's hysterical shrieks, echoed on in the next room. And above these, above all voices far and near, sounded a melancholy whistle, the sibilant lament of some nocturnal train, which seemed to Regina a voice out of other times from a distant place, a cry which called, invited, implored her to — what? She did not know, did not remember; but she was sure she knew that cry, that it had once told her something wonderful, that it was sounding now only for her, having sought her out in the night of the vast, unknown city; — that it was repeating to her things wild, sweet, lacerating —

"At last!" said Antonio, embracing her. "This bed is a limitless desert! Where are you? Oh, what little cold hands! You're trembling! Are you cold?"

"No."

"Then why do you tremble?" he asked, in another tone; "are you not happy, Regina?"

She made no answer.

"Are you not happy?"

"I'm tired," she said, her eyes shut;" I still feel the shake of the train. Do you hear that whistle?"

"Ah!" she went on, as if speaking in a dream, "I know it now! It's the whistle of the little steamer on the Po! Ah! let us start!"

"We have hardly arrived, and already you want to go?" he said, his voice half jesting, half bitter.

She made no response. He thought she slept, and kept motionless for fear of waking her. But presently be heard her laugh and felt quite cheered.

"What's the matter?" he asked, fondling her hand, which was beginning to grow warm.

"That official — was a gravedigger!" she murmured, still dreaming;" if my sister Toscana had been here how she would have laughed!"

"She's still in that old home of hers!" thought Antonio jealously.

Long afterwards he confided to Regina that that night he had been unable to sleep. He wanted to ask how she liked his mother and the rest, but dared not put the question, guessing intuitively that she would not answer him sincerely.

He, too, heard the whistle which had reached the half-slumbering Regina, and had lulled her in memories and hope.

"Go? Is she already dreaming of going?" he thought, bitterly; and remembered, not without resentment, her cold, sad, now and then contemptuous manner during those first hours of communion with her new relatives. Yet he could not but feel the measureless distance which divided those relatives from the thoughtful, delicate creature of a superior race whom he had dared to marry.

"But she knew all about it!" he reflected; "I had told her everything. I said to her: We're a family of working people, descended from working people. My mother is just the housewife, my sister-in-law is a harmless lunatic. She said she did not care — she loved me, and that was enough. Then what more does she want?"

He had a foolish desire to push her away, to distance her from himself in that great, limitless bed; but she was so fragile, so slight, so cold, lying like a dead thing on his warm, pulsing breast!

"I've been wrong in bringing her here! I ought to have prepared our own nest, and taken her there at once. She's like an uprooted flower which must be planted at once in an adapted soil."

He looked at her with profound tenderness, and remained motionless, lest he should disturb the slumber which had descended on her homesickness and fatigue.

CHAPTER II

ON waking next morning Regina found herself alone in the big hard bed.

It was raining; the room was oppressed by a grey, melancholy twilight which seemed thrown from the ceiling. Vehicles were already rolling in the street; screaming trains passed by; there was continued howling of tempestuous wind, the whole making on Regina an impression of unutterable dreariness. The luminous city of her dreams seemed pervaded by this howling wind through which resounded a thousand other voices; a ceaseless booming of toilsome life, dismal under eternal rain.

Presently she looked at the room, screwing up her eyes to distinguish the various objects. The grey ceiling, the three grey windows, especially that one at the foot of the bed, were positively funereal; the rough linen of the sheets and pillow-case, the coarse embroidery of their adornment filled her with horror.

And Antonio, where was he? In her ill-humour Regina resented his having risen silently so as not to wake her, his having left her alone in the immensity of that strange bed; but almost immediately the door was gently pushed open and Antonio looked in.

"There they are, her big eyes!" he said gaily, and came over hurriedly to kiss her lips; "so you've come to, little one, have you? Are you awake?"

"I think so," she murmured rather hoarsely, and threw her arm round his neck. "Is it raining?"

"Yes; it's raining needlessly hard!" he said, heaving an exaggerated sigh, "but it will soon leave off."

"Let us hope so! Open the shutters!"

He moved to obey. "This is Sunday; don't you know that in Rome it always rains on Sunday? — result of the Papal curse! Never mind. It will leave off. I assure you it will! Stay in bed a little longer. I'll ring for your coffee."

"No, no!" she cried, terrified lest the summons should bring her mother-in-law; "I'll get up at once! I'm anxious to write home."

"We'll go out the moment the rain stops," said Antonio. "If you don't mind we'll take Gaspare with us. He knows all about archaeology. We'll go to the Forum."

"To the Forum!" she echoed, her eyes sparkling with revival of joy.

"Yes, my dear — to the Forum. Think of that! To the Forum! Have you realised where you are?"

She smiled at him without answering. He had changed his costume, was wearing a shining collar, a beautiful green tie, had curled his moustache. He was fresh, fragrant, very handsome. Light had come in with him, love, joy. Regina pulled him down to her, kissed his hair, which she said smelt of "burnt flowers," pretended to whisper something in his ear, and made instead a childish shout. He jumped in feigned terror, threatened her and shook her. They laughed, they played, they forgot everything but their own felicity.

"Where have you awaked, *levrottin?*" (leveret), he asked, using one of the pretty pet names he had learned in her country, where he had been for three months on a Royal Commission; "where are you? This time yesterday we were at Parma; to-day we are here. Think, what a distance! And three months ago we didn't so much as know each other! Do you remember the first day we made friends on the river-bank? And that great crimson sun behind the woods? The Master kept looking at us and smiling; he knew we'd have to get married!"

" *'Here is the Signor Antonio Venutelli, junior clerk at the Treasury, and here is the noble Signorina Regina Tagliamari,'* " continued Antonio, imitating the nasal voice of the school-master who had arranged their introduction; " *'she is a real queen of goodness and of genius, fit to reign in the Eternal City, in unequalled Rome!'* "

"Poor old man!" said Regina, more gravely. "Yes, we certainly owe our meeting to him."

"And what do you suppose they'd say in your home, now? They'd say, *'Regina is in Rome, and she's still in bed, the little sluggard, and she hasn't even been to Mass, the little heathen!'* Fancy being in Rome and not going to Mass!"

"But look here!" she began, clapping her hands and imitating her husband's mock-heroic tone. However she was no longer merry. A sweet vision had melted her heart. She saw her mother — her dear, delicate mother, her pretty sister, her youngest brother, her darling, all starting for the nine o'clock Mass. The house on the river-bank was deserted. It stood among poplar-trees veiled in mist, like a fancy house in the background of a stage picture. Inside a fire burned on the great hearth, the black cat sat contemplating the flames, the Baratta painting was illuminated with grey and rosy tints which gave it a suggestive relief. The sound of a bell, singularly pure in tone, was dying on the still air in metallic vibrations; the northern landscape, with the great river winding along like an immense blue vein in the whiteness of that snowy plain, was spread out under the vaporous heaven. Silence — mysterious immensity — the mist of dream!

But this nostalgic vision, which gave her a melancholy pleasure seen thus under the caresses of him for whom she had abandoned all, was snatched from her by the entrance of Signora Anna. The old lady, round and enormous in her red flannel dressing-gown, her hair already dressed, and blacker and oilier than yesterday, advanced with circumspection, puffing and panting as was her wont. Regina blushed, removed her arms from Antonio's neck, and covered herself hastily.

"Why so?" said the young man, taking the coverlet away, "show your lovely little arms at once! Look, mother! see how white my Regina is!"

"No, no! let me alone!" said the girl, hiding under the sheet. But the old lady came nearer, helped Antonio to unbutton the wrist of Regina's jacket, and passed an approving finger over the bride's white and child-like arm.

"Upon my word!" she exclaimed, "you are really lovely!"

"Oh, dear me! Do please let me alone!" said Regina, flattered all the same.

"Isn't she lovely? Isn't she?" insisted Antonio, kissing the fair arms.

"Lovely! Very well made indeed! *Brava!*" said the mother-in-law, almost as if Regina had made herself. "And indeed I was white and shapely enough myself once," she went on; "now I'm an old woman, but in my day I was very much admired, I assure you!"

"Well really!" thought Regina, looking at her mother-in-law's thick hands, brown, chapped, smelling of garlic, and very unlike the blue-veined whiteness of her own delicate members.

"Won't you have some coffee? Do you take it with milk? I'll go and get the coffee and the milk — a little scalded cream — whipped eggs?"

"For pity's sake!" cried Regina. "No, thank you, I don't want anything."

"Get up! Get up!" said Antonio, "the rain's stopping. Let's go out!"

"You're not going to take her out in this weather!" protested the mother-in-law. "You're insane! She shall stay in bed. When I was a girl" (she turned to Regina), "I always stayed in bed the whole morning. But those days were different. The servants *then* were faithful, sensible, active, and the mistress could do the lady even if she wasn't one — thank heaven, I could."

"So you can now. What's to hinder you?" said Regina politely.

"Goodness me! What with such maids as we get now? Dishonest, untruthful, ungrateful hussies! They're the torment of one's existence. There was a time when I loved my servants just as if they were members of the family; now I don't love them at all. They don't deserve it. This girl I have now makes me sick with the worries she causes me."

"Get up! Get up!" repeated Antonio.

But Regina would not stir till she was left alone. Then she jumped out of bed, and, clad in her long white nightgown, stood disconsolately looking at the chaos of objects in the room and at the grey light which penetrated by the three doleful windows. She made also the sad discovery that at Rome it was colder than in her own north country! She washed, dressed, and did her hair awkwardly. Everything was inconvenient from the washstand to the looking-glass, the latter a panel in the wardrobe draped with a heavy curtain. Having tucked this up she saw herself in the glass; pale, worn out, ugly. Her depression reasserted itself.

She was long in appearing, and at last Antonio came to look for her. She had peevishly pulled up all the blinds, tucked away all the curtains, and was engaged settling the things in her trunk

"What on earth are you about?" he asked a little impatiently; and, taking her hand, led her to the dining-room, where Signora Anna was waiting at a table laid for two, but groaning under food sufficient for ten.

"I only want a drop of black coffee," said Regina.

"Only black coffee? My dear, you are crazy — so to speak — I don't mean any offence. But, you know, one must eat at Rome! Here is the black coffee. A little brandy in it?"

"No, thanks. It doesn't agree with me."

"Just try. You'll like it, I'm sure."

"No, no!"

"Yes, yes! If you don't mean to vex me —"

She had to take the brandy in the coffee, and then *café au lait*, and cream, and bread and butter, and biscuits, and the whipped eggs. At last tears rose in her eyes, so overwhelmed was she by her mother-in-law's insistence. By way of comfort Signora Anna at once offered a basin of broth and the wing of a roast chicken.

"But you're trying to kill me!" cried the girl, jesting, though desperate. Antonio laughed, and ate heartily.

Fortunately an alarming noise was heard in the kitchen, and the Signora ran, much agitated and tripping over her red dressing-gown. Regina seized the opportunity and fled to her room.

She put on a beautiful white scarf and a black hat with a pink ribbon, which she thought very smart; powdered herself carefully, and imagined every one was going to admire her as they did at home.

"Behold how lovely my Regina is!" said Antonio, half serious, half amused; "and just you look at her hat!"

Gaspare, buttoned up in his new great-coat, fat, heavy, rosy and pompous, was waiting at the dining-room door. He looked at Regina out of the corner of his eye, then saluted her and said gravely —

"Your hat is like a swallow's nest."

"I'd like to hear what you know about hats, when you know nothing about women," said Antonio.

34

"I shall never marry," declared Gaspare; "but if I should be overtaken by such unhappiness, at least my wife shall not make herself ridiculous."

"Ridiculous?" retorted Regina. "Who? the unhappy one?"

Gaspare deigned no reply. They started.

Regina never forgave her husband for taking Gaspare with them on this their first walk through Rome.

"We'll go down Via Cavour to the Forum, and come back by Piazza Venezia and Via Nazionale," proposed Antonio, consulting his watch; "it's late already."

The weather had cleared. Great drops of shining water fell from the trees in the Via Torino gardens. Santa Maria Maggiore, rose-coloured and grey against the blue sky, towered like a mountain above her broad flight of rain-washed steps. Gaspare pointed to the church with his umbrella and named it. Regina looked indifferently; the edifice seemed to her ugly.

They went down Via Cavour. The wood pavement was drying rapidly, and Regina naïvely remarked that it wasn't polished as she had supposed last night.

"I should hope not!" said Gaspare, who dropped behind now and then to hawk and spit. "What extraordinary things women do suppose! The very opposite of the facts!"

"Men too," retorted Regina.

"Men oftener than women," added Antonio, gallantly.

"Eh! Possibly. *Sometimes,*" said Gaspare, with a disagreeable smile.

Gaspare's rude manners offended Regina, though she had been warned he was "quite a character." Presently, however, she forgot him, and became absorbed in contemplation of the new things she was seeing.

People passed rapidly along the pavements, umbrellas under their arms; vivid light poured from the blue sky still furrowed by metallic clouds; through the bright moist air strayed the smell of roasted chestnuts. Yes! this wide, brilliant street was really fine! In a shop window were exhibited five astonishing hats, which Regina admired more than Santa Maria Maggiore. But presently the brothers made her deviate into a lane, dismal with old houses and old gardens hanging under high bastion-like walls, which went up and down, where there were no pavements, no shops, only a dirty crowd of hawkers, herb-sellers, street arabs. They walked on and on, but this melancholy street seemed endless. Regina grew tired; she leaned on Antonio's arm, and began again to feel a dull weight of sadness. Was this Rome?

The brothers made the blunder of supposing that Regina could walk as far as they. They dragged her on to the Forum, where, her eyes blinded by fatigue, she saw no more than a field of drenched ruins, a sorrow-stricken place, a cemetery over which the metallic clouds brooded, hiding the blue heaven and wrapping arches and columns in veils of doleful shade. Gaspare discoursed learnedly, but she did not listen. The tragic solitude of the vast graveyard was profaned by a great number of persons with eye-glasses and English gowns girded up with pins and dress-fasteners. The columns and the glorious fragments, still soaked with rain, seemed to Regina gigantic marble bones, exhumed by a nation of inquisitive children who amused themselves desecrating this stupendous sepulchre of a dead civilisation.

From the Forum they moved homewards towards Piazza Venezia. It was almost noon; the crowds took the trams by assault; a broad river of smartly-dressed women came down Via Nazionale, spread over the Piazza, and went up the Corso. A confused noise of trams, motors, carriages, human voices, sounded on the air which was still damp, but illuminated by changing light from between the clouds. Regina felt a kind of vertigo. She, who could see little that was distant, began to see even the near things confusedly. The incessant rumble of a thousand noises, among which the motors emitted roars like rampant wild beasts, gave her a vague sensation of terror. She fixed her wide eyes on the crowd, fascinated by the coming and going as by the flowing of a stream. She looked up and saw a network of telephone wires hiding the sky, which renewed her feeling of oppression; and yet, though tired and overwhelmed, she would not admit herself wondering or surprised. The elegance of the women certainly struck her. She felt envious, but also displeased. It was impossible there could be so many shapely and handsome women! They must be painted and padded! Oh, she knew very well! She knew how much corruption, falsity, hidden misery, that crowd carried within itself, the first contact with which on that uncertain autumn morning under the network of metallic threads awoke in her a mysterious sentiment of aversion and pity. Antonio fixed enamoured eyes on his bride's face; but those enamoured eyes failed to perceive the apathy of fatigue which was showing more and more plainly on the beloved features.

"Let's take a carriage," he suggested.

"Why not the tram?" asked Gaspare.

Antonio said the carriage would be quicker, but really he wanted at least for the first day to treat his Regina royally. Gaspare argued for the tram.

"Let's walk," said Regina.

"Walk? When we can't get you along?" exclaimed the brother-in-law.

"Then we'll have the carriage," said Regina to spite him.

"Oh, I see! We've become aristocrats!" said the misogynist.

They found a carriage and drove up Via Nationale, now beginning to empty and a little somnolent. It appeared immense under the white light of a heaven which had become all silver. In the distant and vaporous background of Piazza Termini, the fountains limited like huge crystal flowers. The great street was a thing of exquisite beauty at that hour, under that tender and melancholy sky, with that grand yet delicate background. Antonio looked at his wife, hoping at last to find a ray of admiration in her bewildered eyes. But the great eyes, shadowed and full of weariness, were only following the floating flags, and did not notice the grandeur and beauty of the splendid street. At Via Napoli he said —

"Let's throw a glance into those cross-streets. We'll perhaps find *our* street, Regianotta!"

"It would take me three months to recognise it. I don't know what to look out for."

"But you aren't observing!"

"Very likely not. What's the good of observing?"

"What's the good of having eyes?" put in Gaspare.

"Yes, what's the good? One generally blunders with them."

Gaspare did not appear to understand. He merely spat, and reflected that women are all either fools or flirts.

From that day out, he classed Regina with what he called the "avalanche" of fool-women. She was like Arduina, like Marina the maid, like other women of his acquaintance. Supreme and reciprocal contempt reigned for their whole life between this brother and sister-in-law.

They came in, and Signora Anna declared the lunch "Ready, ready!" yet kept them waiting for half-an-hour. Regina had to give minute descriptions of everything she had seen. The three brothers argued about politics, their ideas being widely apart. Gaspare was a *"forcaiuolo"* [one who favours despotism] of the first water, uncompromising and cruel; Massimo was a Tolstoyan Socialist, as much against war as his brother was against liberty; Antonio was Liberal and a little opportunist. Signora Anna made excursions into her sons' conversation in a manner peculiar to herself. No matter what public character was named, she knew the history of his marriage and could give the name of his mistress. On all such matters she appeared singularly well informed.

After lunch Regina retired to her room, lay down, and slept. When she awoke her ears told her it was again raining, and very heavily. Finding herself once more in the big, hard bed under that detestable ceiling, in the gloom of the chilly room, her depression became almost desperation. She jumped up, and resolved to write her letter home. Antonio established her at the bureau in Signora Anna's room, and she began —

"It's pouring. I am in the lowest spirits."

But come! this was idiotic. Why distress her Mamma with useless lamentations?

"Is it not my own doing?" she thought, tearing the note-paper. "Who forced me to change my state, to leave my family, and my home? For the future I am alone. Alone! Even if I were to explain, no one would ever understand!"

Leaning against the desk, she philosophised bitterly.

"Have I the smallest right to complain? No. And there's no sense in complaining when the cause of discomfort is in oneself. My soul is sick; it's a plant torn from the place where it sprang; every little shock withers it. Why should I lament? It's useless. Nothing can cure me, not even Antonio's love. The rain will stop, the fine days will come, I shall have my own house, and needn't be bothered with any one's company; but shall I even then be happy? Who can tell? Yet, after all, what does it matter? One must just accept life as it is, and resign oneself, and try to live to oneself. I don't understand the mania for company. Isn't it possible to live *alone*? Isn't it better? What company so good as one's own? And," she concluded, "it won't last for ever. We've all got to die."

She took this for resignation, and decided to write a letter full of pious lies. But, searching the pigeon-holes for an envelope, she came upon Antonio's letters to his mother during the three months he had served on the Commission at C—e.

Curiosity prompted her to look into them.

In the beginning of the correspondence Antonio described the place with rapid touches, and praised the inhabitants, whom he found energetic, lively, quick-witted.

"I have established myself," he wrote, "in an excellent family, thoroughly honest and sensible. The father is school-master in a neighbouring village, but lives here that his own children may attend secondary schools. The boy Gabriele is smart, active, and ambitious. Gabriella, the girl, is very clever, and intends to be an authoress. The school-master (nick-named the *guendol* [spindle], because he's never quiet for a single moment) is an excellent fellow. He discourses of Raphael and Michaelangelo, making highly original criticisms. For instance, speaking of Raphael (whose surname he never omits), he says 'the painter of *La Madonna delle Seggiole* (plural), etc.' "

In a postscript to this letter Antonio added —

"The Master has suggested a marriage to me — a young lady of noble family, once very wealthy, now come down in the world — twenty-three — neither pretty nor ugly — clever — fortune, 30,000 *lire*."

In another letter Antonio boasted of tender regards from several young ladies in the neighbourhood, but said the Master still held to his idea.

"The Tagliamari are one of the best families in this part. They still have 200,000 *lire* to be divided into four parts. At present the elder daughter has 30,000. The Signora T— is most distinguished, widow of a noble who in his day ran through half-a-million. The Master paints the young lady as a model of wisdom and goodness. *'E' fine, sa,'* he says to me, *'fine, fine, fine!'* [*Fine* = out of the common — delicately exquisite]. She has been educated at Parma in a school for ladies of rank. 'You ought to take her away from this,' he says, 'to Rome — that's her place.' "

"Poor old man," commented Antonio. "He imagines that I am a prince — I with my small berth at the Treasury! — fit to marry and carry off a young lady who is *fine, fine, fine!*"

"To be sure," he wrote in his letter of September 2nd, "30,000 *lire* are not to be despised; but I must first see the lady."

The next letter described the meeting with Regina on the banks of the Po, near her home.

"She is not beautiful. She has a muzzle like a cat; but she is very attractive, cultured, particularly intelligent. The Master must have talked to her of me, for she got red and looked at me in a shy sort of way. She asked if I was really private secretary to a princess. Evidently she would think that much more interesting than to be merely a junior clerk in the Treasury office!

"Yesterday I went to the Tagliamaris' villa. The mother is the most charming of women, a genuine great lady. She told me the whole story of her life, perhaps with intention, but in the most delicate way. She belongs herself to a distinguished family. Her husband was wealthy, but what she calls unlucky speculations, the floods of —80, and other misfortunes, completely ruined him ———"

"What are you about, Regina?" asked Antonio, appearing at the door.

"Oh!" she cried, looking up, "I've discovered some most curious human documents!"

And she held up the letters. He flushed, and sprang to put them back in their pigeon-holes, then changed his mind and began to read them himself

"Aren't you ashamed?" she said; "a *'signorina fine, fine, fine!'* '30,000 *lire* not to be despised,' 'Private secretary to a princess more interesting in her eyes, etc., etc., etc.' You were horrid!"

"Read here! Read here!" said Antonio. "See what I say afterwards!"

But she got up and looked at herself in the glass.

"I declare it's true! I am like a cat!"

"Read here!" repeated Antonio, pursuing her, a letter in his hand.

"We'll read it later. Now I'm going to write home," she said, reseating herself at the bureau.

Antonio took all the letters and set himself to read them over, buried in a corner of the ottoman. Every now and then, while Regina wrote rapidly, he burst into exclamations and little laughs, then suddenly became serious, as if in the lively recollection of the last days passed at C—e he were living his happiness over again.

Later the pair presented themselves at Arduina's apartment, where they were to dine. The authoress lived on the top floor of the palace in a small suite of rooms furnished in rather strange taste and pervaded by what seemed to Regina affected disorder.

Arduina came to meet her guests screaming with delight. She was dressed in a long white overall, her sleeves tucked up and displaying lean, yellow arms.

"Come in!" she said, hiding her hands behind her back; "give me a kiss, Regina!"

Regina kissed her without enthusiasm, and Antonio said

—

"I've explained that to get time for writing you prepare dinner at 5 a.m. God only knows what sort of meal you'll give us!"

"Here's what will reassure you!" said Arduina, revealing floury hands. "I write easily, you know," she went on, "at any hour and in any place; so it's true, sometimes, when the inspiration comes I do sit down with a pen at a corner of the kitchen table. And I get so wrapped up in what I'm doing that the meat's apt to get burned. But what does it matter?" she added, laughing with her rather silly but apparently conceited laugh; "roast meat is no more than roast meat, and art is art. But come in; sit down; amuse yourself with these papers, dear. I'll be with you in a moment, and then you'll give me that information about female benevolence in Mantua."

"Leave her in peace," said Antonio, as before.

"Don't you interfere with me! There's no one cares for your wife so much as I do. Why, I adore her! Do you hear," she repeated, turning to Regina, "I adore you. It seems as if

I'd known you for years. If for no other reason I love you because of your queenly name. By the way, have you seen the queen yet?"

"Of course! in my dreams last night."

"True; you only arrived last night. Still, you've had time. Where did you go this morning? To the Colosseum? Ah! I adore the Colosseum! I'd like to live in it! Have you read *Quo Vadis*?? What! you have not? — and it's the finest of all modern books! I'll make you read it. I'll make you read all sorts of books. I'll introduce you to ever so many authors. I'll take you to intellectual circles, artistic gatherings, to lectures, to wherever one may live not by bread alone —"

"Are we to have bread alone here?" asked Antonio, in feigned alarm; "well, whatever you do, you're not to make Regina write for your paper."

"Why not?"

"I'd kill you — have you taken up!"

Regina laughed, and Arduina disappeared again into the kitchen.

When they were alone Antonio pulled Regina to the looking-glass. "We mayn't be beautiful," he said, kissing her, "but we make a good group. Look, my queen, and laugh; laugh as you used! You don't know what dumps I fall into when I see you displeased."

"I'm not displeased," she said, putting her hands on his breast.

"But neither are you pleased. You aren't my Regina of the river-side. Your face is long, your eyes are far away. You don't seem to care that you're in Rome — Rome of your dreams."

"It's the weather — the weather," she said in a dull voice.

"The weather will clear up," said Antonio, taking her to the window. "You'll see how beautiful Rome is in fine weather! It's almost always fine, and never cold. Just see all the gardens! Even here in Via Torino there's so much green. Shall we look out a bit? It's not raining now."

He opened the French window. Regina stepped out among the flower-pots — filled with consumptive little plants, on whose sparse leaves the melancholy of the grey sky was reflected. She looked down on the wet and deserted street.

Taking shelter under a doorway was a little old woman, dressed in black, and with a meagre basket of lemons by her side. She was hurriedly wringing out her stockings, and she was pale, huddled up, shaking with cold.

Regina had noticed her in the morning, and now, instead of admiring the palaces and gardens — squeezing up her eyes to see distinctly from this altitude of fifth storey — she looked again at the little old woman with the withered lemons.

Antonio pointed out the Costanzi Theatre, and tried to cheer her by saying that Bellincioni was expected at Carnival time.

"Just think, little one! You shall hear Bellincioni!"

But Regina was looking at the muddy pavement, presided over by that little black figure, whose whole fortune consisted in those seven miserable lemons. It seemed as if she had no right to rejoice in the pleasures offered by a great city, when in that same city, at a street corner, while it rained, that little old woman was to be seen tired and shaking with cold. Her soul must have turned sour and sad like the lemons which made op her ridiculous fortune, all her subsistence, the total of her long life of labour and sorrow.

"To be poor and old!" murmured Regina, trying to express her idea to her husband.

"What is it you've got in your head?" he returned; "do you imagine the old crone is suffering? Not she! She's used to that sort of life. If you altered her habits, even if you offered her a more comfortable existence, she'd be perfectly wretched."

Regina remembered her own case, and questioned whether Antonio were not right. Her thoughts flew to her old home, where the firelight would be just beginning to gild the semi-obscurity of the great parlour. The recollection was enough to make her feel sadder still, here in this cold and untidy little city drawing-room.

She was roused from her homesickness by Arduina, who brought tidings.

"The Princess is coming after all! She had promised, but I feared she'd never turn out a day like this. She is so kind! and so clever. I adore her. I must go and dress. Mario!" she cried, running to her husband, who was entering, "Mario, make haste! Put on at least your —"

Sor Mario entered, very grave, very fat, much out of breath. He pressed Regina's hand, gasped, and in compliance with his wife's insistence went away to dress. Regina could not make out if he were pleased or not that the Princess was honouring his board. As for herself she was curious, even anxious, to meet a lady of authentic rank, or, at any rate, of wealth, however little flattering her portrait as drawn by Antonio. It did not occur to her that the Princess in question could not be a very exalted personage if she deigned to sup with Arduina!

"She's old and deaf," Antonio had said; "she sets up to be a critic, and patronises, or at least receives visits from, the worst scribblers in Rome. But oh! these authors! They penetrate everywhere like flies. It's a fine thing, genius! — worth even more than money."

"Certainly," Regina had answered, "genius can buy even money; or, at any rate, can despise it!"

"I think we'd better dress, too," said Antonio thoughtfully, and added hastily, "not, of course, for her sake — for our own."

They descended the stair again, and Regina put on her prettiest silk, her lace scarf, her jewelled brooch, her rings. She powdered herself, and, following Antonio's suggestion, puffed her hair a little at the temples.

"That's it," he said approvingly, "you look another girl."

He changed his own attire, and curled his moustache.

"A perfect fop!" laughed Regina; "you intend to captivate the lady with that moustache!"

"Surely you don't imagine any one could fall in love with me? — not even that *'vecchia corna'* [scarecrow]!"

"I fell in love with you!"

He caught her and kissed her.

"But is it true you were in love? I don't believe it!"

"It was you who didn't fall in love! A *'signorina fine, fine, fine.'* '30,000 *lire* not to be despised,' 'a muzzle like —' "

"Yes; a muzzle, a muzzle, a muzzle!" he said, like a child persisting in some innocent insult.

As they were going forth the second time Signora Anna ran to see Regina's finery. She examined the stuff of her dress, and looked if it were lined with silk, while deep and painful sighs swelled her capacious bosom. In the kitchen Gaspare was heard scolding Marina.

Regina felt acute pleasure in the thought that Gaspare and the mother-in-law were not coming to Arduina's dinner. However, she was no sooner back in the squeezy drawing-room, where they sat awaiting "Madame," than her low spirits returned.

Evening fell rapidly; the shadows deepened like black impalpable clouds. Arduina was busy with final preparations. Sor Mario grunted benevolently, sunk in an arm-chair, his trousers drawn very tight over the knee. Antonio was thoughtful and silent. No one remembered to light the lamps.

Regina felt a weight of sadness upon her soul. What was it? The gloom, the oppression of twilight in this remote and unknown place to which destiny had carried her, or was it the mere reflection of Antonio's unwonted seriousness? She walked to the window, and again looked for the little old woman with the black raiment; lamps white and yellow pierced the cloudy twilight; the pavement glistened; an infinite sadness, a mystery of fearful shadow fell blacker and blacker from the heavens.

The bell rang. In rushed the servant and lighted the gas, barely in time for the great lady's entrance.

With eyes dazzled by this suddenly kindled light, Regina first saw the Princess, and was at once disillusioned. The tall, stout, flat-chested form, the felt hat, fastened by an elastic under the black chignon stuck at the nape of the neck — suggested something masculine. Thick, colourless lips, a small nose slightly awry, small metallic eyes of yellowish-green, marked the pale heavy face. The whole made up a figure which, once seen, was not likely to be forgotten.

"Bon soir," she said, in a soft, harmonious voice, oddly in contrast with her stout and malformed person. She talked on in French while Arduina hurried to relieve her of her hat and handbag. "I am pleased to see you back, Monsieur Venutelli, I received your letter. This is your bride? She is charming!"

Antonio bowed, and Regina looked at her with wondering eyes, saying shyly —

"You are very kind, Signora."

"Beg pardon?" said Madame, turning her left ear to Regina, who nearly laughed, remembering Antonio's mimicry of the deaf Princess.

But Signora Makuline had taken her hand, and was slipping a sapphire ring on one of its fingers, saying "You will allow me? With a thousand good wishes!"

"Oh, thank you! You are really too good!" cried Regina, delighted, and Antonio also looked at the ring and expressed thanks. Then they all sat down; the Princess removed her dirty white gloves, and, to Regina's surprise, displayed hands small as a child's, and covered with flashing rings.

"What shocking weather," said Madame, her small feline eyes not looking at any one. "I've been many years in Rome, but never remember an autumn like this. It's not manners to talk of the weather; but when it becomes a matter of health, the weather has certainly more influence over us than even the most important events of our lives!"

"Monsieur Antonio, this abominable storm will spoil your honeymoon," said Arduina, trying to joke; but Regina, rather offended, muttered some words of protest.

"Beg pardon?" said the Princess.

"Arduina is right," said Antonio; "my wife is, in point of fact, in the very worst of humours."

"*N'est ce pas?* In the worst possible humour!"

"It's not true!" protested Regina, "quite the contrary; I am extremely cheerful."

However, Madame was tiresome enough to observe that during dinner Regina spoke very little.

"I like to be silent! I like listening," explained the bride, rather shortly.

"Well," said the Princess, "there's a certain cachet about a young woman who doesn't talk. A woman's silence suggests something mysterious, something occult; even something charming. George Sand spoke little. One of my uncles was her intimate friend, and he told me George was designedly silent."

"Perhaps you yourself knew George Sand?" said Massimo ungallantly.

"No," replied Madame, unmoved.

"Her mother, perhaps?" murmured Antonio.

"Beg pardon?"

"I've been reading an article on George Sand's mother," said Antonio louder. "Most interesting! She was a woman of fiery genius, and of fiery heart, too, whose adventures no doubt influenced her daughter's imagination."

"Where did you see that article?" cried Arduina; "we'll reproduce it!"

Sor Mario, bending low over his plate, shook his head, and emitted a perhaps unintentional grunt.

Tedious talk followed of the adventures and romances of George Sand. Arduina declared that the novels were uninteresting. She liked modern books, and *Quo Vadis?* above all others.

"*Dio Mio!*" said Antonio, "do stop about *Quo Vadis?* And really, you know, it's not precisely modern!"

Regina listened and held her peace. The talk was entirely of books, theatres, authors. The Princess told some story of Tolstoy, whom she knew personally. Towards the close of the repast, violent discussion arose between Massimo and Arduina about a great contemporary Italian poet. and novelist — not only about his works, but about his private life. Arduina spoke against the master, hatred darting from her eyes, venom from her lips. She reproached him even for having grown old, bald, and ugly before his time. Massimo, red with fury, withered his sister-in-law with looks of supreme contempt.

"Worms!" he cried, forgetting he sat at her table. "See what you writers are! Merely to blacken the greatest and purest glory of Italy you stoop to absolute nonsense, and don't even know what it is you are saying!"

"Peace! peace!" laughed Antonio.

But now a most extraordinary thing happened. Sor Mario spoke. He had not read one line of the poet's, nor had any scandal to tell of him, but he related: —

"I saw him once at Anzio; he was riding along the shore got up entirely in white; white coat, white hat, white gloves, on a white horse —"

"White gloves on a horse?" queried Massimo, laughing foolishly.

Regina asked the Princess her opinion of the author in question, and the lady replied —

"To tell the truth, I'm not one of his blind admirers; but his prose is certainly lovely — bewitching, like music —"

"True," said Antonio; "but one very quickly forgets what he says."

"That's just my impression," said Regina; "it's music without any echo."

Massimo shook his head; his long hair stood on end like that of an infuriated baby.

"People were coming down to bathe," continued Sor Mario, "and they stared at him and laughed. Some were in hopes the poet would tumble off his white horse —"

About nine, while Arduina was pouring out coffee, the Princess's lady companion arrived; a queer-looking little creature with dark, malignant countenance, a long, pointed chin, and minute, glittering eyes. Small, shrivelled, dressed in grey, this curious person seemed half-animal to Regina, a kind of human rodent. And, really, no sooner had she entered than the room was pervaded and animated by what seemed the scratching and running about of a rat; little cries and exclamations; hand-claspings and kisses which suggested bites, questions, remarks, and, above all, looks which seemed to Regina inquisitive, anxious, mocking, and impudent.

"Take a cup of coffee if you care for it, Marianna," said Arduina, while the companion felt the Princess's forehead with both her hands.

"Why, your head's burning!" she said; "have you been eating a great deal? What have you eaten? Whatever have you made her eat? "she went on, turning to Arduina. "Oh, yes, I'll have some coffee, though I know very well it won't be good! What wretched cups! They're as small as I am!"

Antonio had hinted to his wife that Marianna was commonly supposed to be the Princess's daughter; and Regina, watching her, thought —

"It's clearly the case of the mountain and the mouse."

Apparently, Marianna read her thought, for she turned her little head with the alertness of a mouse, surprised by some slight sound; then came and sat beside the bride, balancing her cup on the palm of her hand, and saying maliciously —

"That husband of yours is a villain; keep your eye on him if you don't want him in every sort of mischief."

"I think you're the villain this time," said Antonio; "what are you insinuating suspicions into my wife for?"

"Because I pity her."

"And pray why?" asked Regina.

"Why? Just because you're married! Here comes another villain," continued Marianna, pointing to Massimo, who had drawn nearer; "for that matter they're all villains, the men! And the good ones are worse than the bad. The good ones are stupid. I don't care if men are bad, terrible even, so long as they have some genius and will-power."

"If I had at least these attributes —" began Massimo, looking at her with his insolent eyes.

"You can't have them," she interrupted; "geniuses never oil their hair as you do. "It's oiled, signora, isn't it?"

"I—don't know," said Regina, "I think not."

"Ah, poor dear! you haven't found it out! You'll never find anything out."

"How silly she is!" thought Regina.

And again she fancied that the young lady read her thoughts.

"Oh, you're thinking me a fool!" she said; "but listen here. I've forgotten to tell you something I always tell people when I meet them first."

"We know what it is," interjected Massimo and Antonio; but Marianna went on —

"Once, seven years ago, at Odessa, the house I was living in went on fire. I was in a top room, all hemmed in by flames — impossible to get me out. The smoke was already blinding and stifling me, and I heard the roar of the flames quite close. I believed in God no more then than now; however, I did feel the need of recourse to some supernatural being, some occult or omnipotent power. So I made a vow. I promised if I were saved, I would henceforth always speak the truth. At that moment the floor fell in. I lost my senses; and when I came to, I found myself safe and sound in the arms of a most hideous fireman. 'How have you managed it?' I asked. 'Like this,' he answered, and told how he had rescued me at great peril of his life. 'Oh, very well,' I said, 'I suspect you're exaggerating; but I'm grateful, all the same, and I'll always remember you; the more vividly that your ugliness is quite unforgettable.' "

Regina laughed. "I seem to be reading a Russian story," she said.

"But is that little tale true?" asked Massimo; and Antonio added —

"You gave me a slightly different version."

"Now you're trying to be witty," said Marianna, "but it's no use. You can't be witty, except for women you wish to please, and you don't in the least wish to please me."

"Oh, yes, I wish to please you," said Massimo; "it's the sole object of my life."

"Well, I don't appreciate your jokes. There are plenty of women very inferior to me, and you won't succeed in pleasing even them."

"I shall succeed with the superior ones, perhaps."

"I don't think there are many women superior to me; if there are, you'll never get within a stone's throw of them."

"Then I suppose I'm one of the inferiors?" said Regina, for the sake of saying something.

"Yes, because you're married. A superior woman never marries. Or if in some spell of unconsciousness she does take a husband, she repents at once. If I wished to pay you a compliment, I should say I believe you are repenting."

"By Jove!" said Antonio, "that's not a matter of joke."

"Do you always tell the Princess the truth?" asked Regina.

"Of course — she keeps me only for that purpose," said Marianna, looking, not without affection, at the Princess. Madame was telling Arduina a story of her aunt.

"— the handsomest and smartest woman in Paris," she said. "I've told you of her marriage, haven't I? They married her at fifteen to the lover of a lady who remained her friend for ten years, her friend, her confidante, her guide. For ten years she never guessed —"

Sor Mario, buried in his arm-chair, was listening, fighting with sleepiness and the desire to pick his teeth.

Marianna began to abuse Nietzsche and his opinion of women, but Regina's attention wandered to the Princess's stories, scraps of which reached her across the screaming and the audacities of the younger lady.

"If women understood him, they'd agree," said Massimo; "they don't approve because they don't understand."

"They do better than approve, they refute him," said Marianna.

"If Gaspare were here," said Antonio, "he'd soon settle the question."

Regina's soul shivered at the mere recollection of Gaspare, and his mother, and the servant.

"Her second husband was a Spaniard," narrated the Princess, "the handsomest man you could see, and acquainted with all the literary personages of his time. But his conduct —"

"The education of women has not even begun," said Marianna, turning to Regina; "women will never have any sense till men begin to tell them the truth."

"But what is the truth?" asked Massimo; "truth between man and woman only comes out when they quarrel."

"That's true up to a certain point. I'm always wondering why truth is so disagreeable to everybody. They tell me I'm cracked because I never tell lies. Nobody cares, because my words don't really interest the person I'm talking to. But let's suppose this lady were to tell her husband all she was thinking, her real impressions, her real idea of him, his family, his friends. I'm certain Signor Antonio would fall quite sick —"

"Regina!" cried Antonio, in feigned alarm, "can this be true?"

Regina laughed, but a shudder as of great cold interrupted her false merriment. The Princess was continuing her story.

" 'Jeanne!' said my aunt, hammering at the door of the room where he was with the lady's maid, 'hand me the *Figaro*, if you please.' My aunt was discreet. That was all she said."

"And what did they reply?" asked Sor Mario, sitting up straight, his toothpick in his fingers.

"My dear!" said Arduina, "what a stupid question!"

Before leaving, the Princess invited Regina to her Friday receptions. Regina promised to go; but that night, when she was comfortably in bed, lulled in the quiet and warmth of the first half-slumber, she said —

"Antonio, do you know what? I've taken a great dislike to that Princess!"

"Why? She's all right."

"Yes, but — you see —"

"What?"

She paused — then went on, her voice rather sleepy: "Do you remember that female lion-tamer we saw at Parma? She looked at women in such a strange way. I couldn't think whom the Princess reminded me of, and I thought, and thought — Her eyes are just like that lion-tamer's! Didn't you see how she stared at me?"

"Well? She liked you. Who knows but she'll leave you something in her will!"

"Is she really rich?"

"The deuce she is! A millionaire."

"Her gloves were so dirty."

"Did you see her rings?"

"What do I care for rings if the gloves are dirty?"

Regina relapsed into silence; then she laughed softly, and presently fell into a light sleep. She dreamt she was in a wood on the banks of the Po towards Viadana. The shining waters were churned by a mill, but the mill was a castle with vast rooms hung with red, and the castle belonged to Madame Makuline. The Princess was dead, but her soul had climbed up a poplar-tree, through the silver leaves of which shone the river, a crystalline blue. The mill wheel roared like thunder, and Regina, seated on the entrance stair of the castle, was washing her feet in a runnel of greenish water which overflowed the steps. A white duck came to peck at the little toe of her right foot, and laughed. Regina laughed herself. She was vaguely aware she was dreaming, for she was analysing her sentiments, and knew that a mill is a mill, that ducks can't laugh, and souls can't climb poplar-trees. None the less, she was oppressed by mysterious fear, by a sense of intolerable repugnance and distress.

Antonio heard her laugh, that vague, strange laugh from the profundity of dream which is like a voice from the depths of a well.

"She's having pleasant visions — she is happy, my little queen!" he thought, much moved.

CHAPTER III

THAT winter was cold in Rome, and the rain seemed endless. Even days which began fine grew suddenly dark; the wind rose, and down came a deluge. Luckily, the showers did not last. Soon the pavements dried, the clouds blew away, the sky became blue, as if smiling at an accomplished jest. The people, however, came home with their clothes drenched, their boots soaking, their chests racked with coughs and their bosoms with evil temper.

"Your famous Roman sky seems to me a lunatic asylum without any warders," said Regina to her husband; "a bedlam where the raging clouds do whatever they like."

And that rainy winter proved one of the saddest in the young wife's whole life. True, she loved Antonio; the first day he left her to resume his work she felt a profound emptiness, and knew herself henceforth attached to him as firmly as the bark to the tree. But existence in the Casa Venutelli, association with her mother-in-law, the presence of Sor Gaspare, the gloomy bedroom with those immense arm-chairs, heavy as vulgar destiny, proved altogether unbearable.

And Rome was horrible under the continuous rain, which had something malicious and mocking about it. People hurried through the streets, their faces livid; the women showed petticoat-edges pasted with mud; the heaven itself was soiled; and Regina's soul made shipwreck amid this ocean of mud and water. She would come in drenched and exasperated; within-doors it was cold; there was no fire, and there was continual annoyance. She was uncomfortable at the table in those high round chairs, opposite the sarcastic countenance of Massimo, Sor Gaspare's red visage, the enormous panting bosom of Signora Anna. At night she was worse off still on that lumpy mattress, in the cold air which was pervaded by the rumble of the trams, and the melancholy rolling of purposeless carriages.

Was this the life of Rome? Nay, was this Rome? What! This the famous Corso — this narrow, smelly, mud-splashed street, with its carriage loads of old and hideous women, its foot-passengers squashing and treading upon each other like flocks of stupid sheep? And was this St. Peter's? Regina had expected it larger. That the Pincio? It was not beautiful. The Colosseum? She had supposed it more sublime. Where were the grandeur and magnificence? She could discover neither; everything appeared melancholy and hollow. She felt no astonishment at anything except her own impressions, and found a dreary pleasure in the thought that among all the provincials who came to Rome to be overwhelmed, she alone saw things in their true light. Sometimes she made exaggerated display of her own superiority; but self-examination convinced her it was tainted by personal rancour, and she felt sadder than ever. What was it she wanted? What did she expect? She felt sick of some deep wound. In vain she told herself the winter would pass, she would soon leave this distasteful house where everything seemed to freeze and suffocate her. Alas! her own sweet home was never, never, to be found again!

After hurried visits to monuments and museums, and a promise of more leisurely re-inspection — promise made by all who fix their dwelling in Rome, and seldom fulfilled under months and years — Regina and Antonio began the (more interesting) round of *appartamenti* to be let.

Between the salary of the one and the dowry of the other, they counted on a fixed income of 3,000 *lire*. Antonio received a small addition from the Princess, who had, however, other advisers, and only consulted him in certain affairs which brought her into collision with the Treasury. The means of the young couple would not therefore allow them more than a small apartment at fifty or sixty lire a month. They began their search in Via Massimo d'Azeglio, where a possibly suitable suite of rooms was to fall vacant in January. Regina, oppressed with doubts, entered a lordly entrance hall, from which led a principal staircase of fine marble. The second stair was perfectly dark at the bottom, but got brighter and brighter as it went up. Regina began to count its steps.

"Eleven, twenty-two, thirty-three, forty-four, fifty-five, sixty-three — you don't tell me there are more?"

She stopped, her heart beating violently. Antonio smiled indulgently; he took his little queen by the arm and helped her up; the higher they went the steeper the steps became.

"Eighty-eight; ninety-nine. Goodness! more? "

"Courage!"

"A hundred and ten!"

By the grace of God they had arrived; but before the door was opened, the trembling and panting wife had said bitterly to herself, "Is this where Regina is to live? Never! never!"

The apartment was suitable and pretty; a real nest in the heart of the city's great forest of stone. Two windows looked out on a garden; the rest on a court none too clean.

Regina declared at once that there was no air and no light, and, in fact, that the rooms would not do at all.

"No air?" repeated Antonio; "no light? I should have said just the opposite! Look! there's a garden down there! And it's so close to my work and in the very centre of the town!"

"No. I want windows on the street."

"Well, then, we'll look for windows on the street; but, mind you, we shan't find a more comfortable little place for our rent."

"You think not?" she said, unbelievingly.

Soon she was obliged to believe. They spent a fortnight in weary pilgrimage, revolving at first about the Esquiline, the Quirinal, and the Villa Ludovisi; and Regina, half vexed, half amused, sang smilingly, *Senza tetto e senza cuna* [With neither roof-tree nor home]. Then she became taciturn and very tired, dragging herself along with an air of desperation. They consulted a house-agent, who proved a delusion and a snare. He gave them a score of addresses, and they gradually went up the Corso exploring all the adjacent streets, as a traveller ascends a river seeking an unknown land and an undiscoverable source. Antonio would have put up with a long walk to his office if he could thus have contented Regina;

but Regina would not be contented. All the suites were either too large and costly, or so cramped and cold that a single glance froze and tightened the heart. Regina saw one *mezzanino* (entresol) of four immense, perfectly dark rooms, inhabited by what seemed an infinite number of smartly attired young ladies. It suggested a tomb for the living, and she fled horrified. It was shocking! And this was Rome! These were the habitations which Rome offered to those who had long dreamed of her! Tombs for the living, obscure caverns, dens for slaves! A thousand times preferable the poorest cabins of the villages on the Po, full of liberty and light!

And still it rained; and Regina, unused to walking, got more and more tired as she wandered about, seeking a nest in which to fold her wounded wings. She had lost her looks, and was thin and pale; as the days passed on she became irritable. Sometimes she looked at Antonio with mocking commiseration. Was there anything more ridiculous than a fine young man dragged round by an ugly little wife, on the search for lodgings at fifty *lire* a month? What a wretched business was civilisation! She gazed enviously at the passers by, thinking feverishly —

"They know where to go! They have houses even if they are dens, and needn't traipse about the streets, like us, looking for a refuge. We are stray dogs, unable to find a hole to die in!"

And she looked yearningly at inaccessible country houses, thinking bitterly —

"I, too, had a home — a home full of poetry and light. I shut myself out with my own hands, and never, never will it be mine again!"

At this thought tears welled into her eyes. Weary and silent she stepped along at her husband's side, and Antonio looked at her with pity, guessing the cause of her discontent. There were times, however, when he also felt irritated. Why had she refused the apartment in the Via d'Azeglio? What more, what better did she want?

They came in, worn out, both of them, and cross. Regina shrank away into remote regions of the big, cold bed, and Antonio sometimes heard smothered sobs which, instead of moving, vexed him all the more. What was the matter with her? Well, really now, what was it? What was the matter? Surely a sensible girl like her couldn't be crying because rooms to her fancy were not discoverable at the first go off?

"No," he told her later, "I thought you didn't love me any longer; I thought you repented having married me. I felt humiliated and wretched like a whipped child."

Regina, far away from him in the great cold bed, had a hopeless feeling of abandonment. She seemed to have lost herself in a boundless, frozen plain; the screaming breath of the tram reproduced the drive of the rain, the roar of the wet wind. All around was cloud, and only far, far, far away shone the crimson of a lighted hearth, glimmered the silver of a river —

"Why did I leave my home?" she asked herself, dully; "I've let myself be rooted up like a poplar; and now, like the poplar-wood, I've been carted here to make part of this odious construction which is called a great city. I also shall warp and rot — get worm-eaten, fall —"

Then she asked herself did she really love Antonio?

There were moments when she answered "No;" other moments when she melted at the thought of him.

"I shall make him miserable! He told me what to expect in Rome; a modest life, a middle-class family. Did I not accept it? Well — well! we shall all die! We must be resigned to our destiny. Every hour will come, and the hour of death is the most certain of all. To die! To have no more suffering from homesickness — never again to see my mother-in-law, Arduina, Sor Gaspare, that maid Marina; to wander no further in the rain seeking an apartment! No — I don't want to torment Antonio any more. Is it his fault that all the miseries of civilisation interfere between him and me? He didn't know it, and neither did I know it. But we shall all die at last! We must be resigned, and go and live in Via d'Azeglio. The days will pass there as they pass everywhere."

She slept, pleased with her philosophy; and, of course, she dreamed of the distant home, the woods, the blazing logs, the windows radiant in the sunset, the kitten on the window-sill contemplating the stem of the poplar-tree. Next morning daylight met her in the detestable Venutelli room; she lay under the incubus of the grey ceiling; she must get up, endure the cold, the rain, the company of Signora Anna! Resignation? It was very well in theory; in practice her nerves revolted fiercely against the reality.

At last, after a month of vain search, more in the end from weariness than from good-will, Regina consented to the suite in the Via d'Azeglio for one year. Yet on the very day of signing the agreement she repented, abandoning all self-control.

"Was it worth while leaving my home and coming to Rome to live in a box? I shall be suffocated! I shall die!" she cried.

Nor could Antonio longer contain himself

"Can't you say what it is you want?" he exclaimed in a fury. "Did you imagine you were marrying a prince? You knew all I had to offer! You told me a hundred times you hadn't corrupted your soul with vain ambitions; you said you were robust and unselfish; you said you didn't ask impossible things of life! Why don't you look back instead of always looking ahead? Didn't you say you were a bit of a Socialist? Well, then, why don't you compare your condition with that of millions and millions of other women?"

She wept, leaning her forehead against the window-pane. Of course it was raining, and it seemed to her that the heavens wept with her. She knew Antonio was right, although he looked at the matter merely on its material side, and did not understand the real causes of her discontent.

However, she laughed through her tears, laughed proudly and ironically.

"If you speak like that, we are done for," she said.

He moderated his voice. "I speak crossly," he said, "but I mean well. I am tired of seeing you so dissatisfied, Regina. What do you want me to do? What can I give you beyond what I have — that is, all my work, all my love, a good position, a morrow without cares?"

"He doesn't understand," she thought; "I shall suffer, but no one shall perceive it, he least of all. I shall be always solitary. Well! I don't need any one, do I? I'm strong, am I not? Are you proposing to let your heart be seen, Regina, by all these odious little people?" And she shook her wings like a little bird which has tumbled into dirty water.

Antonio came nearer, and they made it up.

"You know," he said, stroking her hair, "the agreement is only for a year. Who knows what mayn't happen in a year? I shall apply for a rise, get a step; then we shall have our house rent free. I'll try to get extra work; perhaps Madame will put her whole affairs into my hands. Our position will improve. We'll take a larger flat — with a shorter stair. You'll get used to the stair. Some day you'll laugh at having cried for such trifles. Now wash your face. How ugly you are with those red eyes!"

"Ugly or pretty, I'm always myself!" she said, plunging her face into cold water; then she scrubbed it with the rough towel, powdered herself, put on the lace scarf, and consented to go up and visit Arduina.

They found that lady's door open, and from the vestibule her voice was heard in the drawing-room.

"Who's there?" asked Regina.

There was no one.

"What are you doing? Talking-to yourself?" asked Antonio.

The authoress coloured, laughed, screamed, and con-fessed she was rehearsing a speech for his Excellency the

Minister of Public Instruction, whom she was going to ask for a subscription for her paper.

"Does Mario know? I'll ask him what he thinks of it," said Antonio.

"For pity's sake, don't!" she cried.

"Doesn't it make you shy asking for money?" asked Regina, astonished.

"Why should I be shy? Every one does it. It's not for myself I ask — it's for the journal, which is doing terribly badly. I've asked for a subscription and an audience of the Queen. And to-morrow I must go to my uncle the Senator and learn —"

"I'd sooner die than beg from anybody!" said Regina.

"But why? "asked the other, astounded. "What harm does it do? If you were a literary woman, and ran a paper and had an idea to sustain and to make triumphant —"

"Spare us — my dear goose!" interrupted Antonio.

"And hold my tongue, I suppose? So you never ask for money? Nor take advantage of anything useful which comes in your way? Why do you stare, Regina? It's all a question of getting used to it."

"Getting used to it? That's another matter." Regina felt a flood of contemptuous words rise to her lips, but she kept silence, thinking she would not deign even to reply. She walked to the window and saw the little black-dressed woman with the seven lemons, in the corner by the shut door; but she no longer felt the melancholy this sight had waked in her on her first coming to Rome. *She had got used to it.*

"The Princess often asks for you," said Arduina, "won't you come to her next reception? Now you've found a house and are getting settled, you can begin to return visits and make acquaintances."

"What good are acquaintances to me?"

"What good are they to others? Don't be posing as an oddity," said Antonio, a little sharply.

"Shall I have enough drawing-room to receive them in?" returned Regina in that cold voice of hers which froze her husband's heart.

He was dismayed and silent. Arduina, however, did not understand.

"Your drawing-room will be small," she said, "that means you can't have a large circle. But you'd better come to the Princess's. It's in your husband's interest."

"No. I don't know what to make of your princesses," said Regina; but immediatcly she repented, remembering her vows of a few minutes before. She laughed, joked, turned everything upside down in the little drawing-room, and promised to go with Arduina to see the Senator uncle.

"I'll tell him I'm a poetess, and ask him to get me an audience of the Queen," she said gaily.

"My dear child, capital!" cried Arduina in ecstasy. "Yes! yes! we'll go together!"

But Regina made a roguish gesture, moving her hand like a fan with her thumb on the point of her nose; and the other laughed, more than ever sure that her sister-in-law was half imbecile.

Next day they went together to the distinguished uncle, who turned out only a second cousin of Arduina's mother. The authoress had dressed herself up. She wore a black dress much wrinkled on the shoulders, a yellow straw hat trimmed with poppies; a feather boa so thin and worn that people turned their heads to look at it. Regina, also in black, with her inevitable lace scarf, seemed beside her almost a beauty.

The Senator lived in Via Sistina on a fourth floor. That comforted Regina greatly. If a senator could exist on a fourth floor she might get accustomed to a fifth. Still more was she comforted when she saw the Senator's apartment. It was very dark, and furnished with a meagreness nearer to discomfort than to simplicity. A few aspidistras, whose large leaves glistened feebly in the chiaroscuro, adorned the ante-room and the two dreary reception-rooms through which the ladies were conducted by an elderly chambermaid. There was a portrait in oils of an old man, lean and red, with protruding blue eyes and beautiful white hair (suggestive, however, of a wig), who smiled sarcastically out of his yellow background. The portrait was reflected in a cracked mirror; and the vast, dreary, dark room seemed animated by the two figures — immobile against the yellow background of the picture and the mirror — looking at each other, smiling sarcastically, sharing some half mocking, half melancholy thought.

Regina glanced at herself in the glass, and fancied that the two figures, the one in front and the one behind, had fixed their mocking eyes upon herself; then she turned suddenly, for she saw advancing silently against the yellow background of the room a third figure exactly like the other two. It was the Senator.

"Oh, *brava!*" he said briskly, turning to Arduina and looking at Regina.

"Let me introduce my sister-in-law," said Arduina; "she has been married one month."

"How stupid she is!" thought Regina, but had herself nothing to say when the old man congratulated her on having been married a month.

"Oh, *brava! brava!*" he repeated; and Arduina quickly explained the occasion of her visit.

The old Senator again said *"Brava! brava!"* but Regina understood perfectly that he was out of sympathy with the entire affair.

"Oh, *brava! brava!* It's your paper, to be sure; and devoted to the woman question?"

"No, no! Still — yes! to women's questions, properly understood."

"I see! — women's questions properly understood. Well, teach the women to work. Habituate them to the idea of work, of earning their living, of independence. When I go abroad, especially when I go to England, I am immensely struck by the 'moral physiognomy' of the women — so different from our women at home — from you —"

"But I do work!" protested Arduina.

"Your work is not sufficiently profitable if you require subscriptions!" cried Regina.

"Oh, *brava! brava!* And you, I suppose, write too? "

"Oh, no! I don't do anything!"

The Senator looked at her with his mocking and melancholy blue eyes; and she blushed, remembering she had never worked in her life.

"I want subscriptions," said Arduina, "because in Italy work is not yet remunerative. But in the future — the generations we shall educate —," etc., etc., etc.

She made a long speech about the future generations, and returned to her starting point: the urgent need for a subscription.

"Bless the girl! She shall have the subscription!" said the Senator, who was still looking at Regina.

"And the audience also?"

He promised the audience. At that moment he was smiling just as he smiled in the portrait and in the mirror; and Regina perceived that he pitied the poor Italian journalist and was thinking of the moral physiognomy of the working Englishwomen.

"But why the audience?" asked, Regina, emboldened and imitating the Senator's smile; "subscriptions are all very well — up to a certain point — but the audience —"

"It's a moral support. With reference to my principles —"

"Yes, yes; a moral support," interrupted the Senator, still smiling.

Regina felt rebellious. This man who found the moral physiognomy of the women abroad so different from the moral physiognomy of the incapable, enslaved Italians — why did he not make Arduina understand the errors of her method?

"But," she cried, almost angrily, "if you can't do without assistance, moral or material, it's better — to do nothing at all! We are always despoilers; and it's all one if we despoil fathers, husbands, lovers, or royalty and the Government!

"My dear, you don't understand!" said Arduina, who, had not taken in Regina's meaning; "you talk like that because you've never felt the need —"

"You are from Lombardy?" asked the Senator, who, with his hands folded on his breast, amused himself twiddling his thumbs.

"I'm an incapable and useless Italian," she replied, very contemptuous of herself.

"But you are young. Why don't you write?"

"What's the use of writing," she asked, meeting his eye mockingly, "if it's only to ask for subscriptions and audiences?"

The old man, still twiddling his thumbs, rose and took a step towards the young lady.

"What's your impression of Rome?"

"Bad! It bores me! Town life is so wretched and gloomy. Besides, it does nothing but rain," said Regina, and laughed.

"What makes him stare so?" she thought; "can I possibly have the moral physiognomy of the English ladies?"

The old man stood in front of her, his back to Arduina, whose presence he seemed to have forgotten.

"Town life is wretched," he said, "because it's empty. Our women are full of useless aspirations, and, as you say, despoil their men, who deteriorate working too hard for their families. In those societies where the woman works also, the man has a free margin for the development of his abilities. In England —"

"But what can we do," repeated Regina, "if we haven't been brought up to work?"

The Senator did not appear to hear her. He drew a picture of English society where the whole middle class, the professional and the working sections alike kept themselves up in literature, art, politics, and promoted free discussion on all subjects; where the women were not bored, because they worked.

"They have hundreds of authoresses, translators, newspaper correspondents, who make more than 10,000 *lire* every year, some a great deal more. Mrs. H. W. — do you know how much she gets for each of her books?"

Regina did not know.

"More than seven or eight thousand pounds." Arduina hastily made the calculation.

"More than 200,000 *lire?*" she said, awe-struck. "Dear me! I shouldn't like to make all that!"

"Why not?"

"Because I should go off my head!"

"But in Italy —" began Regina.

"In Italy, too, a woman may earn a great deal. Work! work! there's the secret."

Regina left the old Senator's dark and melancholy house with a new ray of light in her mind. Work! work! Yes, she also wanted work! She would begin to write. If she was no good for anything else, at least she might make some money.

She wanted work; she wanted money; above all she wanted to live.

"I'll escape from this narrow circle which is strangling me. I'll look life in the face. I'll lose myself in the great streets of Rome, feel the soul of the crowd, write descriptions of the lives of the poor, of those who are bored, of those who seem happy and are not — life as it is —"

When she got home she looked round with pitying eyes. Yes! Signora Anna and the maid, Arduina and the brothers-in-law, the whole environment and the souls set in it, all moved her to pity. And this pity gave her a feeling of soft sweet warmth, of profound well-being.

Antonio had not come in, and Regina stayed in her room. She took a book and sat by the closed window. Evening came on. Little by little the warmth which had been the result of the expedition died out. The light failed. Great impalpable veils fell down round her, slowly, one after the other. The book she held in her hand was so futile that she had not been able to read two pages. She shut it up and looked at the sky. But the line of sky above the ugly opposite facade was so ashen and heavy that it gave her the impression of a sheet of metal. Only one little red cloud, a wandering flame, illuminated the ashes of this dead heaven.

Suddenly Regina felt a great emptiness, a great cold within herself. That little cloud had reminded her of the distant hearth fire in her home; of all the little, simple, voiceless things which yet were greater and brighter than all glory, all riches. She thought —

"Work! Money-making! Even if it were possible it couldn't give me back my home, my past, my atmosphere! One little reality is worth more than the greatest of ideals."

"What is the Ideal?" she thought further, still watching the slow passing of the cloud; and she copied the old Senator's smile, remembering how he also imagined he had such lofty ideals!

CHAPTER IV

ON Christmas Eve Regina went early to bed, complaining of an indisposition which made Signora Anna thoughtful, but was not suggestive to Antonio. He knew, or thought he knew, the subtle malady which was consuming his wife. He knew its name: Nostalgia; and he left to time the responsibility of its cure.

Regina was no sooner in bed than she began to remember and to meditate. Christmas in Rome! She saw over again the carts of live fowls being drawn through the streets; the ladies passing quickly along with parcels in their hands; the fat pork-butchers looking out from their nauseating shops with the importance of Roman emperors; his Excellency an Under-Secretary of State standing in front of Dagnino's window with a visage of terrible perplexity.

She reflected upon the quarrel which had broken out among Signora Anna, Gaspare and the maid about wax candles. Marina had gone up and down the stair at least twenty times, each time coming back with parcels, but each time forgetting something. During the whole of lunch and the whole of dinner the brothers, their mother and the girl had discussed the supplies of food.

Well! it had all produced in Regina a sort of spiritual indigestion. Alone in the great bed, shivering, crumpled up, she was conscious of an unspeakable depression. She felt like a little snail which hears the rain pattering on its shell. And she thought continually of the distant hearth, the grey night illumined by the snow. Behind the voices and the laughter which vibrated from the dining-room, behind the painful screech of the trams, behind the buzz of the merry-making city, she heard the whistling of trains in the station. Some of the whistles laughed, some wept; one, faint and tender, seemed the voice of a questioning child; one was like a zigzag on a black sky; one mocked at Regina. "Are you ready to go? Not you! not you! It's your own fault. Here you've come, and here you stay! Good-bye! Good-bye!"

She worked herself into a passion. She was angry even with his Excellency, who had looked in at Dagnino's window, fixing his gold eye-glasses. She asked, exasperated, who were all those strange people laughing and joking in the dining-room?

Antonio soon joined her. She pretended to sleep. He was solicitous and touched her gently. Feeling her very cold, he drew nearer to warm her. She was moved, but did not open her eyes.

The hours passed. The city became silent. It slept, like a greedy child to whom dainties are promised. Regina could not sleep, but she was not insensible to the kindness and the warmth. The little snail had looked out from the window of its shell and seen the sun shining on the grass. Melodious sound of bells trembled and oscillated on the quiet night One seemed to come from beyond a river, grave, sonorous, nostalgic. To her surprise Regina found herself repeating certain lines of Prati's, which she was not conscious of having known before. Whence did they arise? Perhaps from the depths of her subconsciousness, evoked by the nostalgic song of the bells on that first Christmas of exile.

> "Dreaming of home and of the country ways,
> The village feastings and the green spring days."

She repeated the lines many times to herself with sing-song monotony, which ended by putting her asleep. She dreamed she was at home. Her young sister played "Stefánia" on her mandoline. Regina saw the mandoline distinctly and its inlaid picture of a troubadour with a mandola. The little black cat was listening, rather bored, and yawning ostentatiously. Outside fell the evening, violet-grey, velvety, silent. Suddenly a perplexed visage with gold-rimmed eye-glasses started up behind the window-panes. Regina laughed so loud that she woke her husband.

"Whatever is it?" he asked in alarm.

"His Excellency," she murmured, still dreaming. Next morning, on awakening, Antonio found Regina in tears.

"You were laughing last night — now you cry," he said, with slight impatience. "Can't you explain what on earth's the matter with you?"

"Nothing."

"Nothing! You're crying! What are you crying about? I can't bear it any longer! Why do you torment me like this?"

She took his hand and passed it over her eyes. He repented.

"What is it? What is it? Tell me — only tell me, Regina, Regina!" he urged, tenderly and anxiously.

"It has nothing to do with you," she said, hiding her face on his breast, "it's all my own fault. I don't know why, but I can't conquer the past — the homesickness — and I'm afraid of the future."

He also felt a mysterious fear.

"Why are you afraid of the future?"

"Because — I suppose because we are poor. Rome is so horrid for the poor."

"But, Regina, we aren't poor!" he exclaimed with increasing alarm, "and, anyhow, don't we love each other?"

"To love — to vegetate — it's not enough — not enough," she murmured.

"But you knew all about it, Regina!"

"I knew and I know. I'm furious with myself that I can't overcome my aversion to this *bourgeois* life."

"But after all — down there at your home — what sort of life were you leading?"

"Oh, Antonio! I had dreams!"

Antonio understood the anguish in that cry, and tried to lull her sorrow for the time being, administering as to a sick person an innocuous soothing mixture.

"Listen," he said, "it's just that you're a bit home-sick. You'll find that in a little time you'll get used to it all. I admit our life is rather cramped, but do you suppose the rich people are happy?"

"It's not riches I want!"

"What is it then? *I*'m not vulgar, am I? or stupid? After all, it's with *me* you've got to live. Be reasonable. You shall make your own surroundings just as you like them. Meantime, to cure you of your homesickness, you can go home to your own country whenever you like."

The soothing mixture produced the desired effect. Regina raised a radiant face.

"In the spring?" she cried impetuously, "in the spring?"

"Whenever you wish. And you'll see that in course of time —"

But the course of time only augmented Regina's trouble.

The night of San Stefano Antonio took her to the Costanzi Theatre, to the *Sedie* [the cheapest reserved seats]. She put on her smartest frock, her best trinkets, and went to the theatre, resolved to be astonished at nothing, for had she not already been to the theatre at Parma? The Costanzi was magnificent; an enormous casket where the most beautiful pearls in the capital shone on feminine shoulders resplendent with *"Crema Venus."* Even the pit was splendid, a field of great flowers sprinkled with the dew of gems and gold. And in spite of her experience at the Parma theatre, Regina felt sufficiently bewildered. Her short-sighted eyes, dazzled by the brilliant light, were half shut; and it was much the same with the eyes of her soul. She raised her opera glass and looked at one of the boxes. The lady there was plain in feature, but extremely fashionable; Regina thought her painted, decked with false hair, her eyes artificially darkened. None the less, she envied her.

She looked round. Little by little her envy swelled, overflowed, became hateful. She would have liked the theatre burned down. Then she perceived that a lady near her was looking at the boxes just as she was, perhaps with the same criminal envy in her heart. She felt ashamed of herself, put down the glass, and after this did not look at the seats above her again. But on her own level, in the furthest row of the *Poltrone* [seats next above the *Sedie*], she saw a long row of smartly dressed men and women who always and only stared at the boxes. No one looked at the *Sedie*. The people there were an inferior race, or actually non-existent for the ladies and gentlemen in the *Poltrone*.

"We are nothing! We are the microbes which fill the void," thought Regina.

Then she perceived another strange fact, that she herself felt for the *Sedie* and the gallery the very same contempt which was felt by the people of the boxes and the stalls.

Antonio thought she was enjoying the music and the spectacle as he was himself; now and then he touched her hand and made some pleasant remark.

"You look a real queen with that necklace!" he said, for instance.

"An exiled queen!" returned Regina under her breath.

CHAPTER V

LATER, when she thought over that first year of marriage, Regina divided it into many little chapters. Amongst them she attached importance to the chapter of her first visit to the Princess Makuline.

It took place on a warm, cloudy evening at the beginning of January. Antonio was missing, having been detained at the Department till nine, doing extra work; but Arduina and Regina waited in the Piazza dell' Indipendenza for Massimo, who was to escort them. The Piazza, almost deserted, was illumined by the pale gold rays of the veiled moon. The bare trees were scarce visible in the vaporous air, the small, motionless flames of the street lamps seemed far away. Regina, standing in the middle of the great square, was pleasantly conscious of silence, solitude, immensity. For the first time since she had been in Rome she caught herself admiring something.

"Come along!" said Massimo, arriving hurriedly, and brandishing a pair of new gloves; "three-fifty they cost me! Woe to Madame if she doesn't pay me with some hope!"

"I believe you'd be capable of marrying her," said Regina, with a gesture of disgust.

"She'd like it," said Arduina.

"Shut up! The point is — should I like it?" said the young man. "I'm not for sale."

Passing the Princess's little garden gate, Massimo said, "This is the entrance for Madame's lovers!"

But they walked on and rang at the hall door of the villa, or rather of the villas, for there were two; small but handsome houses, joined by an aerial terrace or hanging garden.

"Like two little brothers holding each other's hands," said Regina, with a sigh.

A servant in plain clothes opened the polished door, and disclosed two great wolves, apparently alive, lying in ambush on the red rugs of the entrance hall.

The rooms were much overheated. Thick carpets, skins of bears spread before large low divans, themselves covered with furs, exhaled what seemed the hot breath of wild beasts sleeping in the sun — an atmosphere wild, voluptuous, noxious. Huge waving branches of red-berried wild plants rose from tall metal vases. The Princess, richly but clumsily dressed in black velvet and white lace, was discoursing in French to two elderly ladies, telling them the adventures of her aunt, wife of the man who had known George Sand.

"At that time," she was saying, "my aunt was the best dressed woman in Paris. George Sand described one of her costumes in the *Marquis de Villemer*. . . ."

Beyond the two elderly ladies, an old gentleman, shaven and bald, his head shining like a bowl of pink china, lolled in an arm-chair and listened sleepily.

Marianna, in a low pink dress, ran to the new-comers with her little rat-like steps, and surveyed Regina inquisitively.

"You look very well, Madame," she said; "is there no news?"

"What news do you expect?" asked Regina.

Marianna giggled, her little eyes shining unnaturally. Regina could not resist the suspicion that the rat was excited with wine, and she felt a resurgence of the curious physical disgust with which the Princess and this girl inspired her.

Madame at first paid scant attention to the Venutellis. Other guests were arriving, the greater number elderly foreign ladies in dresses of questionable freshness and fashion. Arduina soon got into conversation with an unattractive gentleman whose round eyes and flat nose surmounted an exaggerated jowl. Massimo followed in the wake of Marianna, who came and went, running about, frisking and shrieking. Regina was stranded between a stout lady who made a few observations without looking at her, and the bald old gentleman who said nothing at all. She soon grew bored, finding herself neglected and forgotten, lost among all these fat superannuated people, these old silk gowns which had outlived their rustle. How tedious! Was this the world of the rich, the enchanted realm for which she had pined?

"Regina shall not be seen here again," she told herself.

Presently she saw Arduina smiling and beckoning to her from the distance; but just then the Princess came over, and put her small refulgent hand in Regina's with an affectionate and familiar gesture.

"Won't you come and take a cup of tea?" she said. Regina started to her feet overwhelmed by so much attention.

"How is your husband?" said the Princess, leading her to the supper-room.

"Very well, thank you," said Regina, in a low voice; "he hasn't been able to come to-night because —"

"Beg pardon?" said the Princess.

All the elderly ladies and gentlemen followed the hostess, and seated themselves round the room, in which a sumptuous table was laid. Marianna ran hither and thither, distributing the tea.

"Could you help?" she asked, passing Regina; "you seem like a girl. Come with me."

Regina followed her to the table, but did not know what to do; she upset a jug and blushed painfully.

"Here!" said Marianna, giving her a plate, "take that to the man like a dog."

"Which man? Speak low!"

"The man beside your sister-in-law. He's an author."

Regina crossed the room shyly, carrying the plate, and imagining every one was looking at her. There was consolation in the thought that she was about to offer a slice of tart to an author.

"Oh, Signorina!" he exclaimed, with a deprecating bow.

"Signora, if you please!" said Arduina, "she's my sister-in-law."

"My compliments and my condolences," said the man, insolently; he rolled his great eyes round the room and added, "In this company you seem a child."

"Why condolences?" asked Arduina.

"Because she's your sister-in-law," replied he.

Regina perceived that the author was very impudent, and she retreated to the table. Not finding Marianna she timidly possessed herself of another plate and took it to Massimo, who, also neglected and forgotten, was standing near the door.

"Oh, you're doing hostess, are you?" he said. "Look here I bring me a glass of that wine in the tall, gold-necked bottle at the corner of the table. Drink some yourself."

Regina went for it, but found the Princess herself pouring wine at that moment from the bottle with the golden neck.

"Massimo would like a glass of that," she murmured ingenuously.

"Beg pardon?" said the Princess, who fortunately had not heard.

Regina, however, found a wine-glass ready filled, and carried it to her brother-in-law; exquisite bouquet rose from the glass as perfume from a flower.

"It's port, you know," said Massimo, with genuine gratitude; "thanks, little sister-in-law! You're my salvation! 'Tis the wine of the modern gods."

"You are facetious to-night."

"Hush! I'm bored to death. Let's go. We'll leave Arduina. Who's that baboon-faced person she's got hold of?"

"That's an author."

"*Connais pas*," said the other, eating and drinking. "What a rabble! No one but rabble."

"Just so," said Regina, "and we belong to it."

"On the contrary, we'll snap our fingers at it. No! we are young and may some day be rich. Those folk are rich, but they'll never be young, my dear!"

"Take care! I think you are right though."

"Then bring me another glass of port!" said Massimo, imploringly.

"Certainly not!"

The old ladies and gentlemen, mildly excited by the wines and the tea, raised their voices, moved about, clustered in knots and circles. In the confusion Regina again found herself beside the hostess.

"But you've had positively nothing," said Madame; "come with me. Have a glass of port? How's your husband?"

"The second time!" thought Regina; and she shouted, "Very well indeed, thank you."

"Have you moved yet? How do you like your house? Come, drink this! Have some sweets? The pastry's pretty good to-day. Oh, Monsieur Massimo won't you have another cup of tea? No? A glass of port, then? Tell me, are you also at the Treasury?"

"No, Madame; in the War Office."

Marianna no sooner observed that the Princess was talking to the Venutellis than she thrust her restless face behind Regina's shoulder; and it struck the latter that this girl watched her patroness over much.

"I've a bothersome affair on hand," said Madame, slowly; "some money due in Milan which I want paid to me in Rome. I'm told I must have a warrant from the Treasury. Monsieur Antonio must come and speak to me to-morrow."

"I'll tell him the moment I get in," cried Regina.

Marianna said something in Russian, turning to Madame with an air almost of command. The Princess replied with her usual calm, but quickly afterwards she moved away.

"Now I must pay for the help you gave me," said Marianna to Regina, pouring out a glass of a white liqueur. "Drink this."

"No, thanks."

"It's vodka. The Russian ladies get tipsy with this. See how I drink it! I'm half tipsy already," she went on, raising the glass and looking through it; "I don't mind! It has the opposite effect on me to what it has on every one else. After drinking, I no longer speak the truth."

"I don't observe it," said Massimo, dryly. "So this is vodka, is it? It's nasty."

"Oh, I've had none to speak of to-day!" said Marianna. She laughed and sipped; then held the glass to Regina's lips and made her drink too.

"Now we'll go and interrupt the idyll of the dog and the cat," said Marianna, leading the way to the next room where Arduina and the author were still *tête-à-tête* under the branches of the red-berried plant.

Regina and Marianna sat down opposite to them on a divan of furs, and Massimo remained standing. In the next room one of the old ladies was playing "*Se a te, O cara!*"

Regina now felt an inexplicable content; the gentle yet impassioned music, the warmth of the divan whose soft furriness suggested a pussy cat to be stroked; the indefinable perfume with which the hot air was charged, the vodka, too, which still pulsed in her throat — all gave her the initial feelings of a pleasant intoxication. Arduina also seemed excited. She spoke loud, in the tones which Regina had noted in the flirtatious cousin, Claretta. She seemed no longer to recognise her relations.

"What's the matter with the silly thing?" Regina asked herself, and Marianna must have guessed her thought, for she said slyly, "They're love-making."

Regina laughed unthinkingly. Then suddenly she felt shocked.

"Is it possible?" she murmured.

"Anything is possible," said the rat. "You are such a child as yet; but in time you'll see — *anything is possible.*"

CHAPTER VI

NEXT day Antonio went to the Princess about the collection of her rents. She invited him and his wife to dinner on Sunday, and this invitation was followed by others. Regina accepted them all, but unwillingly. The dinners were magnificent, served by pompous men servants, whose solemnity, said Antonio, spoiled his digestion. Regina found the entertainments dull, and came away out of temper. The guests were elderly foreigners or obscure Italian poets and artists; their conversation might have been interesting, for it touched on letters, art, the theatre, matters of palpitating contemporary life, but only stale commonplaces were uttered, and Regina heard nothing at all correspondent to the ideas sparkling in her own mind.

She was bored; yet no sooner was she back in the atmosphere of Casa Venutelli than she thought enviously of the Princess's saloons, where the servants passed and waited, silent and automatic as machines, where all was beauty, luxury, splendour, and the light itself seemed to shine by enchantment.

At last the day came when Antonio and his wife chose the furniture for their own Apartment in Via Massimo d'Azeglio.

"We'll go on Sunday and settle how to arrange it," said Antonio, and Regina thought dolefully of all the fatigue and worry awaiting her.

"Fancy coping with a servant!" she reflected, panic-struck.

On Sunday morning they went to their little habitation. It was late in January, a pure, soft morning with whiffs of spring in the air. Regina ran up the hundred-odd steps, and when, panting and perspiring, she arrived at her hall door she amused herself by ringing the bell.

"Tinkle, tinkle, tinkle! Who is there? Mr. Nobody! What fun going to visit Mr. Nobody!"

Antonio opened with a certain air of mystery and marched in first. Then he turned and made Regina a low bow. She looked round astonished, and exclaimed, with faint irony, "But I thought this kind of thing only happened in romances!"

The Apartment was all in complete order. Curtains veiled the half-open windows. The large white bed stood between strips of carpet, upon which were depicted yellow dogs running with partridges in their mouths. Even in the kitchen nothing was missing or awry.

Antonio stood at the window, leaving Regina time to get over her surprise. She hated herself because somehow she did not feel all the pleasurable emotion which her husband might justly expect of her. However, she understood quite well what she must do. She thought —

"I must kiss him and say, 'How good you are!' "

So she did kiss him, and said "How good you are!" quite cheerfully. His eyes filled with boyish delight, and at sight of this she felt touched in earnest.

"Antonio," she cried, "you really are good, and I am very wicked. But I'm going to improve, I really, really am!"

And for a week or a fortnight she was good; docile and even merry. She was very busy settling her treasures in the cabinets, her clothes in the wardrobes, altering this table and that picture; never in her whole life had she worked so hard! The first night she slept in the soft new bed, between the fine linen sheets of her trousseau, she felt as if delivered from an incubus, and about to begin a new life, with all the happiness, all the renewed energy of a convalescent. By this time fine weather had come. The Roman sky was cloudless; springtime fragrance filled the air; the city noises reached Regina's rooms like the sound of a distant waterfall, subdued and sweet. In the sun-dappled garden below, a thin curl of water was flung by a tiny fountain into a tiny vase, dotted with tiny goldfish; monthly roses bloomed; and a couple of white kittens chased each other along the paths. The little garden seemed made expressly for the two graceful little beasts.

Regina passed several happy days. But when all the things were safely installed in the wardrobes and cabinets she found she had nothing more to do. The servant, of whom she had thought with so much dread, looked after everything, was well behaved and prettily mannered. She was an expense, but worth it. Regina's only worry was making out the account for the maid's daily purchases. She got used even to this; and again began to be bored. She stood before her glass for long hours, brushing, washing and dressing her hair, polishing her nails and teeth. She looked at herself in profile, from this side and that, powdered her face, took to using *"Crema Venus,"* laced herself very tight. But afterwards, or indeed at the moment, she asked with impatient and disgusted self-reproach, "Are you a fool, Regina? What's all this for? What on earth is the good of it?"

Of her few visitors, almost all were tiresome relations; among them Aunt Clara and Claretta. Aunt Clara, jealous of Arduina's aristocratic acquaintances, had much to relate of banquets and receptions at which she had assisted.

"And Claretta, as I need not say —"

Claretta admired herself in all the mirrors, ransacked Regina's toilet-table, passed through the little apartment like the wind, upsetting everything. Regina hated the mother, hated the daughter, hated the whole connection, including Arduina, who nevertheless took her about, introducing her to countesses and duchesses at whose houses she met others of like rank.

"It's appalling the number of countesses in Rome," said Regina to her husband.

She was partly amused, partly wearied; she was not offended when the grand ladies failed to return her visits; and she no longer wondered at the shocking things said in almost all the drawing-rooms about the people most distinguished in the literary, the political, and even in the private world.

"Anything is possible," said Marianna, "and what is most possible of all is that the things they say are calumnies."

In the early spring Regina had a recrudescence of nostalgia and discontent. The little apartment began to be hot. She stood for hours at the window with the nervous unquiet of a bird not yet used to its cage. From the "Pussies' Garden" rose a smell of damp grass which induced in her spasms of homesickness. Sometimes she looked down through her eye-glass, and saw a certain short and plump, pale and bald young man, strolling round and round the little vase into which the fountain wept tears of tedium. Life was tedious also for that young man. Regina remembered seeing him on the evening of San Stefano in a box at the Costanzi, his face bloated and yellow as an unripe apricot; and she had included him in her incendiary hatred. Now he, too, was bored. Was he bored because he had come down into the garden, or had he come down into the garden because he was bored? Sometimes he stood and teased the goldfish; then he yawned and battered the flowers with his stick, the wistaria on the walls, the monthly roses, the innocent daisies.

"He must beat something," thought Regina, and remembered that she herself was itching to torment any one or anything. On rainy days — frequent and tedious — she became depressed, even to hypochondria. Only one thought comforted her — that of the return to her home. She counted the days and the hours. Strange, childish recollections, distant fancies, passed through her mind like clouds across a sad sky. Details of her past life waked in her melting tenderness; she remembered vividly even the humblest persons of the place, the most secret nooks in the house or in the wood; with strange insistence she thought of certain little things which never before had greatly struck her. For instance, there was an old millstone, belonging to a ruined mill, which lay in the grass by the river-side. The remembrance of that old grey millstone, resting after its labour beside the very stream with which it had so long wrestled, moved Regina almost to tears. Often she tried to analyse her nostalgia, asking herself why she thought of the millstone, of the old blind chimney sweep, of the *portiner* (ferryman), who had enormous hairy hands and was getting on for a hundred; of the clean-limbed children by the green ditch, intent on making straw ropes; of the little snails crawling among the leaves of the plane-trees.

"I am an idiot!" she thought; yet with the thought came a sudden rush of joy at the idea of soon again seeing the millstone, the ferryman, the children, the green ditches, and the little snails.

And outside it rained and rained. Rome was drowned in mire and gloom. Regina raged like a furious child, wishing that upon Rome a rain of mud might fall for evermore, forcing all the inhabitants to emigrate and go away. Then, then she would return to her birthplace, to the wide horizons, the pure flowing river of her home; she would be born anew, she would be Regina once more, a bird alive and free!

Antonio went out and came in, and always found her wrapped in her homesick stupor, indifferent to everything about her.

"Let's take a walk, Regina!"

"Oh, no!"

"It would do you good."

"I am quite well."

"You can't be well. You are so dull. You don't care for me, that's what it is!"

"Oh, yes, I do! And if I don't, how can I help it?"

Sometimes, indeed, she included even Antonio in the collective hatred which she nourished against everything representative of the city. At those moments he seemed an inferior person, bloodless and half alive, one among all the other useless phantasms scarce visible in the rain, through which she alone in her egotism and her pride loomed gigantic.

But the warm and luminous spring came at last, and troops of men, women and flower-laden children spread themselves through the streets, in the depths of which Regina's short-sighted eyes fancied silvery lakes. In the fragrant evenings, bathed it would seem in golden dust, companies of women, fresh as flowers in their new spring frocks, came down by Via Nazionale, by the Corso, by Via del Tritone. Carriages passed heaped up with roses, red motor-cars flew by, bellowing like young monsters drunk with light, and even they were garlanded with flowers.

Regina walked and walked, on Antonio's arm, or sometimes alone; alone among the crowd, alone in the wave of all those joyous women, whose thoughtlessness she both envied and despised; alone among the smiling parties of sisters, companions, friends, by not one of whom, however, would she have been accompanied for anything in the world! One day, as she was going up Piazza Termini, she saw Arduina in the famous black silk dress with wrinkles on the shoulders. Regina would have avoided her sister-in-law, but did not set about it soon enough.

"I've been to your house," said Arduina "why are you never at home? it's impossible to catch you. What are you always doing? Where have you been? Even our mother complains of you. Why don't you have a baby?"

"Why don't *you*? And where are *you* going?" said Regina, with sarcasm.

"I'm going to the Grand Hotel, to see a very rich English *'miss.'* You can come too, if you like. She's worth it!"

Regina went, so anxious was she for something to do. The sunset tinged the Terme and the trees with orange-red. From the gardens came the cry of children and twitterings like the rustling of water from innumerable birds. Higher than all else, above the transparent vastness of the Piazza, above the fountain, which, clear, luminous, pearly, seemed an immense Murano vase, towered the Grand Hotel, its gold-lettered name sparkling on its front like an epigraph on the façade of a temple.

There was a confusion of carriages before the columns of the entrance, of servants in livery, of gentlemen in tall hats, of fashionably attired ladies. A royal carriage with glossy, jet-black horses, was conspicuous among the others.

"It must be the Queen," said Arduina. "I'd like to wait!"

"Good-bye to you, then," returned her sister-in-law, "where there is one Regina there's no room for another!"

"Good heavens! what presumption!" laughed the other. "Well, then, come on."

Arduina led the way through the carriages and through the smart crowd which animated the hall; then humbly inquired of a waiter if Miss Harris were at home. The waiter bent his head and listened, but without looking at the two ladies.

"Miss Harris? I think she's at home. Take a seat," he replied absently, his eyes on the distance.

Regina remembered Madame Makuline's awe-inspiring servants; this man provoked not only awe, but a sort of terror. They went into the conservatory, and Arduina looked about with respectful admiration. The younger lady was silent, lost in the dream world she saw before her.

Apparently they had intruded into a *fête*. A strange light of ruddy gold streamed from the glass roof; among the palm-trees, treading on rich carpets, was a phantasmagoria of ladies dressed in silks and satins, with long rustling trains, their heads, ears, necks, brilliant with jewels. Bursts of laughter and the buzz of foreign voices mixed with the rattle of silver and the ring of china cups. It was a palace of crystal; a world of joy, of fairy creatures unacquainted with the realities of life, dwelling in the enchantment of groves of palms, rosy in the light of dream!

"The realities of life!" thought Regina, "but is not this the reality of life? It's the life of us mean little people which is the ugly dream!"

Just then a splendid creature, robed in yellow satin, who, as she passed, left behind her the effulgence of a comet, crossed the conservatory, and stopped to speak to two ladies in black.

"It's Miss Harris!" whispered Arduina; "she's coming!"

Regina had never imagined there could exist a being so beautiful and luminous. She watched her with dilated eyes, while from the far end of the conservatory breathed slow and voluptuous music overpowering the voices, the laughter, the rattle of the cups. Miss Harris drew nearer. Regina's eyes grew wild, she was overpowered by almost physical torture, by burning sadness. The rosy sunset light brooding over the palms as in an Oriental landscape, the warmth, the scent, the music, the dazzling aspect of the wealthy foreigner, all produced in her a kind of nostalgia, the atavic recollection of some wondrous world, where all life was pleasure and from which she had been exiled. Ah! at that moment she realised quite clearly what was the ill disease gnawing at her vitals! Ah! it was not the regret, the nostalgia for her early home, for her childish past; it was the death of the dreams which had filled that past, dreams which had perfumed the air she had breathed, the paths she had trod, the place where she had dwelt: dreams which were no fault of her own because born with her, transmitted in her blood, the blood of a once dominant race.

Miss Harris approached the corner where sat the two little *bourgeois* ladies, trailing her long shining train, her whole elegant slimness suggesting something feline. The two foreign ladies accompanied her talking in incomprehensible French. Arduina had to get up and smile very humbly before the Englishwoman recognised her, shook her hand, and spoke with condescending affability. Then Miss Harris sat down, her long tail wound round her legs like that of a reposing cat, and began to talk. She was tired and bored; she had been for a drive in a motor, had had a private audience of the Pope, and in half-an-hour was due at some great lady's reception. She did not look at Regina at all. After a minute she appeared to forget Arduina; a little later, the two foreign ladies also. She seemed talking for her own ears; in her beauty and splendour she was self-sufficient, like a star which scintillates for itself alone. From far and near everybody watched her.

Regina trembled with humiliation. In her modest short frock she felt herself disappearing; she was ashamed of her lace scarf; when Miss Harris offered her a cup of tea she repulsed it with an inimical gesture. She felt again that sense of puerile hatred which had assaulted her at the Costanzi on the evening of San Stefano.

As they left the hotel she said to her sister-in-law, "I can't think what you came for! Why are you so mean-spirited? Why did you listen so slavishly to that woman who hardly noticed your presence?"

"But weren't you listening quite humbly, too?"

"I? I'd like to have seized and throttled you all! Good God, what fools you women are!"

"My dear Regina," said the other, confounded, "I don't understand you!"

"I know you don't. What do you understand? Why do you go to such places? What have you to do with people like that? Don't you take in that they are the lords of the earth and we the slaves?"

"But we're the intelligent ones! We are the lords of the future! Don't you hear the clatter of our wooden shoes going up and of their satin slippers coming down?"

"We? What, *you?*" said Regina, contemptuously.

"Mind that carriage!" cried Arduina, pulling her back.

"You see? They drive over us! What's the good of intelligence? What is intelligence compared with a satin train?"

"Oh, I see! You're jealous of the satin train," said the other, laughing good-humouredly.

"Oh, you're a fool!" cried Regina, beside herself.

"Thanks!" said Arduina, unoffended.

Returned home, Regina threw herself on the ottoman in the ante-room, and remained there nearly an hour, beating the devil's tattoo with her foot in time to the ticking of the clock, which seemed the heart of the little room. Her own heart was overflown by a wave of humiliating distress. Ah! even the ridiculous Arduina had guessed what ailed her.

Daylight was dying in the adjacent room, and the dining-room, which looked out on the courtyard, was already overwhelmed in heavy shadow. The open door made a band of feeble light across the passage of the ante-room, while in its angles the penumbra continually darkened. Watching it, Regina reflected.

"The penumbra! What a horrid thing is the penumbra! Horrid? No, it's worse! It's noxious — soul-stifling! Better a thousand times the full shadow, complete darkness. In the shadow there is grief, desperation, rebellion — all that is life; but in this half-light it's all tedium, want, agony. It's better to be a beggar than a little *bourgeois*. The beggar can yell, can spit in the face of the prosperous. The little *bourgeois* is silent; he's a dead soul, he neither can nor ought to speak. What does he want? Hasn't he got the competence already, which some day every one is to have? His share is already given to him.

If he asks for more he's called ambitious, egotistic, envious. Even the idiots call him so! Satin trains green and shining halls like gardens spread out in the sun — motors like flying dragons! And the gardens, the beautiful gardens *'half seen through little gates,'* country houses hidden among pines, like rosy women under green lace parasols! That should be the heritage of the future, of the to-morrow, promised us though not yet come. But no! all that is to disappear! The world is small and can't be divided into more than two parts, the day and the night, the light and the shade. But some day it's to be all penumbra! Every one's to be like us, every one's to live in a little dark apartment with interminable stairs; all the streets are to be dusty, overrun by smelly trams, by troops of middle-class women who will go about on foot, dressed with sham elegance, wearing mock jewellery, carrying paper fans; joyous with a pitiable joy. The whole world will be tedium and destitution. The beggars won't have attained to the dreams which made them happy; the children of the rich will live on nostalgia, remembering the dream which was once reality to them. What will be the good of living then? Why am I living now?"

Then suddenly she remembered three figures, all exactly alike; three figures of an old man in a dreary room, who smiled and looked at each other with humorous sympathy, like three friends who understand without need of words. Work! Work! There's the secret of life!

The voice of the old Senator resounded still in Regina's soul. Since seeing him she had learned his story; his wife, a beautiful woman, brilliant and young, had killed herself, for what reason none could say. Work! Work! That was the secret! Perhaps the old Senator, panegyrising the working woman, had been thinking of his wife who had never worked.

Work! This was the secret of the world's future. All would eventually be happy because all would work.

"No! I don't represent the future as I have fondly fancied. I belong to the present — very much to the present! I am the parasite *par excellence*. I eat the labour of my husband, and I devour his moral life as well, because he loves me — loves me too much. I don't even make him happy. Why do I live? What's the good of me? What use am I? I'm good for nothing but to bear children; and, in point of fact, I don't want any children! I shouldn't know how to bring them up! Besides, what's the good of bringing children into the world? Wouldn't it be better I had never been born? What's the good of life?"

Surely her soul had become involved in the shadow darkening round her! Everything in her seemed dead. And then suddenly she thought of the luminous evenings on the shores of her great river at home; and saw again the wide horizons, the sky all violet and geranium colour, the infinite depths of the waters, the woods, the plain. She passed along the banks, the subdued splendour of all things reflected in her eyes, the water of rosy lilac, the heavens which flamed behind the wood, the warm grass which clothed the banks. Young willow-trees stretched out to drink the shining water, and they drank, they drank, consumed by an inextinguishable thirst. She passed on, and as the little willows drank, so she also drank in dreams from the burning river. What limitless horizons! What deeps of water! What tender distant voices carried by the waves, dying on the night! Was it a call out of a far world? Was it the crying of birds from the wood? Was it the woodpecker tapping on the poplar-tree?

Alas, no! it was her own foot beating the devil's tattoo; it was the clock ticking away indifferently in the penumbra of the little room; it was the caged canary moaning for nostalgia in the window opposite, above the lurid abyss of the courtyard.

Regina jumped to her feet; she was rebellious and desperate, suffocated by a sense of rage.

"I'll tell him the moment he comes in," she thought; "I'll cry, 'Why did you take me from there? Why have you brought me to this place? What can I do here? I must go away. I require air. I require light. You can't give me light, you can't give me air, and you never told me! How was I to know the world was like this? Away with all these gimcracks, all this lumber! I don't want it. I only want air! air! air! I am suffocating! I hate you all! I curse the city and the men who built it, and the fate which robs us even of the sight of heaven!' "

She went to her room, and automatically looked in the glass. By the last glimmer of day she saw her beautiful shining hair, her shining teeth, her shining nails, her fine skin which (softened by a light stratum of *"Crema Venus"*) had almost the transparent delicacy of Miss Harris's. Her resentment grew. She went to her dressing-table, snatched up the bottle of *"Crema"* and dashed it against the wall. The bottle bounded off on the bed without breaking. She picked it up and replaced it on the table.

"No! no! no!" she sobbed, throwing herself on the pillow, "I will not bear it! I'll say to him, 'Do you see what I'm becoming? Do you see what you're making me? To-day a soiling of the face, to-morrow soiling of the soul! I will go away — I will go away — away! I will go back home. You are nothing to me!' Yes, I will tell him the moment he comes in!"

When he came in he found her seated quietly at the table, busy with the list of purchases for the following day. It was late, the lamps were lit, the table was laid, the servant was preparing supper. The whole of the little dwelling was pervaded by the contemptible yet merry hissing of the frying-pan and the smell of fried artichokes. From the window, open towards the garden, penetrated the contrasting fragrance of laurels and of grass.

	lire. cent.
Milk	0.20
Bread	0.20
Wine	1.10
Meat	1.00
Flour	0.50
Eggs	0.50
Salad	0.05
Butter	0.60
Asparagus	0.50
	—
	L. 4.65
	—

Antonio came over to the table, bent down, and looked at the paper on which Regina was writing.

"I was here at six, and couldn't find you," he said.

"I was out."

"Listen. The Princess sent a note to the office asking me to go to her at half-past six; so I went."

"What did she want?"

"Well — she's beginning to be a nuisance, you know — she wants me to keep an eye on the man who speculates for her on the Stock Exchange."

Regina looked up and saw that Antonio's face was pale and damp.

"On the Stock Exchange? What does that mean? "

"What it means? I'll explain some time. But — well, really, that woman is becoming a plague!"

"But if she pays you?" said Regina; "and are you good at speculating?"

"I only wish I had the opportunity!" he exclaimed, tossing his hat to the sofa; "I wish I had a little of Madame's superfluous money! But this isn't a case of speculating. I'm to study the state of the money-market and audit the operations carried out by Cavaliere R— on the Princess's account; take note of the details of daily transactions; get information from the brokers; in short, exercise rigorous control over all the fellow does."

"But," insisted Regina, "she'll pay you well, won't she?"

"Beg pardon?" he said, mimicking the Princess.

"How much will she pay you?" shouted Regina.

"A hundred *lire* or so. She's a skinflint, you know."

"Supper's on the table, Signora," announced the servant with her accustomed elegant decorum.

During the meal Antonio expounded the operations on 'Change, and other financial matters, talking with a certain enthusiasm. She appeared interested in what he told her; yet while she listened her eyes shone with the vague light of a thought very far away from what Antonio was saying. That thought was straying in a dark and empty distance; like a blind man feeling his way in a strange place, it sought and sought something to be a point of rest, a support, or at least a sign.

Suddenly, however, Regina's eyes sparkled and returned to the world about her.

"Why shouldn't *you* be Madame's confidential agent?" she said; "her secretary? I remember what I dreamed the first night I saw her at Arduina's — that she was dead and had left us her money!"

"It would be easy enough," said Antonio.

"To get the money?"

"No — the administration of her affairs. True, one would have to flatter and cringe, and take people in, especially as she employs two or three others in addition to the Cavaliere. One would have to intrigue against them all. I don't care for that sort of business."

"Nor I," said Regina, stiffening.

She rose and moved to the window which overlooked the garden. Antonio followed her. The night was warm and voluptuous. The scent of laurel rose ever sweeter and stronger; patches of yellow light were spread over the little garden paths like a carpet. Regina looked down, then raised her eyes towards the darkened blue of the heavens and sighed, stifling the sigh in a yawn.

"After all," said Antonio, pursuing his own line of thought, "are we not happy? What do we lack?"

"Nothing and everything!"

"What is lacking to us, I say?" repeated Antonio, questioning himself rather than his wife; "what do you mean by your 'everything'?"

"Do you see the Bear?" she asked, looking up, and pretending not to have heard this question. He looked also.

"No, I don't —"

"Then we do lack something! We can't see the stars."

"What do you want with the stars? Leave them where they are, for they're quite useless! If there were anything you really wanted you wouldn't be crying for the stars."

"Then you think I am lacking in —?" She touched her forehead.

"So it seems!"

"Perhaps the deficiency is in you," she said quickly.

"Now you're insulting me, and I'll take you and pitch you out of the window!" he jested, seizing her waist. "If my wits are deficient, it's because you're making me lose them with your folly!"

CHAPTER VII

SHE was not guilty of folly in action, but certainly her words became stranger and stranger. Antonio sometimes found them amusing; more often they distressed him. Though seemingly calm, Regina could not hide that she was under the dominion of a fixed idea. What was she thinking about? Even when he held her in his arms, wrapped in his tenderest embrace, Antonio felt her far, immeasurably far, away from him. In the brilliant yet drowsy spring mornings while the young pair still lay in the big white bed, Antonio would repeat his questions to himself: "What do we lack! Are we not happy?"

Through the half-shut windows soft light stole in and gilded the walls. Infinite beatitude seemed to reign in the room veiled by that mist of gold, fragrant with scent, lulled to a repose unshaken by the noises of the distant world. In the profound sweetness of the nuptial chamber Regina felt herself at moments conquered by that somnolent beatitude. Antonio's searching question had its echo in her soul also. What was it that they lacked? They were both of them young and strong; Antonio loved her ardently, blindly. He lived in her. And he was so handsome! His soft hands, his passionate eyes, had a magic which often succeeded in intoxicating her. And yet in those delicious mornings, at the moments when she seemed happiest, while Antonio caressed her hair, pulling it down and studying it like some precious thing, her face would suddenly cloud, and she would re-commence her extravagant speeches.

"What are we doing with our life?"

Antonio was not alarmed.

"What are we doing? We are living; we love, we work, eat, sleep, take our walks, and when we can we go to the play!"

"But that isn't living! Or, at least, it's a useless life, and I'm sick of it!"

"Then what do you want to be doing?"

"I don't know. I'd like to fly! I don't mean sentimentally, I mean really. To fly out of the window, in at the window! I'd like to invent the way!"

"I've thought of it myself sometimes."

"You know nothing about it!" she said, rather piqued. "No, no! I want to do something you couldn't understand one bit; which, for that matter, I don't understand myself!"

"That's very fine!"

"It's like thirsting for an unfindable drink with a thirst nothing else can assuage. If you had once felt it —"

"Oh, yes, I have felt it."

"No, you can't have felt it! You know nothing about it."

"You must explain more clearly."

"Oh, never mind! You don't understand, and that's enough. Let my hair alone, please."

"I say, what a lot of split hairs you have! You ought to have them cut, I was telling you —"

"What do I care about hair? It's a perfectly useless thing."

"Well," he said, after pretending to seek and to find a happy thought, "why don't you become a tram-conductor?"

and he imitated the rumble of the tram and the gestures of the conductor.

"I won't demean myself by a reply," she said, and moved away from him; but presently repented and said —

"Do the little bird!"

"I don't know how to do the little bird!"

"Yes, you do. Go on, like a dear!"

"You're making a fool of me. I understand that much."

"You don't understand a bit! You do the little bird so well that I like to see you!"

He drew in his lips, puffed them out, opened and shut them like the beak of a callow bird. She laughed, and he laughed for the pleasure of seeing her laugh, then said —

"What babes we are! If they put that on the stage — good Lord, think of the hisses!"

"Oh, the stage! That's false if you like! And the novel. If you wrote a novel in which life was shown as it really is, every one would cry 'How unnatural!' I do wish I could write! — could describe life as I understand it, as it truly is, with its great littlenesses and its mean greatness! I'd write a book or a play which would astonish Europe!"

He looked at her, pretending to be so overwhelmed that he had no words, and again she felt irritated.

"You don't understand anything! You laugh at me! Yet if I could —"

In spite of himself Antonio became serious.

"Well, why can't you?"

"Because first I should have to — No, I won't tell you. You can't understand! Besides, I can't write; I don't know how to express myself. My thoughts are fine, but I haven't the words. That's the way with so many! What do you suppose great men, the so-called great thinkers, are? Fortunate folk who know how to express themselves! Nietzsche, for instance. Don't you think I and a hundred others have all Nietzsche's ideas, without ever having read them? Only he knew how to set them down, and we don't. I say Nietzsche, but I might just as well say the author of the *Imitation*."

"You should have married an author," said Antonio, secretly jealous of the man whom Regina had perhaps dreamed of but never met.

Again she felt vexed. "It's quite useless! You don't understand me. I can't get on with authors a bit. Let me alone now. I told you not to fiddle with my hair!"

"Stop! Don't go away! Let's talk more of your great thoughts. You think me an idiot. But listen, I want to say one thing; don't laugh. You want to do something wonderful. Well, an American author — Emerson, I think — said to his wife, that the greatest miracle a woman could perform is—"

"Oh, I know! To have a baby!" she replied, with a forced smile. "But you see, I think humanity useless, life not worth living. Still, I don't commit suicide, so I suppose I do accept life. I admit that a son would be a fine piece of work. I'd enter on it with enthusiasm, with pride, if I were sure my son wouldn't turn out just a little *bourgeois* like us!"

"He might make a fortune and be a useful member of society."

"Nonsense! Dreams of a little *bourgeois*!" she said bitterly; "he would be just as unhappy as we are!"

"But I am happy!" protested Antonio.

"If you are happy it shows you don't understand anything about it, and so you are doubly unhappy," she said vehemently, her eyes darkening disquietingly.

"My dear, you're growing as crazy as your great writers."

"There you are! the little *bourgeois* who doesn't know what he is talking about!"

And so they went on, till Antonio looked at the clock and jumped up with a start.

"It's past the time! My love, if you had to go down to the office every day I assure you these notions would never come into your head."

He hurried to wash; and still busy with the towel, damp and fresh with the cold water, he came back to kiss her.

"You're as pink as a strawberry ice!" she said admiringly, and so they made peace.

With the coming on of the hot days Regina's nostalgia, nervousness and melancholy increased. At night she tossed and turned, and sometimes groaned softly. At last she confessed to Antonio that her heart troubled her.

"Palpitations for hours at a time till I can hardly breathe! It feels as if my chest would burst and let my heart escape. It must be the stairs. I never used to have palpitations!"

Much alarmed, her husband wished to take her to a specialist, but this she opposed.

"It will go off the moment I get away," she said.

They decided she must go at the end of June. Antonio would take his holiday in August and join her, remaining at her mother's for a fortnight.

"After that, if we've any money left, we'll spend a few days at Viareggio."

Regina said neither yea nor nay. After the first seven months the young couple had only 200 *lire* in hand. This was barely enough for the journey; Antonio, however, hoped to put by a little while his wife was away.

The days passed on; Rome was becoming depopulated, though the first brief spell of heat had been followed by renewal of incessant and tiresome rain.

Antonio counted the days.

"Another ten — another eight — and you'll be gone. What's to become of me all alone for a month?"

Such expressions irritated her. She wished neither to speak nor to think of her departure.

"Alone? Why need you be alone? You've got your mother and your brothers!"

"A wife is more than brothers, more than a mother."

"But if I were to die? Suppose I fell ill and the doctors prescribed a long stay in my home?"

"That's impossible."

"You talk like a child. Why is it impossible? It's very possible indeed!" she said, still vexed; "whatever I say you think it nonsense — a thing which can't happen. Why can't it happen? It's enough to mention some things —"

"But, Regina," he exclaimed, astonished, "what makes you so cross?"

"Well, you just explain to me why it's impossible I should get ill? Am I made of iron? The doctor might forbid me to climb stairs for a while, and might tell me to live in the open air, in the country. If he took that line where would you have me go unless to my home? Would you forbid me to go there?"

"On the contrary, I should be the first to recommend it. But it's not the state of affairs at present. Oh! your palpitation? that will go off. We must see about an apartment on a lower floor — though, to say truth, I've got to regard this little nest of ours with the greatest affection. We're so cosy here!" he said, looking round lovingly.

She did not reply, but stepped to the window and looked out. Her brow clouded. What was the matter with her? Detestation of the little dwelling where she felt more and more smothered? or irritation at her husband's sentimentality?

"This is Friday," she said presently; "I suppose I ought to go and bid your Princess good-bye. When is she going away?"

"Middle of July, I think. She's going to Carlsbad."

"Well, let her go to the devil, and all the smart people with her!"

"That's wicked! Aren't you going to the country yourself? Think of all the folk who have to stay in the burning city, workmen in factories, bakers at their ovens —"

"Precisely what made me swear!" said Regina.

Later she dressed and went to Madame Makuline's; not because she wanted to see her, but in order to occupy the interminable summer afternoon.

She pinched her waist very tight, and put on a new blue dress with many flounces and a long train; she knew she looked well in it and far more fashionable than on her first arrival in Rome, but the thought gave her little satisfaction.

As she was passing the Costanzi she saw the yellow-faced gentleman who strolled in the "Pussies' Garden." He was talking to a friend, plump as himself with round, dull blue eyes, a restless little red dog under his arm. Regina knew this personage also. He was an actor who played important parts at the Costanzi. Regina fancied the two men looked at her admiringly, and she coloured with satisfaction; then suddenly conceived something blameworthy in her pleasure, and felt angry with herself, as a few hours earlier she had been angry with Antonio for "talking like a child." She arrived at the Princess's in an aggressive humour, and came in with her head very high. She did not speak to the servant nor even look at him, remembering that he always received her husband and herself with a familiarity not exactly disrespectful, but somehow humiliating.

Madame Makuline's drawing-room, though its furs and its carpets had been removed, was still very hot. Branches of lilac in the great metal vases diffused an intense, pungent, almost poisonous fragrance. Only two ladies had called; one of them was abusing Rome to Marianna, and the girl, unusually ugly, in an absurd, low red dress, was protesting ferociously and threatening to bite the slanderer. The

Princess listened, pale, cold, her heavy face immobile. Regina came in, and at once Marianna rushed to meet her, crying —

"If *you* are going to say horrid things, too, I shall go mad!"

Regina sat down, elegantly, winding her train round her feet as she had seen Miss Harris do; and, having learned the subject in dispute, said with a malicious smile —

"Most certainly Rome is odious."

"I'll have to scratch you!" cried Marianna; "and it will be a thousand pities, for you're quite lovely to-day! Now you're blushing and you look better still! Your hat's just like one I saw at Buda-Pesth on a grand duchess."

"Rome odious?" said the Princess, turning to Regina, who was still smiling sarcastically; that's not what you said a few days ago."

"It's easy to change one's opinion."

"Beg pardon?"

"It's easy to change one's opinion," shouted Regina, irritated; "besides, I said the other day that Rome was delightful for the rich. It's altogether abominable for the poor. The poor man, at Rome, is like a beggar before the shut door of a palace, a beggar gnawing a bone —"

"Which is occasionally snapped up by the rich man's dog," put in Marianna.

The other laughed nervously.

"Just so!" she said.

The Princess raised her little yellow eyes to Regina's face and studied it for a moment, then turned to the lady at her side and talked to her in German. Regina fancied Madame had meant her to understand something by that look, something distressing, disagreeable, humiliating; and her laughter ceased.

"June 28, 1900.

"ANTONIO, —

"You will read this letter after I am gone, while you are still sad. You will perhaps think it dictated by a passing caprice. If you could only know how many days, how many weeks, how many months even, I have thought it over, examined it, tortured myself with it! If you knew how many and many times I have tried to express in words what I am now going to write to you! I have never found it possible to speak; some tyrannous force has always prevented me from opening my heart to you. I felt that by word of mouth we should never arrive at understanding each other. Who knows whether, even now, you can or will understand me! I fancied it would be easy to explain in a letter; but now — now I feel how painful and difficult it must be. I should have liked to wait till I was there, at home, to write this letter to you; but I don't want to put it off any longer, and above all I don't wish you to think that outside influences, or the wishes of others, have pushed me to this step. No, my best, dearest Antonio we two by ourselves, far from every strange and molesting voice, we two, alone, shall decide our destiny. Hear me! I am going to try and explain to you my whole thought as best I can. Listen, Antonio! A few days ago I said, 'Suppose I were to fall ill and the doctors were to order me to return to my native air and to stay for a short time in my own country, would you forbid me to obey?' And you ended

121

by confessing you would be the first to counsel obedience. Well, I am really ill, of a moral sickness which consumes me worse than any physical disorder; and I do need to return to my own country and to remain there for some time. Oh, Antonio my adored, my friend, my brother, force yourself to understand me; to read deep into these lines as if you were reading my very soul! I love you. I married you for love; for that unspeakable love born of dreams and enchantments which is felt but once in a life. More than ever at this moment I feel that I love you, and that I am united to you for my whole life and for what is beyond. When you appeared to me there, on the green river-banks, the line of which had cut like a knife through the horizon of all my dreams, I saw in you something radiant; I saw in you the very incarnation of my most beautiful visions. How many years bad I not dreamed of you, waited for you! This delicious expectation was already beginning to be shrouded in fear and sadness, was beginning to seem altogether vague when you appeared! You were to me the whole unknown world, the wondrous world which books, dreams — heredity also — had created within me. You were the burning, the fragrant, the intoxicating whirlwind of life; you were everything my youth, my instinct, my soul, had yearned for of the maddest and sweetest. Even if you had been ugly, fat, poorer than you are, I should have loved you. You had come from Rome, you were returning to Rome—that was enough! No one, neither you nor any one not born and bred in provincial remoteness, can conceive what the most paltry official from the capital — dropped by chance into that remoteness — represents to an ignorant visionary girl. How often here in Rome have I not watched the crowds in Via Nazionale, and laughed bitterly while I thought that if the lowest of those little citizens walking there, the meanest, the most anaemic, the most contemptible of those little clerks, one with an incomplete soul, dropped like an unripe fruit, one of those who now move me only to pity, had passed by on that river-bank before our house — he might have been able to awaken in me an overwhelming passion! My whole soul revolts at the mere thought. But do not you take offence, Antonio! You are not one of those; you were and you are for me something altogether different. And now, though the enchantment of my vain dreams has dissolved, you are for me something entirely beyond even those dreams. You were and you are for me, the one man, the good loyal man, the lover, young and dear, whom the girl places in the centre of all her dreams — which he completes and adorns, dominating them as a statue dominates a garden of flowers.

"But our garden, Antonio, our garden is arid and melancholy. We were as yet too poor to come together and to make a garden. My eyes were blindfolded when I married you and came with you to Rome; I fancied that in Rome our two little incomes would represent as much as they represented in my country. I have perceived, too late, that instead they are hardly sufficient for our daily bread. And on bread alone one cannot live. It means death, or at least grave sickness for any one unused to such a diet. And love, no matter how great, is not enough to cure the sick one!

"Alas! as I repeat, I am sick! The shock of reality, the hardness of that daily bread, has produced in me a sort of moral anaemia; and the disease has become so acute that I can't get on any longer. For me this life in Rome is a martyrdom. It is absolute necessity that I should flee from it for a time, retire into my den, as they say sick animals do, and get cured — above all, get used to the thought, to the duty, of spending my life like this.

"Antonio! my Antonio! force yourself to understand me, even if I don't succeed in expressing myself as I wish. Let me go back to my nest, to my mother! I will tell her I am really ill and in need of my native air. Leave me with her for a year, or perhaps two. Let us do what we ought to have done in the first instance, let us wait. Let us wait as a betrothed couple waits for the hour of union. I will accustom myself to the idea of a life different from what I had dreamed. Meanwhile your position (and perhaps mine, too, who knows?) will improve. Are there not many who do this? Why, my own cousin did it! Her husband was a professor in the Gymnasium at Milan. Together they could not have managed. But she went back home, and he studied and tried for a better berth, and presently became professor at the Lyceum in another town. Then they were re-united, and now they're as happy as can be.

"'But,' you will say, we *can* live together. We have no lack of anything.'

"'True,' I repeat, 'we don't lack for bread; but one cannot live by bread alone.' Do you remember the evening when I asked you whether from our habitation you could see the

Great Bear? You laughed at me and said I was crazy; and who knows! perhaps I am really mad! But I know my madness is of a kind which can be cured; and that is all I want, just to be cured — to be cured before the disease grows worse.

"Listen, Antonio! You also, unintentionally I know, but certainly, have been in the wrong. You did not mean it; it's Fate which has been playing with us! In the sweet evenings of our engagement, when I talked to you of Rome with a tremble in my voice, you ought to have seen I was the dupe of foolish fancies. You ought to have discerned my vain and splendid dream through my words, as one discerns the moon through the evening mist. But instead you fed my dream; you talked of princesses, drawing-rooms, receptions! And when we arrived in Rome, you should have taken me at once to our own little home; you shouldn't have put between us for weeks and months persons dear, of course, to you, but total strangers to me. They were kind to me, I know, and are so still; I did my best to love them, but it was impossible to have communion of spirit with them all at once. Above all, you ought to have kept me away from that world of the rich of which I had dreamed, which is not and never will be mine.

"Do you see? It's as if I had touched the fire and something had been burned in me. Is it my fault? If I am in fault it's because I am not able to pretend. Another woman in my place, feeling as I feel, would pretend, would apparently accept the reality, would remain with you; but — would poison your whole existence! Even I, you remember, I in the first months worried you with my sadness, my complaints, my contempt. I knew how wrong I was, I was ashamed and remorseful. If we had gone on like that, if the idea which I am broaching now had not flashed into my mind, we should have ended as so many end; bickering to-day, scandal to-morrow; crime, perhaps, in the end. I felt a vortex round me. It is not that I am romantic; I am sceptical rather than romantic; but everything small, sordid, vulgar, wounds my soul. I am like a sick person, who at the least annoyance becomes selfish, loses all conscience, and is capable of any bad action. Again I say, is it my fault? I was born like that and I can't re-make myself. There are many women like me, some of them worse because weaker. They don't know how to stop in time, on the edge of the precipice; they neither see, nor study how to avoid it. And yet, Antonio, I do care for you! I love you more, much more than when we were betrothed. I love you most passionately. It is chiefly on this account that I make the sacrifice of exiling myself from you for a while. I don't want to cause you unhappiness! Tears are bathing my face, my whole heart bleeds. But it is necessary, it is fate, that we separate! It kills me thinking of it, but it's necessary, necessary! Dear, dear, dear Antonio! understand me. Beloved Antonio, read and re-read my words, and don't give them a different signification from what is given by my heart. Above all, hear me as if I were lying on your breast, weeping there all my tears. Hear and understand as sometimes you have heard and understood. Do you remember Christmas morning? I was crying, and I fancied I saw your eyes clouded too: it was at that moment I realised that I loved you above everything in all the world, and I decided then to make some sacrifice for you. This is the sacrifice; to leave you for a while in the endeavour to get cured and to come back to you restored and content. Then in my little home I will live for you; and I will work; yes, I also will bring my stone to the edifice of our future well-being. We are young, still too young; we can do a great deal if we really wish it. Neither of us have any doubts of the other; you are sure of me; I also am sure of you. I know how you love me, and that you love me just because I am what I am.

"Listen; after two or three weeks you shall come to my mother's as we have arranged. You must pretend to find me still so unwell that you decide to leave me till I am better. Then you shall return to Rome and live thinking of me. You shall study, compete for some better post. The months will pass, we will write to each other every day, we will economise — or, what is better, accumulate treasures — of love and of money. Our position will improve, and when we come together again we shall begin a new honeymoon, very different from the first, and it shall last for the whole of our life."

Having reached this point in her letter, Regina felt quite frozen up, as if a blast of icy wind had struck her shoulders. This she was writing — was it not all illusion? all a lie? Words! Words! Who could know how the future would be made? The word *made* came spontaneously into her thought, and she was struck by it. Who makes the future? No one. We make it ourselves by our present.

"I shall make my future with this letter, only not even I can know what future I shall make."

Regina felt afraid of this obscure work; then suddenly she cheered, remembering that all she had written in the letter was really there in her heart. Illusion it might be, but for her it was truth. Then, come what might, why should she be afraid? Life is for those who have the courage to carry out their own ideas!

It seemed needless to prolong the letter. She had already said too many useless things, perhaps without succeeding in the expression of what was really whirling in her soul. She rapidly set down a few concluding lines.

"Write to me at once when you have read this — no, not at once! let a few hours pass first. There is much more I should like to say, but I cannot, my heart is too full, I am in too great suffering. Forgive me, Antonio, if I cause you pain at the moment in which you read this; out of that pain there will be born great joy. Reassure me by telling me you understand and approve my idea. Far away *there* I shall recover all we have lost in the wretched experience of these last months. I will await your letter as one awaits a sentence; then I will write to you again. I will tell you, or try to tell you, all which now swells my heart to bursting. Good-bye — till we meet again. See! I am already crying at the thought of the kiss which I shall give you before I go. God only knows the anguish, the love, the promise, the hope, which that kiss will contain.

"Whatever you shall think of me, Antonio, at least do not accuse me of lightness. Remember that I am your own Regina; your sick, your strange, but not your disloyal and wicked

"REGINA."

The letter ended, she folded and shut it hurriedly without reading it over. Then she felt qualms; some little word might have escaped her; some little particle which might change the whole sense of a phrase. She reopened the envelope, read with apprehension and distaste, but corrected nothing, added nothing. Her grief was agonising. Ah! how cold, how badly expressed, was that letter! Into its lifeless pages had passed nothing of all which was seething in her heart!

"And I was imagining I could write a novel — a play! I, who am incapable of writing even a letter! But he will understand," she thought, shutting the letter a second time, "I am quite sure he will understand! Now where am I to put it? Suppose he were to find it before I am off? Whatever would happen? He would laugh; but if he finds it afterwards — he will perhaps cry. Ah! that's it, I'll lay it on his little table just before I go."

With these and other trivial thoughts, with little hesitations which she had already considered and resolved, she tried to banish the sadness and anxiety which were agitating her.

She pulled out her trunks, for she was to start next morning by the nine o'clock express, and she had not yet packed a thing. The whole long afternoon had gone by while she was writing.

"What will he do?" she kept thinking; "will he keep on the apartment? And the maid? Will he betray me? No, he won't betray me. I'm sure of that. I'll suggest he should go back to his mother and brothers. So long as they don't poison his mind against me! Perhaps he'll let the rooms furnished. How much would he get for them? 100 *lire*? But no! he's sentimental about them. He wouldn't like strangers, vulgar creatures perhaps, to come and profane our nest, as he calls it. And shouldn't I hate it myself? Folly! Nonsense! I have suffered so much here that the furniture, these two carpets with the yellow dogs on them, are odious to me. I never wish to see any of the things again! And yet — Come, Regina! you're a fool, a fool, a fool! But what will he do with my *trousseau* things? Will he take them to his mother's? Well, what do I care? Let him settle it as he likes."

Every now and again she was assailed by a thought that had often worried her before. If he were not to forgive? In that case how was their story going to end? But no! Nonsense! It was impossible he should not forgive! At the worst he would come after her to persuade or force her to return. She would resist and convince him. Already she imagined that scene, lived through it. Already she felt the pain of the second parting. Meanwhile she had filled her trunk, but was not at all satisfied with her work. What a horrid, idiotic thing life was! Farewells, and always farewells, until the final farewell of death.

"Death! Since we all have to die," she thought, emptying the trunk and rearranging it, "why do we subject ourselves to so much needless annoyance? Why, for instance, am I

130

going away? Well, the time will pass all the same. It's just because one has to die that one must spend one's life as well as one can. A year or two will soon go over, but thirty or forty years are very long. And in two years — Well," she continued, folding and refolding a dress which would not lie fiat in the tray, "is it true that in two years our circumstances will have improved? Shall I be happier? Shall I not begin this same life over again — will it not go on for ever and ever to the very end? To die — to go away — Well, for that journey I shan't anyhow have the bother of doing up this detestable portmanteau; There!" (and she snatched up the dress in a fury and flung it away), "why won't even *you* get yourself folded the way I want? Come, what's the good of taking you at all? There won't be any one to dress for *there!*"

She threw herself on the bed and burst into tears. She realised for the moment the absurdity, the *naughtiness* of her caprice. She repeated that it was all a lie; what she wanted was just to annoy her husband, out of natural malice, out of a childish desire for revenge.

But after a minute she got up, dried her eyes, and soberly refolded the dress.

When Antonio came in he found her still busy with the luggage.

"Help me to shut it," said Regina, and while he bent over the lock, which was a little out of order, she added —

"Suppose there's a railway accident, and I get killed?"

"Let's hope not," he replied absently.

"Or suppose I am awfully hurt? Suppose I am taken to some hospital and have to remain there a long time?"

This time he made no reply at all.

"Do say something! What would you do?"

"Why on earth are you always thinking of such things? If you have these fancies why are you going away? There! It's locked. Where are the straps?" he asked, getting up.

She looked at him as he stood before her, so tall, so handsome, so upright, his eyes brilliant in the rosy sunset light

"To-morrow we shall be far apart!" she cried, flinging herself on his neck and kissing him deliriously; "you will be true to me! Say you will be true to me! Oh, God! if we should never see each other again!"

"You do love me, then?"

"So much — so much —"

He saw her turn pale and tremble, and he pressed her to him, losing all consciousness of himself, overwhelmed by the pleasure and the passion which intoxicated him each time Regina showed him any tenderness.

They kissed each other, and their kisses had a warmth, a bitterness, an occult savour of anguish, which produced a sense of ineffable voluptuousness. Regina wept; Antonio said senseless things and implored her not to leave him.

Then they both laughed.

"After all you aren't going to the North Pole," said Antonio. "I declare you are really crying! Pooh! a month will soon pass. And I'll come very soon. At this hour we'll go out together in a boat, when the Po is all rosy —"

"If there isn't a railway accident!" she said bitterly. "Well! here are the straps. Pull them as tight as you can."

PART II

CHAPTER I

THE crazy little carriage belonging to Petrin il Gliglo rattled along by the river-side towards Viadana. Regina was seated, not particularly comfortably, between her brother and sister, who had come to meet her at Casalmaggiore station. She laughed and talked, but now and then fell silent, absent-minded, and sad. Then Toscana and Gigino, being slightly in awe of her, became also silent and embarrassed.

The night was hot; the sky opaque blue, furrowed by long grey clouds. The big red moon, just risen above the horizon, illumined the river and the motionless woods with a splendour suggestive of far-off fire. The immense silence was now and then broken by distant voices from across the Po; a sharp damp odour of grass flooded the air, waking in Regina a train of melancholy associations.

Now she had arrived, now she was in the place of her nostalgia, in the dreamed-of harbour of refuge, it was strange that her soul was still lost to her. Just as at one time she had seemed to herself to have taken only her outward person to Rome, leaving her soul like a wandering firefly on the banks of the Po, so now it was only her suffering and tired body which she had brought back to the river-side. Her soul had escaped — flown back to Rome. What was Antonio doing at this hour? Was he very miserable? Was he conscious of his wife's soul pressing him tighter than ever her arms had pressed him? Had he written to her? Antonio! Antonio!

Burning tears filled her eyes, and she suddenly fell silent, her thoughts wandering and lost in a sorrowful far-away.

She had already repented her letter, or at least of having written it so soon. She could have sent it quite well from here! He would have felt it less — so she told herself, trying to disguise her remorse.

"And the Master? And Gabri and Gabrie?" she asked aloud, as they passed Fossa Caprara, whose little white church, flushed by the moon, stood up clearly against the blackness of the meadow-side plane-trees. At the other side of the road was a row of silver willows, and between them the river glistened like antique, lightly oxidised glass. The whole scene suggested a picture by Baratta.

Toscana and Gigi both broke into stifled laughter.

"What's the matter?" queried Regina.

The boy controlled himself, but Toscana laughed louder.

"Whatever is it? Is the Master going to be married?"

"*Lu el vorres, se, ma li doni li nal reul mia, corpu dla madosca* (He'd be willing enough, but the women won't have him)," said Petrin, turning a little and joining in the "children's" talk.

"They want to go to — to Rome! Gabri and Gabrie!" said Toscana at last, and her brother again burst out laughing.

"Why do they want to go to Rome?"

"Gabri wants to get a place and to help Gabrie in her studies, as she intends to be a Professor ———"

"Ah! Ah! Ah!"

Then they laughed, all four, and Regina forgot her troubles. The boy and girl thought of going to Rome, as they thought of going to Viadana, without help and without money! It was amusing.

"And what does the Master say?"

"He's mad!" interrupted Petrin, turning his face, which was round and red like the moon. "*El diss, chi vaga magari a pe: i dventarà na gran roba* (He says let them go if it's even on foot! they'll turn out great!)"

Then Gigi mimicked Gabri, who talked through his nose:—

"We could go to Milan, of course, but there's no university there which admits women, like the universities of Florence and Rome. Rome is the capital of Italy; we'll go there. I'll be a printer, and Gabrie shall study."

And Toscana mimicked Gabrie:—

"My brother shall print all my books."

"My dear children, I think you are jealous," said Regina.

"Oh!" they cried, cut to the quick, for Gigi did verily want to go to Rome for his college course, and Toscana, who had a pretty mezzo-soprano voice, had a plan of living at her sister's to learn singing.

Regina became thoughtful, guessing their own and their friends' dreams, and remembering her own earlier illusions. She vainly sought to shake off the sadness, the remorse, the presentiment of evil, which was weighing her down.

"And you, Petrin, I suppose you want to go to Rome too? Couldn't you bring Gabri and Gabrie in this chaise?"

"I'm going to Paris," the man answered, stolidly.

"To be sure! I remember you thought of it last year. You said you had enough money."

"So I have still. I can't spend it here, and my uncle in Paris keeps writing 'Come! Come!'"

Regina was not listening. She was caught up in a pleasure, expected indeed, which yet took her by surprise, soothing her sick heart as a balsam soothes a wound. For there, in the hollow behind the row of black trees bordering the viassolin (lane), was the little white house, a lamp shining from its window! Already she heard the scraping voice of the frogs, which croaked in the ditch beside the lane. Shadows of two persons were spread across the road, and a soprano voice resounded in a prolonged call, like the shout of a would-be passenger to the ferryman on the opposite bank of the river —

"Regina—a—a—"

"It's that fool Adamo," said Gigi; "he's always calling you like that. He says you ought to hear him in Rome. She shouts, too," he added, pinching Toscana's knee.

"And so do you," said Toscana.

The voice rang out again, sent back by the water, echoing to the farther shore. Regina jumped from the carriage, and ran towards the two dear shadows. One of them separated itself from the other and rushed madly. It was the boy, and he fell upon Regina like a thunderbolt, hugging her, squeezing her tightly, even pretending to roll her into the river.

"Adamo! Are you gone mad?" she cried, resisting him. "Do you want to break my bones?"

Then Adamo, whose great dark eyes were brilliant in the moonlight, remembered Regina had written something about being ill, and he too became suddenly shy of her.

"How you've grown!" she exclaimed. "Why, you're two inches taller than I am!"

"Ill weeds grow apace," said Gigino. Then Adamo, who for fifteen was really a giant, gave Toscana a push *en passant*, and sprang upon his brother, trying to roll him down the bank. Shouts of laughter, exclamations, a perfect explosion of fun and childish thoughtlessness filled the perfumed silence. Regina left the children to forget her in this rough amusement, and hurried on to her mother.

They embraced without a word; then Signora Tagliamari asked for Antonio.

"I thought he would have come to take care of you!" she said. "Frankly now, how are you getting on together? You haven't had any little difference —"

"Oh dear no!" cried Regina. "I told you he couldn't get away just now. I've been bothered with a lot of palpitation — we've more than a hundred steps, you know. Fancy having to climb a hundred steps three or four times every day! Antonio got anxious and took me to a specialist — an extortioner — who demanded ten *lire* for just putting a little black cup against my chest! 'Native air,' he said; a few months of her native air!' But now I'm all right again. It's almost gone off. I'll stay for a month, or two months at the outside. Then Antonio will come for me —"

Mother and daughter talked in dialect, and looked each other fixedly in the face. The moon, white now and high in the heavens from which the clouds had cleared, illumined their brows. Signora Caterina, not yet forty-five years of age, was so like Regina that she seemed her elder sister. Her complexion was even fresher, and she had great innocent eyes, more peaceful than her daughter's. Regina, however, thought her much aged, and her black dress with sleeves puffed on the shoulders, which a year ago she had believed very smart, now seemed absurdly antiquated.

"He's coming to fetch you?" repeated the mother; "that's all right."

Regina's heart tightened. Would Antonio really come? Suppose he were mortally offended and refused to come? But no — no — she would not even fancy it!

Before traversing the short footpath which led between hedges to the villa, she stood to contemplate the beautiful river landscape bathed in moonlight. A veil seemed to have been lifted. Everything now was clear and pure; the air had become fresh and transparent as crystal. The dark green of the grass contrasted with the grey-green of the willows; the ditches reflected the moon and the light trunks of the poplar-trees, whose silver leaves were like lace on the velvet background of the sky. The house, small to her who was returning from the city of enormous buildings, was white against the green of the meadows. Round it the vines festooned from tree to tree, following each other, interlacing with each other, as in some silent nocturnal dance. The great landscape, surrounding and encompassing like the high seas seen from a moving ship, the wide river, familiar from her childhood, with its little fantastic islands, shut in by the solemn outline of the woods, by the far-reaching background, where a few white towers gleamed faintly through the lunar mist, relieved and expanded Regina's soul by pure immensity.

Swarms of fireflies flashed like little shooting stars; the mills made pleasant music; the freshness and sweetness of running water vivified the air; all was peace, transparence, purity. Yet Regina felt some subtle change even in the serenity of the great landscape, as she felt it in the countenance of her mother, in the manners of her brothers and sister. No, the landscape was no longer *that*; the dear people were no longer *those*. Who, what had changed them thus? She descended the little path, and the frogs redoubled their croaks as if saluting her passage. She remembered the damp and foggy morning in which she had gone away with Antonio. Then all around was cloud, but a great light shone in her soul; now all was brilliant — the heaven, the stream, the fireflies, the blades of grass, the water in the ditches — but the gloom was dark within herself.

Another minute, and she was inside the house. Alas! it also was changed! The rooms were naked and unadorned. Dear! how small and shabby was Baratta's picture over the chimneypiece in the dining-parlour! It was no longer *that one!*

They sat down to supper, which was lively and noisy enough. Then Regina went out again, and, in spite of the fatigue which stiffened her limbs, she walked a long way by the river-side. Adamo and her sister were with her, but she felt alone, quite alone and very sad. He was far away, and his presence was wanted to fill the wondrous solitude of that pure and luminous night. What was be doing? Even in Rome at the end of June the nights are sweet and suggestive. Regina thought of the evening walks with Antonio, through wide and lonely streets near the Villa Ludovisi. The moon would be rising above the tree tops, and sometimes Antonio would take his inattentive wife in by saying —

"How high up that electric light is!"

The fragrance of the gardens mixed with the scent of hay carted in from the Campagna, and the tinkle of a mandoline, moved the heart of the homesick Regina. Yes; even at Rome the nights had been delicious before the great heat had come, when already many of the people had gone away. Now she too had gone, and who could know if she would return? Who could tell if Antonio would want her ever again! Lost in this gnawing fear, she suddenly started and checked her steps. There, on the edge of the bank, abandoned in the lush grass, was that despised old millstone, which so often had stood before her eyes in her attacks of nostalgia. Now she saw it in reality, and she noticed for the first time that it lay just exactly where a little track started, leading to the river through a grove of young willows and acacias. One evening, last autumn, standing on that little sandy path in the rosy shadow of the thicket, Antonio had sung her the song "The Pearl Fishers," and presently they had exchanged their first kiss. Now still she heard his voice vibrating in her soul.

"Mi par d'udire ancora."
(Still meseems I hear thee.)

And now she understood why she had always remembered the old stone. It would have meant nothing to her if it had not lain exactly at that spot, on that little tree-shadowed pathway, which was full of memories of him.

She stepped down it, standing for a minute among the willows, which had grown immensely, then approaching the water, now all bluish-white, gleaming under the moon. But the Po had made a new island, as soft and frothy as a chocolate cream, and even the river-side seemed to her changed.

Adamo and Toscana descended also to the water's edge, and the girl began to sing. Her voice trembled in the moonlit silence like the gurgle of a nightingale. Why she knew not, but Regina remembered the first evening at the Princess's and the voice of the elderly lady who had sung

"A te, cara."

How far off was that world! So far that perhaps she might never — never enter it again!

Ah! well! that mattered nothing! In this moonlight hour, in face of the purity of the river and of her native landscape, she seemed to have awakened from some pernicious intoxicating dream. Yet she was tormented by the doubt, the fear, that never again would she see the personages of her fevered dream, because never would Antonio come to lead her back into that far-off world. The days would pass, the months, the years. He would never come. Never! not after the three years of her suggesting, nor after ten, nor after

twenty! How was it she had not thought of this when she
had secretly planned her flight, even as a bird schemes to
leave its cage without considering the perils to which it must
expose itself? How could she help it? Which of us knows
what we shall think or feel to-morrow? She had been
dreaming; she was dreaming still. Even her increased terror,
her fear that Antonio would forget her, was perhaps no more
than a dreadful dream. But — if her dread should prove
reality —

"What would become of me?" she thought, seemingly
fascinated by the splendour of the running water. "There is
no longer any place for me here. Everything is changed;
everything seems to mistrust me. I have been a traitor to my
old world, and now it pushes me from it! And I — I did not
foresee that!"

"Come! Let us go!" she said, shaking herself and returning
to the main path. She walked along, her head drooping,
thinking she was surely mistaken. Her old world could not
betray her! It was too old to be guilty of any such crime!

"Life is certainly quite different here, but I'll get used to it
again. To-morrow, by daylight, when I am rested, I shall see
everything in its old sweet aspect!"

For the present she dared not raise her eyes, lest she should
see the willow which had protected their first kiss. She
hurried past, fearful of an unforgettable spectre.

Toscana followed her singing, while Adamo, whose figure
showed like a black spot on the glistening enamel of the
water, amused himself shouting —

"Antonio—o—o. Antonio—o—o."

The sonorous tones echoed back from the river, and Regina hastened her steps lest her sister should see her scalding tears.

Ah! *He* made no response. Never again would he answer, never again!

But the next morning's sun dispersed Regina's childish fears, her anxiety, and her remorse.

"I shall hear from him to-day or to-morrow," she thought, waking in her old room, the window of which gave on the river. A swallow, which was used to come in and roost on the blind rod, flew round the room and pecked at the shut window. Regina jumped out of bed and opened it. The sight of the swallow had filled her heart with sudden joy, which increased at sight of the smiling landscape. Irresistibly impelled, she left the house and wandered through the fields, refreshing her spirit in the intoxicating bath of greenness and morning sun and lingering dew. She followed little grassy paths, at the entrance to which tall poplars reared their white stems like gigantic columns, their tops blending into one shimmering roof. She passed along the ditches populated by families of peaceful ducks; the little snails crept along, leaving their silvery tracks upon the grass; woodpeckers concealed in the poplars marked time with their beaks in the serenity of space and solitude.

As in the moonlit evening, so now in the sunshine, every blade of grass, every leaf, every little stone, sparkled and shone. The river rolled on its majestic course, furrowed by paths of gold, flecked here and there by pearly whirlpools.

The islands, covered with evanescent vegetation, with the lace of trembling foliage, divided the splendours of the water and of the sky. Spring was still luxuriant over the immensity of the plain — spring strong as a giantess, kissed by her lover the river, decked by the thousand hands of the husbandmen, her slaves.

But when she was tired Regina threw herself upon the clover, still wet with dewdrops, and at once her thoughts flew far away. In the afternoon she began again to feel anxious and sad.

That very day visits began from inquisitive, tiresome, interested people — relations, friends, persons who wanted favours. They all imagined Regina influential to obtain anything, just because she lived in Rome. She was amused at first, but presently she wearied. All these people who came to greet and to flatter her seemed to have changed, to have grown older, simpler, less significant, than she had left them.

The Master himself came, with Gabriella, a small fair-haired creature, with pale, round face, and steely eyes, very bright, very deep, very observant.

"And so here is our Regina!" said the Master, buttoning his coat across his narrow chest. "Oh, *bravissima!* I got the postcard with the picture of the Colosseum. That really is a monument! Oh, brava, our Regina! I suppose you have visited all the monuments, both pagan and Christian? And seen the works of Michaelangelo Buonarotti? Oh, Rome! Rome! Yes, I wish my two children could get to the eternal Rome."

146

"Papa!" said Gabrie, watching Regina to see if she were laughing at him.

But Regina was merely cold and indifferent — an attitude which relieved but slightly intimidated the future lady-professor. A little later came a young lady of a titled family from Sabbioneta. She had a lovely slender figure, and was very pale, with black hair dressed *à la* Botticelli; she was smart also, wearing white gloves and tan shoes with very high heels.

Toscana, Gabrie and this young lady were all the same age — about eighteen — clever and unripe, like all school-girls. They were nominally friends. Regina, however, saw they envied and nearly hated each other. The aristocratic damsel gave herself airs, and spoke impertinences with much grace.

"Good gracious! What heels!" said Gabrie, whom nothing escaped. "But they're quite out of fashion!"

"They're always in fashion among the nobility," explained the other, condescendingly. Then they talked of a little scandal which had arisen the day before, in consequence of two Sabbioneta ladies having quarrelled in the street.

"Wives of clerks!" said the Signorina, contemptuously. "Women of the upper aristocracy would never behave like that!"

"But," said Regina, "where have you known any women of the upper aristocracy?"

"Oh! one meets them everywhere!"

"Look here, my dear; if you were to find yourself beside a lady of the upper aristocracy, and if she deigned to look at you at all, you would be frozen with humiliation and alarm."

The other girls giggled, and the Master asked eagerly —

"Regina, I wonder do you know the Duchess Colonna of San Pietro?"

"*Chi lo sa?* There are no end of duchesses in Rome!" "We have an introduction to that great lady from a friend of ours at Parma."

"Papa!" cried Gabrie, red with indignation and pride, "I don't require any introductions! I snap my fingers at great ladies one and all! What could they possibly do for me?"

"My dear child," began Regina, pitying and sarcastic, "great ladies rule the world; and so —"

She stopped and turned pale, for there was a loud knock at the door. She fancied it the bicycling postman, who brought telegrams to the villages between Casalmaggiore and Viadana. But no; it was not he.

Evening fell — red and splendid as a conflagration. The three girls went out, and Regina lingered at the window, scrutinising the distance and looking for the telegraph messenger's bicycle.

The Master and Signora Tagliamari sat on a blue Louis XV sofa at the end of the room, and talked quietly. Now and then they threw a glance at Regina, who scarcely tried to conceal her sadness and disquiet. The Master, hoping she was listening, talked of the dreams and ambitions of his children.

"Well, as they wish it, we must let them work and conquer the world. What can they do here? Be a school-master? A school-mistress? No, thank you!"

"But if they go away, won't you miss them very much?"

148

"That's not the question, Signora Caterina! It's like a tearing out of the vitals when the young ones leave the parents. But the parents have brought them into the world to see them live, not vegetate. Ah, my children!" said the Master, stretching out his arms with great emotion, "the nest will remain empty and the old father will end his days in sorrow as, in truth, he began them; but in his heart, Signora Caterina, in his heart he will say with great joy, 'I have done my duty. I have taught my little ones to fly! Oh, that my parents had done as much for me. Ah!' "

Regina still looked out. She heard the Master's babble; she heard the fresh voices and the laughter of the three young girls who were strolling along the river; she watched the sky grow pale, diaphanous, tender green like some delicate crystal, flecked with little wandering clouds like a flight of violet-grey birds. She began to feel irritated. She knew not why. Perhaps because the girls made too much noise, or the Master was talking nonsense, or the postman did not appear out of the lonely distance.

The Master pulled a note-book from his pocket, and, interrupting himself now and then to explain that he did it without his daughter's knowledge, began to read aloud some of Gabrie's sketches.

"Listen to this! See how cleverly she observes people! It's a character for a future novel. My Gabrie is always on the look-out. She sees a character, observes, sets it all down. She's like those careful housewives who preserve everything in case it may come in useful. Listen to this!"

And he read: " 'A young lady of eighteen, of titled but worn-out family, anaemic, insincere, vain, envious, ambitious; knows how to hide her faults under a cold sweetness which appears natural. She is always talking of the aristocracy. Some one once told her she resembled a Virgin of Botticelli's, and ever since she has adopted a pose of sentiment and ecstasy.' Isn't it excellent, Signora Caterina?"

"Yes, indeed; quite excellent!" said the lady, with gentle acquiescence. "Regina, come and listen. Hear how Gabrie is going to write her novel. It's quite excellent."

Regina remembered the novel she also had wished to write, with which she was quite out of tune to-day. Her irritation increased. She had recognised the signorina from Sabbioneta in Gabrie's sketch, and resented the pretensions, the ambitions, the dreams of the Master's little daughter. The simple father's delusions were pitiable. Better tear them away and bid him teach his child to make herself a real life, refusing to send her forth into the world where the poor are swallowed up like straws in the pearly whirlpools of the river. But in the faded eyes of the humble school-master she saw such glow of tenderness, of regret, of dream, that she had not the heart to rob him of his only wealth — Illusion.

"It's so dreadful to have no more illusions," she said to herself, and added that to-day there would come no telegram from Antonio.

As evening came on she again fell a prey to puerile terrors and unwholesome thoughts. She was wrapped in frozen shadows — a mysterious wind drove her towards a glacial atmosphere, where all was dizziness and grief. She seemed suspended thus in a twilight heaven, wafted towards an unknown land, like the little wandering clouds, the violet-grey birds, migrating without hope of rest. The old world to which she had returned had become small, melancholy, tiresome. She was no longer at her ease in it. But at last she was driven to confess a melancholy thing. It was not her old world which had changed; oh no! it was herself.

CHAPTER II

THAT night she dreamed she was standing on the river-bank in the company of Marianna, Madame Makuline's companion, who had come to hurry her back to Rome.

"Monsieur Antonio is in an awful rage," she said. "He came to Madame and told her all about it, and has borrowed 10,000 *lire* to set up a finer house. Then he sent me to bring you back."

In her dream Regina shook with shame and anger. She set off with rapid steps to Viadana, intending to send Antonio a thundering telegram.

"If he has still got the money," she sobbed, "I wish him to give it all back this very moment. I don't want a finer house. I don't want anything! I'll come home at once. I'd come back, even if we had grown poorer, even if we had to live in a garret!"

And she walked and walked, as one walks in dreams, vainly trying to run, crushed by unspeakable grief. Night fell; the mist covered the river. Viadana seemed farther and farther. Marianna ran behind Regina, telling her that the day before in Via Tritone she had met the ugly fireman who had rescued her at Odessa.

"He had turned into a priest, if you please; but coquettish, and under his cassock he had a silk petticoat with three flounces, which made a *frou-frou*." And she laughed.

Her unpleasant expression exasperated Regina almost to fits. She was not laughing at the fireman, but at something else, unknown, mysterious and terrible. Suddenly Regina turned and tried to strike her, but the *signorina* started backwards and Regina tumbled down.

The shock of this fall wakened the dreamer, whose first conscious thought was of the fireman priest with the silk flounces. In the dream this detail had disgusted her horribly, and the disgust remained for long hours. Sleep had deserted her. It was still night, but already across the deep silence which precedes the dawn came the earliest sounds of the quiet country life — a tinkling of tiny bells trembling on the banks of the streams, going always farther and farther away. The silvery, insistent, childish note seemed to Regina the voice of infinite melancholy.

A thousand memories started up in her mind, insistent, puerile, melancholy, like that little silvery tinkling.

"My whole life has been useless," she thought, "and now, now, just when I might have found an object, I have flung it away like a rag! But what object could I have had?" she asked herself presently. "Well, family life is supposed to be an object. Everything is relative. The good wife who makes a good family contributes no less than the worker or the moralist to the perfection of society. I have never made anything but dreams. I remember the dream I had the second night after our arrival. I thought Madame Makuline had given me a castle."

Just then she heard a faint rustle, and something like a scarce perceptible but tender groan emitted by some minute dreaming creature.

"It's the swallow! Does it also dream? Do birds think and dream? I expect they do. Why, I wonder, is this one all alone? And *he!*"

She felt a sudden movement of joy, thinking that this day the letter from Antonio would surely come!

The hours passed. Post hour came, but there was no post. Regina went out of doors to hide her agitation, to forget, to flee from the extravagant fears which assailed her! As on the preceding day, she wandered in the woods and lanes, by the river-side, upon which beat the full rays of the sun. Everywhere fear followed her like her shadow.

"He has not forgiven me. He will not write. In his place I would do the same. He wants to punish me by his silence, or he is coming to take me back by force. A wife has to follow her husband, otherwise he can demand a legal separation. What would become of me if he did that?"

Pride would not allow her to confess that if Antonio insisted on her return she would go to him at once merely to be forgiven. But as the slow hours rolled on her pride weakened. Memory assailed her with consuming tenderness. She sickened at the thought of passing her life's best years deprived of love.

"Oh, why didn't I think of all this before?" she asked herself. And she remembered she had thought of it, but so vaguely, so lightly, that her faint fears had not held her back from folly. In an opposing sense she reasoned thus.

"It's my character made up of discontent and contradiction which tosses me hither and thither like a wave of the sea. Why have I changed so soon? If I go back to Rome I shall be sorry immediately that I didn't carry out my project, which is perhaps better than I am now thinking it. Perhaps after all he thinks it reasonable, and is delaying to write that I may see he accepts it. Oh! there's a bit of four-leaved clover! Yes; that's what it is. He accepts my plan."

She stooped, but did not pick the four-leaved clover. What luck could it bring to her?

She felt hurt and saddened by the idea that Antonio was not broken-hearted; that he would not try by all means in his power to get her back; would not reproach, punish, coax her, move her to agonies of despair and love.

"He has not written. He isn't going to write," she said again. "He will come himself to-morrow, or the next day, at the first moment he can. What shall I say when I see him?"

And in the joy of renewed confidence she forgot everything else.

He neither wrote nor came. The days went by; the slow, cruel hours passed in a waiting increasingly apprehensive. Regina wondered at the presentiment she had felt from the very moment of her arrival — the presentiment that her husband would write to her no more. Yet still she waited.

She perceived that her mother, observant of Antonio's silence, was watching her with those beautiful serene eyes now disturbed and unquiet. So one morning she feigned to have met the postman and brought back a letter. She came into the house, an envelope in her hand, crying —

"He's not well! He's laid up with fever!"

The mother was opening a silvery fish from the Po, and she looked at her daughter, scarcely raising her eyes from her work. Regina saw that her mother was not deceived, and that wistful maternal glance agitated her to the very depths of her soul. And the silver fish, in whose inside was discovered another little black fish, reminded her of Antonio's promise —

"We will go out together in a boat. We will fish together in the beautiful red evenings —" and of all the torturing tenderness of that last afternoon they had spent together.

She went to her room and wrote him a letter. Pride would not let her set down her real thoughts; but between the lines he might read all her stinging anxiety, her fear, her penitence. He did not reply.

Suppose he were really ill? Regina thought of writing to Arduina, but quickly felt ashamed of the idea. No. All those people whom Antonio's unfortunate notion had thrust between her and him on the first days of her arrival — all those people, the prime cause, perhaps, of their present misery, were repugnant to her, positively hateful.

But what was he doing? Had he shut up the apartment in Via d'Azeglio and gone back to his family? The mere recollection of the marble stair which led to that place of suffering, to that low, grey room where a mysterious incubus had weighed down her soul, was enough to darken her countenance.

She wrote again. Antonio did not reply.

Then Regina felt something rebound violently within her, like a rod which straightens itself with a whirr after breaking the fetters which have tied it down. It was her pride. She thought Antonio must have guessed her unspoken drama of grief, lament, tenderness and remorse, and that he was passing the bounds of just punishment.

"He is taking advantage of me," she thought, "but we will see which is the stronger!"

"Antonio," she wrote to him, "I have been here for a whole fortnight of patience and suffering. What is the meaning of your silence? If you have neither understood nor pardoned the letter I left for you, surely you must have written to tell me so? If you have understood, and have forgiven, or, better still, if you have consented to what I ask, equally in that case you must have written. You cannot be ill, or one of your people would certainly have informed me. Your conduct is so strange that now I am more offended than grieved by it. Am I a child that you punish me in this childish way? Perhaps it has been a caprice on my part; but, mind, it is not the freak of a child! It is one of those caprices which, punished too severely, may end fatally. Antonio, don't suppose your silence will bring me back to your side like a whipped and famished hound. If you think you can take advantage of my love for you, you are altogether mistaken. I will never go back unless you call me; and whether this return is to be soon or not for a long time, that is what we must decide together. Either write or come to me at once. If within eight days you have not replied, I shall not write again — not until you have written yourself. But don't imagine that my answer *then* could be what it would be *now*. After all, Antonio, we are husband and wife; we are not mere lovers who can allow themselves jesting and nonsense, because their passion is perhaps destined to come to nothing and to remain for them only a memory. You and I are united by duty, and by more serious, stronger, more tragic fetters than passion. If I have been —let us admit it — thoughtless, romantic, even childish, this is no reason why you should be the same. And if you wish to be like that, I, at any rate, don't wish it any longer. This is why I am writing to-day. This is why I still wait. I repeat —write to me or come. We will decide together. And now it all depends upon you whether the fault is to be all mine or all yours, or to belong partly to us both. I am waiting.

"REGINA."

Two days later Antonio replied with a telegram:—

"Starting to-morrow. Meet me at Casalmaggiore. Love and kisses!"

Love and kisses! Then he forgave! He was coming! He would forget — had already forgotten! Regina felt as if she had awakened from an evil dream. Ever afterwards she remembered the immense joy — melancholy perhaps, but on this very account soothing and delicious — which she experienced that day. She seemed to have come off victorious in the family battle. It was she who, just to save appearances, had recalled her husband. He was apparently defeated. But in reality it was she, it was she! And by her own wish and without repentance. Still, by this first victory she had tested her hidden strength and had found it great. Henceforth she could rely upon it as a safeguard in all the dangers of life.

"Life belongs to the strong," she thought, "and who knows, who knows but that I too may succeed in achieving fortune? From this out I am a different person. What has changed me I do not know!" she exclaimed, wandering along by the river as if lovelorn.

"How full of strange incoherence and contradiction is the human soul! Who is it says that inconsistency is the true characteristic of man? Certainly the greater part of our disasters come from punctiliousness, from pride, as to letting ourselves be inconsistent. We often ought to be, we often wish to be, inconsistent. Well!" she continued, increasingly surprised at herself, "it's very strange! A month, a fortnight ago, I was another person! Why, how have I changed like this? Here I am ready, without the smallest complaint, to leave this world which held me so tight. Here I am ready to follow my husband and to take up again the modest monotonous life which I did detest, but which now I do not mind in the least. Is it because I love Antonio? Yes; certainly; but there is some other reason as well — something which I can't make out. I don't want to make it out. I won't torment myself any more. I will understand only that happiness lies in love, in domestic peace, in the picture which life makes, not in the picture's frame. But how wonderfully changed I am!" she repeated, in astonishment. "Such a strange, sudden metamorphosis would seem unnatural in a novel. Yet it is true! the soul — what a strange thing it is! Well, I won't think any more! *He* is coming, and that is all the world!"

She walked on and on, analysing, and, at the same time, enjoying her happiness. Rays of pleasure flashed across her spirit as she remembered Antonio's eyes, lips, hands. Hers! Hers! Hers, this young man! his love, his soul, his body! She had never before rightly realised this great, this only happiness!

She walked and walked. The sunset hour came. Though it was mid-July, the country was still fresh. Now and then a transparent cloud veiled the sun. A *gabbia* [a special cart used in the Mantuan district for carrying wheat, maize etc.] passed her. The driver, fair complexioned and careless as a child, was singing to himself. The wheels seemed mere diaphanous clouds of dust, rosy lilac in the sunset. Quietly the great river rolled in from the horizon; quietly it vanished to the horizon, passing along, calm, luminous, solemn. In its omnipotent force the river also appeared beneficent and happy, bringer of peace to its fertile shores. In the very depths of her soul Regina was stirred by the peace of the wide-stretched valley, by the far-reaching beauty of the horizon, by the sublime, health-giving tranquillity of the fields, the woods, the shores, by all the emanations of grace from what she fancied a god transformed into a stream. She had renewed her youth. Everything within, everything around her was poetic, beautiful, stainless. Sorrow and evil had fled far off, carried away by the river, vanished below the meeting line of earth and heaven. The western sky had become all one soft yet burning rose colour; the Po grew ever redder and more resplendent; the woods were drawn out in long black lines against the flaming background; the pungent perfume of grass hung on the air. Regina, vaguely watching a laden boat as it descended the sunlit water from Cicognara, became pensive and even sad. She asked herself whether all the enchantment of this peace did not hide something insidious, whether it were not like those mock islands covered with evanescent verdure, amorously encircled by the river which yet reserved the right of swallowing them at the first flood; enchanted islets for the eye, unstable and engulfing for the unwary foot.

There were three mills on the river close to where Regina was standing. She had often admired the most ancient one, the lower walls of which were rudely decorated with prehistoric pictures, red and blue scrawls representing the Madonna and St. James, a bush, and a boat. The mill was surrounded by silvery-green water, which dashed against the shining wheel. Boats came and went laden with white sacks. On the platform stood the white figure of the miller, a young woman sometimes by his side.

Regina had often seen those two figures. The man was elderly but still erect, his face shaven, lean and sallow, his cynical green eyes half shut. The young woman also had half-shut, light eyes. She was tall and lithe, pretty, in spite of too rosy a face, and hair dishevelled and over red. She must be the miller's daughter, Regina had supposed, probably in love with the mill servant. Life at the mill must be happy as in a fairy tale.

But later she had heard that the girl was the miller's wife, that he drank, that he was jealous, and kept his wife imprisoned with him in the mill. Evidently a tragedy was being played in the interior of this prehistoric habitation! The running water, the turning wheel, were reciting the eternal tale of human grief — were singing of the jealous, tipsy, disagreeable old man, and of the girl, fiery as her curls, brooding continually over rebellious and sinful thoughts.

The boat, laden with workmen, touched the shore, and Regina recognised one or two whom she knew. They invited her to go with them to the mill, to eat *gnocchi*.

She agreed.

The Po was becoming more and more splendid, reflecting the whole west, the great golden clouds, the reversed woods. An enchanted land seemed to be submerged there in the water. Regina admired and was silent, listening to the lively chatter of her companions. They were talking of ghosts. Old Joachin, the rich miller — big, purple-faced, goggle-eyed — one night, when he was passing along the bank in his cart, saw a huge white dog, which jumped out of a bush and silently and obstinately followed him. Who could believe this dog a dog? It was a spirit.

And one moonshiny night Petrin the boatman had seen from the river a most strange, glistening creature flying along the shore.

"A bicycle," pronounced old Joachin, beating his empty pipe against the palm of his hand.

"Oh, very well! Then your white dog was just a white dog!"

Presently the party arrived at the mill. The miller came forward, all smiles, and stretched out his hand to Regina.

"*Ma benissimo!* This is an honour, Signora Regina! I know you well; and here is my wife, who knows you quite well too!"

The ruddy young woman hung back shyly.

"How do you do?" said Regina, looking at her curiously. She noticed that the miller was not quite so old nor the woman so young as they had seemed from the distance.

The inside of the mill was very clean. A fire was burning at the foot of the plank bed. Pots and pans of red earthenware were arranged on the dresser. The mechanism of the mill was of the most primitive pattern. Two large, round stones of a bluish hue were revolving one upon the other, moved by the wheel. The flour slipped out slowly, falling into a sack.

And the wheel turned and turned, pursued, battered, lashed by the noisy water. Wheel and water seemed to be whirling in a fight, merry in appearance, pitiless and cruel in reality.

Old Joachin took his wife by the shoulder and shook her.

"Go and make the *gnocchi*, woman! Make them as fat as your fingers!"

She giggled, looking at her hands, which were enormous, then took flour and kneaded it with river water.

Regina, finding her presence embarrassed the woman, went to the platform and sat down on a sack of flour. She lost herself in contemplation of the wonderful sunset. Already the sun was touching the river, making a great

column of gold. The water came burning down from that
magic spot, but upon reaching the mill its fire began to go
out, and it disappeared into the east, pallid as mother-o'-
pearl.

Regina saw the whirlpools all luminous like immense
shells; the mill wheel flapped in the golden water like a huge
metallic fan; the falling drops, in which the slant rays of the
sun were refracted, showed all the rainbow colours.

The miller drew near Regina and bent towards her. His feet
were bare, his thin legs and arms naked. His little green eyes
smiled cynically.

"If I may, I'll speak two words with you," he murmured,
respectfully.

"Yes?" said Regina.

Instead of two words, he told her a great number of
interesting things. For instance, that he had all his teeth; that
he paid 100 *lire* tax on his *richezze mobili*; that the wheel could
be stopped with a rope; that his wife was timid and diffident,
and always wanted to be tied to her husband's coat tails.
Regina listened, half-disappointed that her tragedy had been
wholly imaginary.

"You know," said the miller, who, while he talked, never
stopped rubbing his arms and scratching one foot with the
other, "I wish to goodness she'd go away for a fortnight or
a month."

"Why?" asked Regina, ingenuously.

"Why, Signora Regina —" said the man, embarrassed, and
scratching with all his might — "well, you have no baby
either, have you? And you want one, I suppose? You'll be

certain to have one now, after being away for a month. Well, if you'll come with me, I'll show you how we stop the wheel," he said, alarmed lest he had offended her.

Regina followed him. The old man stopped the wheel with the rope and asked his guest to examine the flour, the sack, the mill stones. In the sudden silence of the wheel he laughed without any reason. A dense cloud involved everything. The miller's wife, quite confounded by Regina's presence, turned scarlet as she fried the *gnocchi*. The figures on the platform were silhouetted against the golden background.

The miller looked at Regina and laughed, and suddenly, without knowing why, she laughed herself.

CHAPTER III

AGAIN the crazy little carriage belonging to Petrin il Gliglo rolled along the river-bank. The night was hot, dark, and damp. After a few sentences on indifferent matters, Antonio and Regina had fallen silent, as if overcome by the quiet of the country and the night. They were silent, but Regina spoke within herself, as was her habit, and made note of a sad discovery. Antonio was changed! No; this time it really was not fancy! He was changed.

"He kissed me almost in a frenzy the moment he got out of the train — as if he had feared he would never see me again. Then all of a sudden his expression changed. Something gloomy, something deprecating, came into his eyes. Has he lost his faith in me? Is there something between us now? Well! of course it's like this at first. To-morrow the constraint will have passed off."

To drive away all vestige of fear she spoke to him again; but her heart was thumping uncomfortably, and when she pressed his hand and found it inert and cold, unexplained anxiety again took possession of her. It was almost as bad as her terror during those days when she had been vainly expecting a letter from him.

"Oh, what is it?" she thought. "Has he not forgiven me?"

"Feel!" she said, putting Antonio's hand against her side. The hand became suddenly animated.

"Is your heart still bad?" he asked, as if bethinking himself.

"No! It's beating for joy!" she replied, and talked on very fast. "Yesterday I went to the old painted mill, to eat *gnocchi*. It was such fun! There was a splendid sunset. What a character that old miller is!"

She told the miller's prophecy, then went on to describe a visit to the Master and his family.

"He's a character too! But he's really quite mad. He wants to send the children to Rome — the boy to make his fortune, the girl to become famous. He says —" and she mimicked the Master's speeches and voice.

Antonio laughed, but his laugh was cold and contemptuous, and seemed far away.

"Oh, what is it?" thought Regina, overwhelmed by unexpected sadness. That scoffing laugh was new in Antonio. He was scornful. Was it of herself?

Fancies! Folly!

"As soon as we're alone, I'll take him by the shoulders, shake him and cry, 'What on earth's the matter with you? Haven't you forgiven me? Don't let us have any more nonsense, please! There has been more than enough!' "

They were silent again. The chaise rolled on through the dark warm night, through the pungent perfume of the motionless vegetation. The young trees along the river were black in the darkness, blacker even than the darkness. Everything was silent, everything exhaled sweet odours. From the hot ground, from the damp wayside weeds, from the paths bathed in dew, rose an intoxicating scent, a silent breath, dreamy and voluptuous. Beside every bush seemed to stand a woman waiting for her lover, her desire and her joy filling the emptiness of the hot, rich night.

"To-morrow we'll go out by moonlight," said Regina, who could not keep quite silent. "The night I arrived there was a beautiful moon, wasn't there, Petrin?"

The driver made no reply.

"He's asleep. We shall be upset," said Antonio.

"Oh, no! The old horse is quite used to it," returned Regina, and sure now that Petrin was not listening, she added, softly, "How wretched I was that evening!"

"Were you?" said Antonio, as if remembering nothing of what had passed.

Regina turned round, astonished and trembling. She had no strength left.

"Antonio," she whispered, her arm round his neck, "Why are you like this? What is it? What's the matter?"

"Do you ask?" he murmured, not looking at her. His voice was hardly a breath, but a breath in which Regina felt the raging of a storm of resentment. Again she was afraid.

"You don't mean to forgive me!" she said, separating herself from him. But already he had turned and pressed her to him, his lips seeking hers with a fervour which seemed rather of despair than of passion.

Adamo's voice rang out from the bank.

"Antonio—o! Regina—a!"

Then Petrin's broad back swayed from right to left, and his whip cracked.

"*Quel ragass m'ha fatto ciappar pagura* (That boy made me jump)," said the man, as if talking in his sleep. Antonio and

Regina moved apart, and she blushed in the darkness as if new to love.

Her heart was beating strongly, but between its strokes of joy were shudders of sickening grief.

After supper, as on the night of Regina's arrival, they all went out, except Signora Caterina. Toscana and her brothers ran about as usual, leaving their sister and her husband far behind.

"Yes," said Regina; "my mother is right. You look ill! Surely you've been having fever!"

He did not answer at once. He was thinking. He seemed seeking an appropriate beginning for a speech and un-successful in finding it.

"Your mother herself looks out of sorts," he said at last. "What distress you must have caused her, Regina!"

"I? But I never told her a word!"

"Didn't you?"

"Don't you believe me? To explain your silence, I said you were ill."

"Oh, did you?" he repeated, still incredulous. "Well, I was imagining it was her advice had made you less — unkind."

"Unkind? What do you mean?" she asked, coldly.

Antonio was perhaps frightened in his turn. Had he deceived himself, thinking Regina penitent and ready to come home? He became animated, and found that beginning of speech which he had sought. The hour of explanation had come.

Regina asked nothing better; but to her surprise she did not feel the commotion, the joy, the tenderness, which she had anticipated. She was distressed. Antonio had forgiven her; he had suffered; he had come, resolved to take her back at all costs; he loved her more than ever, with true passion; he was united to her by all the strong ties of his heart and his senses. But she was not content; she was not properly stirred. Something was standing between her husband and herself — something inexorable. They walked as of old, their arms round each other, their fingers interlaced; but there was a whole gulf between them, a whole immense river of cold, colourless water, perfidiously silent, like that river down there below the road, scarce visible between the black trees in the black night.

Regina was certainly the clearer-sighted of the two, and she now saw a mysterious thing. Once it was her soul which had escaped Antonio, hiding itself behind a world of littlenesses, of vanity, of vain desires and ambitions; now, on the contrary, it was his soul which some occult and violent force was trying to wrest away from her. She attempted to fathom this mystery.

"What is it? He loves me; he has forgiven me! But he mistrusts, is afraid of me. Why is this?"

"Regina," said Antonio, "you must explain to me what you are intending to do."

"You know already."

"I don't. I don't understand. Your last letter was even worse and uglier than the first. I am not going to reproach you — as you say, it would be useless; but another man in my place — well, never mind! You have told me more than a hundred times that I don't understand you. Now, to show you at least my good-will, I ask you to explain."

"But didn't I write it?" she cried, half humble, half pettish. "I wrote, 'It all depends upon you.' "

"Do you mean you will come back with me to Rome?"

"Yes."

"Oh, very well. I am quite ready to forget all that has taken place. But now I must know one thing more. Why have you given up your idea so soon? I say *idea*, not caprice, because it has seemed to me, and seems still, a very serious matter."

"How can I tell? Are we able to explain our ideas or caprices, or whatever you choose to call them? Have you never contradicted yourself? One thinks one way to-day, another to-morrow. Are we masters of ourselves? You said a minute ago, 'If I were another man.' I understood what you meant; that if you had been another man you would have ill-treated, insulted me. But, on the contrary, you are very kind — perhaps kinder than before. Can you explain to yourself why, instead of hating me for the trick I have played you, you care for me perhaps more than before?"

She spoke not entirely of conviction; but she wished to suggest to Antonio the line he had better take. She believed she had succeeded, for he became thoughtful as if repeating her questions to himself, and presently said with a slight smile —

"Well, I dare say you are right!"

"Don't let us say any more about it," cried Regina, imitating the Master again. "It has been a freak — a folly of youth. Let us draw a veil over the past."

"You know you have humiliated me," urged Antonio; "it was a blow in my face — a betrayal — and besides ——"

"Oh, don't we all make mistakes? What about all the other women? Those who really betray their husbands?"

"Yes," he answered her, quickly, "and the husbands who betray their wives! Generally it's the bad husband who makes the bad wife. But I never gave you any cause, Regina! What had you to complain of in me? True enough I am not a lord, but you knew that from the first. Had I promised you more than I could give? Well, you should have had patience — confidence. Our circumstances may improve any day. I shall never be rich, but, of course, in a little time my position must alter to a certain extent ——"

"Oh, that'll do! That's enough," protested Regina. "You did not guess that my fancy would pass away so soon?"

"Did you think it yourself when you wrote? My dear, things seriously done have serious effects. Well, we will cancel the past, as the Master says. I've got one good thing to tell you, however. Your letter has done us some good after all. I saw at once that in one sense you were right. Everybody has to try to get on, to push, to solicit, to intrigue, *Out with you, sir, in with me!* and all that. 'Come,' I said to myself, 'isn't it just possible I might do something?' Well, I began my solicitations. I set Arduina to work. I had her running about the town all day. I sent her to the Senator, the Princess, to her journalists and deputies ——"

"Of course you didn't tell her ——" interrupted Regina.

"I told her no more than this: 'I want to be secretary to some Minister. Find me a berth, and I'll get you six subscribers to your paper among my colleagues.' She laughed and went to work, and I set others in motion too. But it was all no good; there wasn't a vacant post anywhere. Then Arduina gave me an idea. You remember how the Princess sent for me one day to ask information about the Stock Exchange, and how I saw she was beginning to be suspicious of Cavaliere R——? Well, Arduina, who is no fool at bottom, sounded Marianna. She found out it was just as I thought. She wanted to put some one to look over his shoulder. 'Why shouldn't you become her confidentail agent?' said Arduina. So I went to the Princess and offered my services. I said the office of a spy did not seem to me very delicate, but that I would accept it, as it was a case of urgent necessity. She convinced me that the indelicacy was on the Cavaliere's part, and said that if I succeeded in being useful she would be most grateful. That was on the 5th. Four days later I proved that the Cavaliere R—— was speculating with her money more for himself than for her."

"How did you manage it?" asked Regina, vaguely uneasy at Antonio's relation.

"I will explain. You must know that Madame, for all her riches, is as ignorant as a child about money affairs. She doesn't understand a thing about banking, stocks, shares, book-keeping, and so forth, and naturally has to put herself entirely into the hands of some person who acts for her, and to accept all propositions and all results of operations without any control. The Cavaliere R—— has been serving her in this way for many years, and no doubt at first he was perfectly scrupulous in his operations and in the statement of accounts. But presently, aware that she knew nothing whatever about these affairs and accepted with her eyes shut whatever he chose to say, he thought he might profit without even risk of being found out. Marianna, however, has been observing for some time that the proceeds of the speculations have kept continually diminishing, which the Cavaliere accounted for by the special conditions of the money market, by monetary crises, by the rupture of commercial contracts, by the war, etc. At her instigation, Madame made me the proposition I told you of. Well, as she pressed me, I accepted the job, and told her to put me in full possession of some recent transaction that I might verify it. Next morning Madame sent me one of his statements, on which I read, among other things—

" 'Exchange of 10000.00 *marks*, at 123.20 *lire*; acquired 8 shares of Acqua Marcia at 1465.00 *lire*.'

"I consulted at the office the prices on the Exchange reported in the *Gazzetta Ufficiale* and found it was different from what he had put down. Not satisfied with this, at lunch-time I went to the Chamber of Commerce and got a list of the Exchanges of the preceding day, and made certain of the difference I had already made out: the Berlin Exchange was at 123.37 *lire*, and the shares of Acqua Marcia were quoted at 1460.00 *lire*. Consequently, Cavaliere R—— had put 57 *lire* into his own pocket. Then I made Madame give me all his statements up to the end of June, which she had kept mixed up with her private letters and newspapers. By the help of the bulletins of the Exchange and other publications which

174

I got through a stock-broker I know, I proved that in these operations alone the man had made a profit of 137.45 *lire*."

"And then?"

"Oh, then Madame thanked me very warmly and said she'd take the opportunity of her going away to relieve the Cavaliere of his services, and on her return would ask me to undertake the speculating. She left home on the 12th, and has given me a whole lot of matters to disentangle before her return. I must look up my German a bit, for she has no end of business with Germany."

Instinctively, Regina took her hand away from Antonio's, and said—

"Well?"

"Well?" repeated Antonio.

"How much is she able to pay you?"

"For the present, a hundred *lire* a month; but a little later, you see, I'm to become her *factotum*. I must grind at the German," he repeated, seeming much pre-occupied with this question of the language. He talked on about it, but Regina was no longer listening.

"Let's go back!" she said, turning suddenly. "You must be tired! Toscana! Gigi! Shall we go in? Here they come! Antonio, it's a funny thing, but, do you know, I dreamt something very like this the first night I was here."

She told her dream of the ten thousand *lire*, Marianna, and the fireman.

"There's no doubt at all that dreams are very queer things!"

He made no reply.

"And why," asked Regina, after a moment of hesitation, "why didn't you write to me?"

"What was I to write to you? You had settled the question for yourself. I wished to settle it in another manner, and a discussion by letter seemed useless. Besides, I had decided to come to you here."

Antonio's explanation was rather lame, but Regina did not insist. He went on to describe his plans for the future.

"Next year I'll go up for the examination and pass at latest in October. Meantime, we can count on 325 *lire* the month, net and certain. You see, our position is already a little better. I have sub-let the apartment, and I've seen a capital *mezzanino*, in Via Balbo, for 80 *lire*. Three first-rate rooms looking on the street, and one, a large one, on the courtyard; all very light and sunny. We can have two drawing-rooms."

Regina listened, but she felt something which was not joy. Antonio's news was not altogether cheering, and his voice seemed entirely changed. It was the monotonous, distant voice of one not the merry and happy Antonio of old. It moved her to positive pity.

Two drawing-rooms! Yes, she understood his pre-occupation. He wanted to give her something of what in her infatuation she had dreamed, in her foolishness had asked. He wanted to give her at least the illusion that she was a fine lady, prosperous and fashionable. And he made his offer quite humbly, as if he were the guilty one, ready for any weakness, if only he might be forgiven! She would have preferred a tragedy of reproaches, and then the sweetness of pardon; a storm which would leave their domestic heaven clearer than before.

On the other hand, she realised that Antonio's love was blinder, more abject, than she had imagined; in this, at least, there was some satisfaction.

They walked towards the house, so absorbed in their prosy talk that they no longer noticed the mystery of the hot, sweet night brooding over the colourless river, the dark sky, the motionless black woods, like the profile of a forest sculptured on a bronze bas-relief.

From time to time flashed the violet gleam of a bicycle lamp, which went silently by, preceded by a big butterfly of shadow. At intervals a few voices vibrated in the silence and immobility of the sleeping world. The magic of dream floated in the warm, soft air. But the young pair no longer felt the magic. Antonio was hot about his plans; Regina overcome by pity for the man whom her folly had so miserably and so profoundly changed.

CHAPTER IV

THEY returned to Rome about the middle of August, and changed their dwelling. The *mezzanino* was really charming, but one of the rooms remained almost empty for lack of furniture.

"We might let it," suggested Regina.

"Fie! Who's the little *bourgeoise* now?" cried Antonio, indignant.

"Oh, one changes as life goes on," she said, not without bitterness; "one gets older, gets whipped, ends by adapting oneself to anything."

She did in fact adapt herself — without knowing why. In herself and in her surroundings, in the quiet life which she and Antonio had resumed, she was sometimes conscious of an emptiness like that in the new apartment, but she no longer rebelled.

After dinner they would go out arm in arm in the good *bourgeois* fashion, stifling the gentle tedium of their existence at the Café Aragno or in Piazza Colonna, oftener in the streets and avenues round Piazza della Stazione. The little tables in front of the Café Gambrinus or Café Morteo were always surrounded by people who at any rate seemed very lively. Crowds tramped the broad streets, bright with electricity and moonlight. Beyond the great white square, where the twin lights of the trams shone like drops of water, the station carriages looked like files of monstrous sleeping insects.

After the long silences and solemn solitudes of the Po, back now in the crowd, in the cold, sharp splendour of the electric lights hidden like little moons among the black ilices, Regina felt herself in a dream. The cafés were overflown with light. Livid reflections came from some empty table. Vestiges of lunar rays made their way through the green shadows, the strange semi-darkness of the trees. The crowd rolled past and looked into the café, merry with a second crowd reflected and multiplied by mirrors. Now and then, in the smoke-wreathed background of the Morteo, hovered the moving and screaming figure of a singer, whose coarse notes were mixed with the melancholy scraping of violins and the buzz of the people. A hundred faces, derisive but brutally pleased, looked at the swaying, strident figure. Regina found a curious interest in watching the crowd, the faces, the light dresses of the women, the physiognomy of the men who ogled the singer, the pitiable arms of this pitiable creature.

One evening a little girl with thick hair falling in a red plait over thin shoulders, with a green hat and a short green dress, which left half-bare her meagre legs and big feet cased in yellow shoes, reminded her of a water bird. Then suddenly, under those trees blackened and burnt up by the heat of a thousand burning breaths, she thought of her great river, of the poplars rising at this hour like candles lighted by the moon, of the white line of the river-banks cleaving the immense circle of the plain; and she marvelled that she no longer felt the nostalgia which she had known of old.

Antonio proposed to sit down at the café, but Regina preferred moving round with the crowd, going as far as Via Volturno, where the voices of the melon-sellers crossed, followed, answered each other jealously, like the crowing of cocks.

"*Favorischino, Signori! Favorischino!*"

On the black, damp tables, cut melons showed rosy in the trembling lamp-light, and diffused a fresh and agreeable odour like great red flowers. Children, workmen, a pair of students, a woman or two, bent over the pink flesh of the juicy slices.

"*Favorischino, Signori!* Behold what beauties! Real blood! Will you buy one, lady?"

There was a stall at the corner of the street against the wall, and the vendor looked condescendingly at the people clustered round his banks of melons; but if any one noticed his money-box, he turned anxiously and put on an air of preternatural solemnity.

"Do you intend to buy, madam?"

And from an ambulant gramophone, whose red trumpet rose in the shadow like a coral cup, issued a strange, hoarse music, a metallic and rapid laughter, now near, now far, which streamed forth from an unknown and alarming profundity, expressing a false joy, a cry of misery, grief, derision, of wickedness and roguery, of pity and sadness — a voice at once mocking and imploring, empty and portentous, unconscious, and supremely melancholy.

To Regina it seemed the voice of the surrounding crowd. Yes! the voice of the pale young daughter of joy, with the auburn hair under the great black hat, seated alone and thoughtful before one of the tables at the Morteo; the voice of the child like the water bird of the famished singer, of the rough melon-seller, of the bright-eyed old man in the pink shirt, of the gentleman with the thick lips and brutal looks, of the melancholy fat man, of the lady in the red dress lifted to show a trim ankle, of the wet-nurse with the Jewish profile, of the yellow infant which she held in her arms, of the little woman in black with floating veil who ran after the tram, of the pair of lovers leaning romantically against the garden gate.

"And it's my voice too, and Antonio's!" thought Regina, and sometimes the crowd still disgusted her, but her disgust was tempered by compassion. Returning home, she still saw the melon-seller, the fat misanthrope, the nurse, and the girl with the red frock; but above all the thin singing woman, who was probably hungry, and the daughter of joy with the thoughtful, the pure face. She fancied that Antonio had glanced at the latter with a certain interest, and she thought: "Can they have known each other once?" But she felt no resentment, only great compassion for the lost girl, for Antonio, for herself, and for all the unconscious ones, the rich or the wretched, for all the sadness and the weariness of men, which gurgled forth from the blood-coloured cup of the ambulating gramophone.

Sometimes Antonio and Regina sat on a bench at the bottom of the avenue in the shadow. He seemed overcome by depression and fatigue. She watched dreamily the great coloured eyes of the tram, the course of the newspaper carts, carrying to the station their load of glory and of gossip, the going and coming of the people, the shadows of the trees, the clouds which rose up from the silver depths of the horizon. White and tender the moon looked down from heaven. Music of mandolines and violins throbbed and vibrated, a neighbouring bell tolled, a distant trumpet sounded.

"They all make music!" observed Regina. "The whole world seems holiday-making and merry."

"On the contrary, according to you it's sad," said Antonio, not without irony.

"No; it's worse than sad! It's miserable, and I am very sorry for it!"

He made no reply. Since their re-union he did not controvert the melancholy speeches of his wife on those occasions, infrequent now, when she allowed herself to be depressed.

In September Regina perceived that the old miller's prophecy had come true. She was to be a mother.

The fact was not particularly agitating, certainly not displeasing, either to her or to her husband. It occasioned, however, a small dispute between them, for Antonio declared at once that the child must have a nurse, while Regina was for bringing it up herself.

"Too much worry," he said, almost roughly.

"Well, have we the means to pay for a nurse?"

"We have," he affirmed, shortly.

The year passed. Nothing extraordinary happened. During the winter Regina went out little and scarcely saw any one. She did not visit her mother-in-law, finding an excuse in the stairs. When Arduina came to look for her, she bade the maid say she was not at home. She was aware of her own ingratitude, since after all it was Arduina who had got Antonio his post with the Princess; but she could not overcome her antipathy to her husband's whole family.

Before the child's birth she fell into a sort of moral lethargy. In spite of the physical disturbances her prospects did not displease her; on the other hand, the idea of motherhood woke in her little enthusiasm. During the winter she devoured an immense number of novels, which her husband brought from the library. Hour after hour she sat over the fire, which Antonio had arranged in one of the drawing-rooms — quite alone and very quiet.

Antonio went out in the morning often while she was still asleep. He ran in for lunch, went out again, came back towards evening after an extra hour or two in the office, studying or dispatching business for the Princess. Regina had got used to solitude.

All was going on well; perhaps too well. In addition to his two salaries, Antonio said he had made a little by extra work in the Department. Then one evening towards the middle of April, when the birth of the baby was imminent, he told Regina a somewhat curious story.

"If you won't scold," he began, "I'll confess my sins to you."

"I needn't scold if you have upbraided yourself and repented."

"Repented? No; the serious thing is, I haven't repented! Look here. The day you ran away last year I got dragged by a friend of mine into a gambling-house ———"

"Ah ———!" cried Regina.

"Don't be frightened. It was the one only time. I was irritated, naturally; infuriated — almost desperate. But, you know (I never spoke of it, but I want to tell you now once and for all) I was far angrier with myself than with you. You were perfectly right. I had been imprudent, improvident. I hadn't properly forewarned you of all the little annoyances of middle-class life in a big town. We needn't go over it. It's enough that I was furious with myself for not having the sense to find some way out of my subordinate position. Well, I went with the fellow, and I played. You remember I had 100 *lire*? I put them all on the green table. I saw I was still a great baby, fancying I understood others and myself, while, on the contrary — why, I saw two or three of my colleagues there, and I even observed one of them cheating! Another had that day gone down from our Department into that of the Intendance, and the man who superseded him had paid him 2000 *lire*. He (my colleague) had three children and another coming. His wife hadn't been out for two months because she hadn't a decent frock. He had made the exchange because he wanted to get away from Rome, pay his debts, provide for his wife's confinement. That night he had his 2000 *lire* in his pocket, and, would you believe it, he lost them all! As for me, I began by winning. I got up to 1800 *lire*;

then I lost till I was down to 50. I won and lost again. That's how it always is. Towards morning I had made about 2000 *lire*. I was worn out, sleepy, nauseated. I thought of you. I thought: 'If Regina only knew!' All at once a quarrel burst out between one of the players and my colleague, who had been cheating. They came to blows. The manager of the house intervened. There was pandemonium! I got up and came away with my fine 2000 *lire*."

Regina listened, seated by the window, against which Antonio was leaning. It was almost night. From the beautiful hushed street, where the lamps shone pale in the last rosiness of the long twilight, from the gardens of the opposite houses, from near, from far, came that warm and grateful perfume of the spring evenings in Rome. The new moon, pale green like a slice of unripe orange, was going down in a violet-pink sky, above the already darkened houses in the far part of the street. Regina remembered the night when she had leaned against the window of their first apartment and complained that she could not see the stars. What changes within and around her! That night she had formulated to herself the plan of flight and separation. Now — now all that seemed a dream. Why does life change one in this way? And neither was Antonio what he had been that evening. He confessed it himself. He said, "I was a great baby and did not know it."

Now — now he was telling her a story, and Regina was listening, but with an inexplicable conviction that it was not true. Why should he say what was not true? She did not know, did not try to explain her incredulity. She just felt that the story Antonio was telling her was an invention. She was

vaguely distressed. She would much rather have thought
Antonio had really been gambling, had lost or won — it
mattered little which — so long as he were not telling her
lies.

He went on —

"Now hear the best of it. When I found myself with the
2000 *lire* I formed at least two thousand projects. I thought
of going to you. I thought of gambling again. What I did was
to hand the money over to Arduina and tell her to get me a
post as secretary. Then came the days in which I was going
to the Exchange about the Princess's matter, and presently
I purchased five shares in the Carburo Italiano Company.
They were at 300 *lire* just then. Do you know what they are
worth now? Do you know, Regina?"

In spite of herself, Regina was excited. Antonio was
bending over her, and though his voice was calm, almost
indifferent, she felt in him some unaccustomed agitation.

She forgot the doubts which had assailed her. No; Antonio
was no longer lying. The expression of his eyes, brilliant in
the light of the window, was truly a sincere expression, on
fire with audacity. His eyes, once so soft, so amorous, were
now those of a man intent on making a fortune at all costs.

"Do you know?" he repeated.

"How should I know?"

"Guess."

"500 *lire*?" she hazarded.

"More."

"600?"

"More — more."

186

"1000?" she suggested, timidly.

"More still."

"Then we are rich!" she exclaimed, with forced irony, angry at her own excitement.

"We are not rich yet, but we can be. It's the first step, which is everything, my dear! Our five shares are each worth 1200 *lire*. They may go up even higher, but I intend to sell out to-morrow. Half the money I shall give to you; with the other half I'll make another venture. Fortune, it seems, is only a matter of will. But you mustn't be frightened!" he ended, for Regina had turned pale.

"Why did you never tell me about it?"

"What was the use? Suppose the shares had gone down?"

As on that former evening, which rose obstinately before Regina's memory, the maid interrupted by announcing dinner, and the young pair went into the next room. By the lamplight Antonio again noticed Regina's pallor, but he jested.

"Don't fly away on the wings of Pegasus!"

They talked a little of the morality and the opportunities of speculation, of risks and lotteries.

"Nonsense!" said Antonio. "All life is a lottery. We must risk something or die. And now we'll go out for our walk."

Next day he sold the shares, after having shown them to Regina, and gave her 3000 *lire*. She put 2000 in the savings bank; with the rest she bought furniture, and provided for the birth and christening of her baby.

"Perhaps I shall die," she said, in the last days of waiting. "You'll see that now, just when we've got a little luck, I shall die."

"Don't talk nonsense," said Antonio, almost angry.

She did not die, but she gave to the light a miserable little being, its life hanging by a thread, a baby like a kitten, ill-formed, ill-coloured, with an enormous head.

When she first saw this little misery she wept with disappointment and repugnance.

"If it would only die!" she mourned, cruelly. "Why oh! why have I given it life!"

"Young lady," she was answered by the nurse, a peasant woman, like a statue, with a bronze face in an aureole formed by a turquoise head ornament, "leave the infant to me. You have brought her into the world, and now you have no more to do. Leave her to me, *Signurì*."

Regina appeared to have little confidence, so the big woman was offended. She sulked, she quarrelled with the servant, who insisted the baby was dying. Next day she fell out with Marianna, who had come to inquire for Regina, and made the remark that the child seemed a kitten.

"Just let her grow a bit," cried the indignant peasant, "and she'll be clawing at you! Little Miss Catharine may be like a kitten, but you're for all the world like a rat!"

By the middle of May Regina had recovered; she had regained her beauty and felt strong and happy. The nurse kept her promise; her rich country milk gave life and vigour to the poor little city infant The distorted black little face cleared and acquired a profile; the immense heavy eyes began to be human. Sometimes the baby smiled, and her whole little face became animated. Then Regina felt certain her daughter was beautiful; but presently she laughed and thought she must be deluded — a victim of that mania which attacks all mothers.

However, she was happy, happy in her freedom, her health, her life. After the few first delicious walks on Antonio's arm she began to go with the nurse and the baby. The mornings were splendid; breaths of perfumed wind gave stimulating sweetness to the air; bands of shining silver furrowed the luminous heights of the heaven.

How different from the spring of a year ago! Now Regina felt impulses of tenderness for everything and everybody. The warm surging of that breeze which came from the summer of the southern plains and passed on to her northern home still stung by the sharpness of winter, ravished her soul, sending it forth in flight like a bird drunk with light and space.

One day she sallied forth quite alone. She felt like that hero of Dostoievsky's, who, unexpectedly obliged to cross the principal streets of the great city in which he had long lived without attention, seemed to himself born again to a new life. Roaming in the immensity of Via Nazionale, Regina looked about her with childish curiosity. For the first time she perceived that the Hotel Quirinale was a soft grey, while to her it had always seemed mustard colour; she saw the tower of the American Church striped and elegant like a lady's dress; she admired the fine perspective of Via Quattro

Fontane; she stood on the sunlit carpet which covered regally the steps of the Exhibition. A red-faced cabman raised two fingers, thinking her a foreigner seeking a carriage; a Moor in European dress passed near her and stared; a flower-girl offered her roses. It was all interesting; but a year ago she would have been annoyed.

She descended Via dei Serpenti, and as she advanced saw the arches of the Colosseum open to the deep sky, and she fancied them huge blue eyes looking at her and full of eternal dream. She found herself alone before the great dead sphinx; only a boy — fair-haired, rosy, dressed in green — was watching the entrance from between two baskets of oranges. The broken columns lying in the sun showed metallic reflections; the voluptuous wind brought whiffs of country fragrance; cries of love-making birds came from the trees of the Palatine; the outline of the trees was soft against the feathery silver clouds which veiled the sky.

Regina descended, almost running. She penetrated under an archway and paused, checked by a sudden chill. A priest passed close to her, black and fluttering, like a melancholy bird. She moved on, opened her guide-book, but did not read. Play of sun and shade painted the background of the Colosseum's immense emptiness. The walls, dotted with wild plants and yellow flowers, suggested a mountain-side; shady corners, green with moss, seemed little damp pastures; mysterious caverns opened great black mouths. Hoarse cawing of rooks came from behind the huge blue eyes which the great sphinx fixed on its own ruin. From the hopeless profundity of heaven rained a dream of solitude and death.

"I have never cared for history," thought Regina. "There are persons who come miles to gush about a stone on which possibly some Roman warrior set his dirty foot! That seems silly to me. Why? A stone is for me only a stone! Nothing speaks to me by its past, but by its present significance. The past is death; the present is life. Here am I, and here once laboured twelve thousand slaves — or how many was it?" (Again she opened the guide-book, but did not read.) "Here the lions devoured the Christians, and cruel eyes of emperors, women, plebeians, with less conscience than the lions, enjoyed the horrid spectacle. But all that is past, and it doesn't move me a bit. Oh, dear! Here come the foreigners, bursting into this dream of death, chattering like ducks in a stagnant pond! Let me escape!"

She went away. The Palatine trees trembled in the breeze against a sky ever brighter and brighter. The campanile of Santa Francesca Romana was clear-cut, bright, and dark. The Arch of Constantine framed the bright picture of the roadway with its background of silvery cloud. Regina followed the road and seated herself on the highest step of the stair of San Gregorio. Everything she could see in front of her, from the pine-trees, noisy with birds, to the rosy vision of the city's edge, all was light, life, joy; behind her, in the damp cloister, green with moss, in the portico guarded by tombs, in the abandoned garden, all was silence, sadness, death. Always the great contrast! Vibrating with life, she nevertheless entered into that place of death and allowed herself to be taken round by a friar, who seemed a skeleton wrapped in a yellow tunic. They visited the chapels, in whose silence the beautiful figures of Domenichino and Guido grow pale, like persons condemned to solitude. Regina crossed the desolate garden and watched the friar, with profound pity, wondering he could still walk, though he was dead to life.

She thought of her baby, the little Caterina. Ah! she should be taught to appreciate, to enjoy, to adore life!

"How many dead people there are in the world!" she thought. "I myself was dead till a few months ago. Now I have revived a little, but I am not so much alive as my baby shall be! I am only a resuscitated person with the memory of the grave still in my soul."

As she went out she put a small coin in the friar's yellow palm, and, from the manner in which he thrust the money into his pocket and looked at the donor, she perceived that he had still some life in him, this little yellow skeleton of a friar!

Then she went out, hurrying from the sepulchre-guarded portico, thirsting for the sun, for noise, and for immensity.

PART III

CHAPTER I

ON Christmas Eve (Old Style) Regina and Antonio went to the Princess's reception. They were accompanied by a little blonde lady, modestly attired in black. It was Gabrie, the Master's daughter, who had realised her dream of finishing her studies in Rome at the *Scuola di Magistero*. For two months, courageously and quietly, she had lived on study and privation in a garret of Via San Lorenzo, in the family of a strolling musician, who had once been an organist near her home. The Venutellis had offered her hospitality, but she had refused it, contenting herself with visiting at their house and allowing them occasionally to take her to the theatre. To-night, chiefly out of curiosity, she had condescended to go with them to Madame Makuline's. She wanted to see a rich lady close, that she might excite the envy of her puffed-up young friend at Sabbioneta.

Innocently, or sarcastically (Regina had not yet made out if Gabrie were innocent or malicious), she said —

"I've been sending her picture cards of the fox hunt, the meet, the motors, the smart people. That young woman has no ideas beyond all that." (She said *that young woman* in accents of profound contempt.)

"Nor have many others," muttered Antonio.

He was stepping a little in advance of the ladies, and seemed lost in thought, very erect and fashionable, however, in his dark, smooth overcoat.

"Do you mean that for me?" said Gabrie, after a pause. Then, without waiting for a reply, almost as if penitent, she added, "Dear me, Signor Antonio, aren't you crushed by that coat? The history professor has one like it, and the girls say whenever he goes out he has to come home and lie down — he's so worn out by it."

"Indeed!" said Antonio, absently.

They arrived at the Villa. The night was warm and still; the blue splendour of the moon eclipsed the lamps. The street was empty. Regina remembered the first night she had come to this house, and she sighed and smiled. She did not know why she sighed nor why she smiled, but she rapidly recalled how unhappy she had been then, while now she was so extremely happy, with a husband who loved her so much and worked for her so hard, with her pretty baby, her home, her heart-felt peace and assured prosperity; and yet — And yet? Oh, nothing! A mere cloud, the shadow of a cloud, passing over the depths of her soul!

The great doors opened. The servant did not smile, but his pale, impassive face lighted up amiably at sight of the new-comers.

"Are there many people?" asked Antonio, as the servant took Regina's cloak.

"A few," replied the big youth, in a bass voice.

Regina looked at Gabrie, who, after a rapid glance at the wolves in the porch, was covertly scrutinising the servant. He carried the wraps into an adjacent room, and Antonio familiarly opened the door to the right.

"Wait one moment," said Regina, who was smoothing her hair. It was beautifully arranged. She was rosy, and a little plumper than she had been a year or two ago. Her light dress with its neck garniture of foamy white was becoming. She looked young and almost a beauty. Indeed, she thought so herself, and entered the Princess's drawing-room quite satisfied.

"How's the little one?" asked Madame.

"Quite well, thank you. May I introduce my friend?"

Gabrie bowed to the hostess, who scarcely noticed her. Then she sat down in the corner of a sofa and stayed there the whole evening, shy, quiet and silent

The usual old ladies and old gentlemen filled the rooms, which, as usual, were overheated.

The only person at all young was a lady dressed childishly in blue, with big blue eyes and long, downcast golden lashes. She sat near the hostess, in a circle of two old ladies and three old men, amongst whom was he of the pink-china bald head.

Madame was silent, listening to a German traveller who was giving an account of his recent tour in India. Fatter than ever, paler, more dowdy in her clumsy black velvet gown, the Princess looked like one of the many old women of remoter ages whose ugliness has been immortalised by the painters of their day. Her eyes alone seemed alive in her swollen, corpse-like face.

The lady in blue asked the German if he had read Loti's article on Inia (without the English) in the *Revue des Deux Mondes*.

"Oh, he exaggerates, as usual. To read Loti, you'd suppose the burial in the Ganges a poem. On the contrary, it's a great ———"

"——— a great *saleté*," said Marianna, sitting near Gabrie, and whispering so as not to be overheard by Madame, who often reproved her for her coarse language.

Gabrie, who had understood from her Sabbioneta friend that great ladies never said ugly words, stared at Marianna, then dropped her eyes and remained quiet in her corner.

"Whatever Loti says is false," continued the German. "I once heard Madame Ciansahma, a Japanese authoress, say that when she wanted a laugh she read a book of Loti's."

"And don't we laugh when Madame Ciansahma takes us off, and tries to look like an European?" asked the lady in blue.

"How can she know what Madame Ciansahma looks like?" whispered Marianna, leaning forward.

Regina also leaned forward and indicated the blue lady.

"She's blind, isn't she?"

"Stone blind. For that matter," added Marianna, "the blind sometimes see more than those with eyes."

Gabrie, mute and stiff, wedged in between the two young ladies, looked and listened. Every one was talking except herself — her small, colourless self in her little black frock. The blind lady, moving and talking as if she could see perfectly, became the special object of her attention.

The Princess was talking. Antonio also, very handsome but preternaturally grave, was talking to an elderly young lady who had stuck a golden fringe on top of her scanty red hair.

Scraps of phrases, laughter, isolated words in the midst of the general hubbub, reached the corner where sat Regina, Gabrie and Marianna.

"Do you know that lady's history?" asked Marianna. "Blind as she is, she tried to murder her husband, who was the cause of her calamity."

"How was that?"

"I'll tell you afterwards. Now I must talk to those people over there."

She moved off with a great rustling of her petticoats. But suddenly she stopped and said, looking back to Regina —

"I met your baby out with that demon of a nurse. I put the woman in a fury telling her we were going to have an earthquake."

"I know," said Regina laughing; "you frightened her to death."

"Frightened her? Won't that poison the baby? But it's quite true about the earthquake. I read it in print."

"Really? What fun!" said Gabrie.

Marianna seemed to see her for the first time.

"Is this a relation of yours?" she asked Regina.

"More or less," said Regina.

"I observe a likeness. But bless me! I'm forgetting my duties."

She started again, but again turned back.

"Oh! I've been wanting to tell you something, Signora. Come with me. How grand you are to-night! It must be because —"

"What do you want to tell me?"

"Come with me," said Marianna, taking her hand.

"Gabrie, you come too," said Regina.

Gabrie rose, but, bethinking her that Marianna probably wished to speak to her friend alone, she begged to be allowed to remain where she was.

"You won't be lonely?"

"No, no. I like this corner. Go."

Regina went, but soon came back and took Gabrie to the supper-room. The table was laden with plate, and the company stood round it eating and drinking. Marianna, seated at the *Samovar*, was pouring tea into Japanese cups, delicate and transparent as flowers. Antonio was carrying them to the guests. He gave one to Gabrie, who smiled at him quietly.

"Are you enjoying yourself?" asked Antonio.

"Yes, very much. Only I can't understand all they say. Even Regina talks French. She speaks very well."

Antonio looked at his wife, so fair, delicate, graceful. She drew nearer and said —

"What are you staring at me for?"

"Am I not allowed to look at my wife? Why are you pale? You were quite rosy when we came. What's the matter?"

"The matter? Nothing. Am I pale, Gabrie?"

"A little. But it's very becoming," said Gabrie, tasting the tea.

"Thank you, dear!"

"You're much the prettiest here. Isn't she, Signor Antonio?"

"The prettiest and the best dressed."

"You're overwhelming me, you two," said Regina; "you're a pair of flatterers, that's what you are!"

"She's grown fatter, hasn't she," said Antonio to Gabrie. "Do you remember how thin she was? By Jove, she was a fright!"

"Thank you, my dear!" said Regina.

"No, she wasn't a fright. She was thin, certainly. But when she came home last year she was thin then. And quite *green*, she was! And always in a bad humour! She was afraid you had run away from her, Signor Antonio, and was always watching for the post-man —"

"Who told you that?" asked Regina, astonished.

"I saw it. But the moment Signor Antonio arrived —"

"Upon my word, if you fail as a novelist it won't be for want of observation, my dear!"

They were standing all together at a short distance from their hostess. The latter suddenly turned and came towards them. In her small be-gemmed hands she held a plate and a silver fork. She was eating slowly, munching at a slice of tart, and she had smeared her mouth with chocolate. Never had she looked more hideous.

"Is your friend from Viadana?" she asked Antonio, pointing to Gabrie with her fork.

"From the country — from my home!" cried Regina, looking affectionately at the girl.

It seemed to her that Gabrie's little face wore a look of ineffable disgust.

The days and the months rolled on.

A morning came when Regina woke to see a thread of gold coming through the closed shutters and falling on the blue wall across the corner of her room. It was the sun beating on the window. Spring had come, and Regina felt a profound gladness. Time had run on, and she had not noticed it, so happy she thought herself. Sometimes she felt quite afraid of her happiness, and even this morning, after her quick joy at sight of the sunshine, she looked at the sleeping Antonio and thought —

"Suppose he were to die! Any one of us, I, or he, or baby, might die at any moment! This great light which shines in my soul might be put out in one instant."

She raised herself on her elbow and surveyed her husband. His fine head, motionless on the pillow, illuminated by the gold ray from the window, had the severe beauty of a statue. Blue veins showed on his closed eyelids. His whole aspect was of suavity and gentleness.

Last night he had come home late, later than usual, even though most nights he was late. Regina was not jealous. He worked hard all day. Every hour was absorbed by feverish activity. Only in the evening could he amuse himself, walk, do what he liked. His wife knew this and asked for no account of these hours. Besides, did he not always tell her where he had been? There were days in which husband and wife hardly saw each other, except in the morning when they first woke; and sometimes, if he woke late, Antonio had to jump out of bed, dress in a hurry, bolt his breakfast, and run to the office.

For all that, perhaps because of that, their life went on smooth and tranquil as a limpid and quiet stream. Nurse (always relating how she had lived with a pair who used to beat each other even in bed — "and when I wanted to make peace between them I took a stick too!") used to say —

"We can't go on like this, Mistress! Do quarrel with Master a little, or you'll see we shall get some bad luck."

"I defy the prophecy!" said Regina.

"Well, I hope I'll get through bringing up the little angel first! See what a beauty she is! See!"

Antonio woke, and before opening his eyes felt that Regina was looking at him, and he smiled.

"It must be very late!" he exclaimed, seeing the ray of sunshine.

"No; it's the sun which is earlier. It's a quarter to eight. Shall I ring for baby?"

"Wait one minute! Give me a kiss! We hardly ever see each other!"

He took her in his arms and kissed her, hugging her like a child. She kissed his smooth brow, his hair, and, feeling him all her own, so loving, so young, so handsome, so trusting, her heart throbbed with a tenderness that was almost pain. Thus for several minutes they remained embraced, in the silence, in the luminous penumbra of the warm, blue room.

Outside the street was becoming animated; but the noises vibrated softly, as if blended in the deep serenity of the air.

"I feel as if we were lying in a wood," said Antonio. "I'm still half asleep, and I'd like to sleep on like this to the end of time."

"It's the spring!" said Regina. "I also see the wood, and through the wood the river, and, oh, so many flowers!"

"Are you going to the Pincio to-day?"

"No; I'm going to see Gabrie. She has been three days in bed, poor child."

Antonio made no remark. He did not require his wife to account for her time, just as she did not demand it of him.

Regina wanted to go and see her mother in June, and he asked, suddenly, "When is the exam.?"

"What exam.? Gabrie's? July, I think."

"Then you aren't going back together, as she said the other day?

"No."

They were silent. So much time had passed, so many things had changed — Regina had left home twice, and twice she had come back — that the caprice of her first going away now seemed a mere childishness, far off, obscured by subsequent events. Still, every time they spoke of parting, even if, as to-day, it were at one of the sweetest and most intimate moments of their life, they felt embarrassed, separated, torn asunder by some extraneous force. But this did not last. To-day spring was beating at the window. It was the time not of clouds, but of sun. Young, at ease, in love with each other, Regina and Antonio forgot the winter with the birds, and with them sung their hymn of joy.

He called her his little queen, and squandered on her a thousand extravagant pet names. She admired him — meaning it, too — and told him he was the most beautiful husband in the whole world. From the wall the sun's eye watched them, pleased and peaceful.

Regina went with the nurse and baby to the station gardens, then set off to visit Gabrie. She was taking her a book, a bunch of violets, and a packet of biscuits; and she walked along lightly and briskly, imagining herself engaged in a work of charity. She glanced at the station clock and saw it was ten. Not a leaf fluttered, and the motionless air was perfumed by narcissus and young grass. In the distance the mountains were the colour of flax-blossom, and scarce visible, as if seen through the transparence of water. A bird-seller stepped just in front of Regina, and so intense, so insistent was the joy of spring, that even the little half-fledged sparrows, the redbreasts stained with blood, the canaries yellow as daffodils, twittered with delight in the two swinging cages carried by the melancholy man. Regina thought of buying a baby sparrow for Caterina; but what would Caterina make of it? She would choke it without even amusement. No; Regina would not accustom her little one to senseless pleasures and cruel caprices.

"But," she reflected, "if I buy the bird I shall give one moment of pleasure to this sorrowful seller, who probably hasn't taken a penny to-day. Yet why should I suppose the man sorrowful? He may be quite happy. We are always imagining the griefs of others, and probably they don't exist.

Once I thought everybody was unhappy; now — now — I see I was wrong."

Spring penetrated even into the big house where Gabrie lived. Regina had always seen the stairs damp, greasy and muddy; but to-day they were quite dry, the landings washed; an open door revealed a passage with polished floor. From the first storey, which represented the luxury of a book-keeper, to the fourth, inhabited by the ex-organist, the inhabitants had cleaned up the house to receive the Easter warmth — enemy of that great enemy of the poor, winter. Regina had an undefined feeling of pensive pleasure as she heard her green silk petticoat rustling up the silence of the stairs. She was not consciously thinking of her silk petticoat, nor of the comfort of her life, the short, well-lighted stair of her own dwelling, her two drawing-rooms, her Savings-bank book, her subscription to the Costanzi; but the certainty of all these possessions illumined her heart, and made her a little sentimental. She felt herself a person of consequence, sun-warmed like Easter, violets in her hand, bringing the breath of spring up that stair of poverty, of workers, students, failures. She would have liked to leave a violet on the threshold of every apartment. She remembered an anaemic young student whom she had once seen coming out of N.8, his lips blue, his eyes pale as faded hyacinths, buttoned up in a threadbare though clean overcoat; and she wished she might meet him to-day to greet him and make him understand that she loved the poor, whom once she had despised.

But the young man did not come out, and she climbed on till she had reached a door where a card, fixed with four wafers, informed the visitor that this apartment had the good fortune to shelter

MARIO ENNIO COLORNI,
Ex-Organist and
Professor of the Violin.

It was not impressive to Regina, as she had seen it already. She had visited Gabrie several times. In the first instance the Master had written praying her to "scrutinise whether the environment were dangerous or doubtful, as all the houses in the San Lorenzo quarter were reputed to be."

Signora Colorni opened the door, a little woman with a black cap and blue spectacles. She did not immediately recognise the visitor, and hesitated childishly about allowing her to enter. Regina made her smell the violets, and said, in the Mantuan dialect —

"Don't you know me? How is Gabrie?"

The little woman, whom typhus fever had left bald, dumb, and nearly blind, smiled gently. Her little face was the face of a child who has put on Grandmother's cap and spectacles for fun. Regina walked on into the apartment, crossed the passage, which was very clean and in which was a great smell of cooking, went into the little parlour, the half-shut window of which was veiled by a curtain of yellowish muslin. Through the open door she saw that Gabrie's room, in process of arranging by Signora Colorni, was empty.

She turned. The dumb woman smiled, and waved her hand to the window.

"What? Out? But she wrote to me she was ill in bed!"

The little woman shook her head, coughed, and touched her forehead to signify that Gabrie had certainly been ill. Then she smiled again, pointed to the window, took a chair, for they had come into the little room, and placed it before Regina.

"Will she soon be back? Where is she gone?"

The woman took an envelope from Gabrie's table and held it to the wall.

"Gone to post a letter, is that it? Well, I'll wait a few minutes, as I am tired. And how's Signor Ennio?"

Again the woman smiled, made the gesture of violin-playing, then opened her arms very wide, perhaps to intimate that he had gone a long way, and that his instrument was speaking tenderly and humbly to some German bride and bridegroom in that hour of sun, in the poetry of some suburban inn, lively with chickens and pink with peach-blossom.

Regina sat down, and the little woman went away.

For some minutes profound silence reigned in the clean little apartment, full of peace and the odour of baked meats. Gabrie's tiny room, with its pink-flowered yellow paper, its narrow white bed, its little table littered with books and copy-books, its window open on a sky of pearl-strewn azure, gave Regina the idea of a nest on the top of a poplar-tree. Yes! life was lovely even for the poor! Everything was relative. This strolling fiddler, who at night brought two, three, sometimes even five *lire* home to his little hard-working, dumb wife, and found his little home clean, a good piece of *abbacchio* (kid) in the oven, and a soft bed waiting for him, was happier than many a millionaire. And Gabrie, with her pluck and her dreams, who saw her life before her long but luminous, like that depth of sky behind her window — who could say how happy she must be! "Happiness is not in our surroundings, but in ourselves," thought Regina. "I declare I once thought myself wretched because I lived on a fifth floor in a house which was in quite a good quarter. Now I believe I could be happy even here — in this house of poor people, in the outskirts of the kingdom of the most miserable!"

Still Gabrie did not come in. So much the better, if it meant she was cured. Regina looked at her tiny clock; it was half-past ten. She could wait a little longer. She got up and walked to the window. On the right, on the left, overhead, that dazzling sky; down below the railway, the tall houses tanned by the sun; bits of green, the vague breathing of life and of spring, the immense palpitation of a distant steam engine. All, all was beautiful.

Still no Gabrie. Regina left the window and approached the table to set down the violets which she still held in her hand. Her silk petticoat made a great rustling in the silence of the tiny room.

Yes; everything was beautiful; not least that little table covered with foolscap and note-books which represented the dream, the essence, the finger-marks of a soul clear and deep as a mirror. Regina took up an open note-book.

She remembered the time when she, too, had thought of becoming an authoress. She had never succeeded in writing the first line of her first chapter. How far would Gabrie get? Further, it was to be hoped, than Arduina! Regina's thoughts wandered to her husband's relations. They had disappeared, or at least faded from her life, like personages in the opening chapters of a novel who find no opportunity of coming in again. Regina often sent nurse and baby to visit the grandmother, and she listened to Antonio when he talked of his family. Herself, however, she hardly ever saw any of them, and though now she regarded them as neither more nor less agreeable than a thousand others, she could not resist a feeling of resentment whenever she found herself in their society.

But why should she think of them now when she was turning the leaves of Gabrie's note-book? She sought the sequence of ideas. This was it. Confusedly she was thinking that if Antonio, instead of taking her to his relations in that odious apartment, choked up with lumber and horrible figures like an ugly and ill-painted picture, had brought her to a little, silent, sunny home as humble as even this of the ex-organist, she would not have suffered so acutely during her honeymoon.

She put down that note-book and picked up another. Her thoughts now changed their shape like clouds urged by the wind.

"No; I should probably have suffered more. I had to suffer, to pass through a crisis. I suppose all wives of any intelligence have to go through it. And now, now it's easy for me to think everything beautiful, because I am happy, because my life has become easy. Ah! What's this?

"A young lady of seventeen, of noble though fallen family, anaemic, insincere, vain, envious, ambitious; knows how to conceal her faults under a cold sweetness which seems natural. She is always talking of the upper aristocracy. Some one told her she was like a Virgin of Botticelli's, and ever since she has assumed an air of ecstasy and sentiment. This does not prevent her from being ignobly enamoured of a sign-painter."

Regina recalled the enthusiasm with which the Master had read part of this extract to Signora Caterina. She saw again the big Louis XV room, flooded with the burning twilight, the clouds travelling like violet-grey birds over the greenish sky, over the greenish river.

"See what a spirit of observation! It's a character for a future story, Signora Caterina. My Gabrie picks up, picks up. She sees a character, observes it, sets it down. She is like a good housewife who keeps everything in case it may come in useful ——"

The Master talked, and Regina pitied him. The Master read, and Regina recognised in the figure drawn with photographic minuteness the young lady from Sabbioneta.

Gabrie's note-book was almost filled with these little figures. Regina turned the leaves without scruple, and in the later pages she found characters of professors, students, that of Claretta (a flirt, hysterical, corrupt), whom Gabrie had met in Regina's drawing-room a few days before.

She was terrible, this future novelist; not a looking-glass, but a Röntgen apparatus!

Regina, impelled by curiosity, continued to turn the leaves and to read, standing by the little table.

"A young wife, short-sighted, dark, all eyes and mouth, clever, rather original, a little enigmatical. Of noble but fallen family; imagines she doesn't value her blue blood, and, perhaps, does not think about it; but her blood is blue, and she feels it, and would like to be aristocratic. She is fond of luxury and of rich people. She is married to a poor man, but has succeeded in making him largely increase his income."

"Good gracious! This is myself!" thought Regina, amused but slightly offended. "She doesn't treat me very kindly, this girl! What does she mean by that last phrase?"

Suddenly she remembered that Gabrie had once told her certain stories she has got from her fellow-students.

"But it's a fire of calumny, that college of yours!" Regina had protested, and Gabrie had answered —

"A fire? It's a furnace!"

She read on —

"An authoress: tall, thin, yellow, with little, milky eyes, small mouth, black teeth, yellow hair, hooked nose. Moves pity by the mere sight of her. When she's with men she also tries to flirt."

"That's Arduina, slain in three lines," thought Regina.

Then she found Massimo, Marianna — ("short, with malicious olive face, little black eyes, pretends always to speak the truth, but a sculptor would entitle her, 'Statuette in bronze representing Malignant Folly' "), the blind lady, other persons who frequented the Princess's receptions, to which Regina had taken Gabrie several times. At last —

"A foreigner: very rich, tall, and stout; very black hair (dyed), lips too thick, pale, almost livid. Eyes small and sharp; mysterious as those of a wicked cat. Never laughs. Impossible to guess her age. Deaf. Always talking of an uncle who knew George Sand. Type of the sensual woman. Has a young lover ——"

And immediately after —

"Government clerk: private secretary to an old Princess. Young. Fair. Very handsome. Tall, athletic; long, fascinating eyes; good mouth; fresh complexion. Lively. Good-hearted. Deeply in love with his young wife. Nevertheless, *he is the Princess's lover.*"

CHAPTER II

REGINA had once dreamed of an eclipse of the sun. Reading Gabrie's page, she remembered that dream, because there was reproduced in her the same feeling of fearful darkness, of portentous silence and terrible expectation.

For a moment. When the moment had passed she again saw the light of the sun, felt again the vibration of life, perceived that everything in the outer world had retained its proper aspect and position, and that nothing was changed. But she was no longer the same. Around her, far and near, the light had returned; within her darkness remained.

She laid the note-book on the table, took up the violets, the biscuits, the book, and she went. Later she saw she had fled from the vulgar temptation to question Gabrie, to force her, even by violence, to tell how she had guessed, whom she had heard speak of the hideous secret. As always, she was sustained by pride, stiff and cold as the iron which sustains the clay of the statue.

The dumb woman ran after the visitor as she departed, and made signs which Regina did not understand. That little figure, like a disguised child, woke in her a kind of ferocious repulsion. Why did such beings exist? Why did not nature or society suppress all maimed, useless, weak persons?

For the rest of her life Regina remembered that quiet little apartment of the strolling musician, the uneven stair, the equivocal landings, the dusty hall of the big house in Via San

Lorenzo; but it was with profound disgust, as if she had there come in contact with all the most foul and miserable things of life. She never returned to it.

Again she traversed the sunny street, the Piazza, the avenues, without noticing any one or anything, though she forced herself to remain calm and not to believe that nonsense which she had read. She would speak of it to Antonio. They would laugh at it together

However, she was aware that agitation was gaining upon her, and, instead of going back to the garden where nurse and baby were waiting, she sat down on the first bench of the avenue on the right, opposite the Terme.

Why did she not go back to the garden? Why not call the nurse, that they might return home together? *She could not.*

Suddenly she seemed to hear a distant rumble like that of the immense palpitation of a train passing on some remote and invisible path.

"My God, what is it?"

A lady, with a great roll of red hair twisted at the nape of her neck, passed, looking at her curiously and turning her head as she went by. Regina drew a hand over her face, and understood that she was pale and visibly upset. The distant rumble, the breathless palpitation, came from her interior world, from her own agitated heart.

Then she shook herself all over like a bird just awakened, and tried to return to reality. The violets, the packet and the book were still on her lap. Why had she brought these away? Well, yes; by an instinctive vendetta against Gabrie, who had thrust this thorn into her heart.

"How small I am!" she thought. "What fault is it of hers if *that* is true? But can it be true? And why? And why did I not ask that at once, that *Why?*"

Ah! because it was useless to ask!

She knew the answer to this terrible *Why*. Even before the useless question had shaped itself on her lips the reason *Why* had sounded in her blood from vein to vein, out of the echoing abysses of her heart.

He had sold himself. Regina did not doubt it for a single instant, nor did the absurd thought pass for a single instant through her mind, that before his marriage he could have been the disinterested lover of that rich old woman.

He had sold himself. He had sold himself for her, for Regina, precisely as women sell themselves, to get money, to get a fine house, light and air, bits of silk, gewgaws, gloves, silk petticoats — all the things she had asked, all the things for lack of which she had reproached him.

"Oh, wretched, stupid boy! to be so weak, so vile. I will come home, I will take you and punish you as one punishes a wicked child! You ought to have understood me — you ought to have understood me!"

But while in her heart she sobbed out these and other recriminations, she felt them vain. Words of a very different truth were resounding in her soul, turning it into a threatening whirlwind.

It was she who had been weak and vile; she who had not understood the seriousness and fatality of life; and now life was punishing her like the wicked child which she had been.

Her head burned and throbbed as if she had literally been beaten. How long had she been sitting on this bench? People passed and stared at her. Young men turned their heads. One of them smiled after a glance of admiration at her green shoes and the edge of her green silk petticoat showing under the flounces of her dress.

She remembered that nurse was waiting in the gardens, but she could not move. Through the veil of her anguish she saw the people passing, the trees, the ruins in their spring clothing of weeds. There was a yellow awning among the ruins, and two doves with grey plumage were kissing in the ivy. The telegraph wires engraved the vivid azure of the heavens. She saw the advertisements on a corner of the Terme, a hunting scene, notice of a sale. She read senseless words, "Odol! Odol! Odol!" which afterwards remained strangely impressed on her memory. Builders were at work in the Piazza, and never afterwards could she forget the earthy red colour of their shirts. She followed with her gaze the scintillations of the wheels of the vehicles.

The simple scene, familiar after having been seen a hundred times, woke in her a profound disquiet, attracted, absorbed her. Then she suddenly realised that she herself was creating this curious interest in it, as an excuse for not moving from the bench, not going back to the gardens, delaying the hour for returning home.

She feared the return home to the house, the thought of which roused in her a sense of horror. All in it was lurid! All! all! all!

She would have liked to strip herself, to strip her baby —
to tear from the little soft body, pure as a rose-bud, the robes
of shame, of prostitution, and take her thus naked on her
naked breast, and fly with her, fly, fly ———!

Fly! The old idea came back; but this time Regina would
have wished to fly to some spot far distant from her native
province, away beyond the river which never, never, would
she cross again!

CHAPTER III

FOR more than half-an-hour Regina remained sitting on the bench. People passed, hurrying homewards. The children had come away from the gardens; even Caterina and her nurse must have left. The scent of grass became oppressive; a hot and enervating breath passed through the air. Like plaintive music, that odour of grass, that voluptuous warmth which undulated in the perfumed air, sharpened Regina's memories and emotions. Thoughts, stinging and ungovernable, rolled in waves through her perturbed mind. Only one recollection was insistent; it disappeared and returned, more definite than the others, burning, portentous. It, and it alone, was a revelation, for the other memories, however she might call them up, try to fix and interrogate them, did not suggest to her that which she desired and feared to know.

How, she asked herself, could Gabrie have penetrated to the secret? The intuition of an observant mind was not enough, nor the keen vision of two sane and cruel eyes. What manifest sign had appeared to Gabrie? Where had she found out the secret? On Madame's impassive face? Antonio's? Marianna's? Or was it a thing already public? Yet Regina had never even suspected it, nor did she remember the smallest revealing sign. True, a few words, a few phrases, now returned to her memory, taking a significance, which, even in her agitation, she thought must be exaggerated. "Anything is possible," Marianna had once said to her with her bad smile."The blind see more than those with eyes." Who had said that? She did not remember, but she had certainly heard it in the Princess's drawing-room. Even the blind — could they, did they see? Who could tell? *She* had not seen, perhaps because, in her foolish confidence, she had never looked. Now she remembered the almost physical disgust which Madame Makuline had caused her the very first time they had met. She remembered Arduina's untidy, depressing little drawing-room, the wet sky, the melancholy night; the little old woman dressed in black, sheltering under a doorway, with her meagre basket of unripe lemons. In the shadow, dense as the blackness of pitch, Antonio's face had become suddenly sad, overcast, mysterious. The Princess's pallid, expressionless face, with its thick, colourless lips, appeared in that depth of shade like a dismal moon floating among the clouds of dream. Who could guess how long the evil woman, the outworn body of a dead star, had been attracting into her fatal orbit, her turbid atmosphere, the winged bird, instinct with life and love, which was unconsciously fluttering round her?

Unconsciously? No. Antonio had become sombre that evening when he saw the woman. As yet she disgusted him. But an abominable day had come later. His wife had left him, reproaching him for his poverty; and he, blind, humiliated, and defeated, had sold himself!

And the most insistent of Regina's recollections, the one which came as a revelation of the accomplished fact, was just that arrival of Antonio at Casalmaggiore, that drive along the river-bank, that strange impression she had received at sight of her husband. Now all was clear. This was why he was changed; this was why his kisses had seemed despairing, almost cruel. He had returned to her contaminated, shuddering with anguish. He had kissed her like that for love and for revenge, that he might make her share in the infamy to which she had driven him, that he might forget that infamy, that he might purify himself in her purity, and gain his own forgiveness.

Afterwards — well, afterwards he had *got used* to it. One gets used to everything. She herself had got used —— Would she get used to this?

A whip would have stung her less than this idea. She leaped to her feet, hurried down the Viale, and entered the garden. It was deserted; already somnolent, scarcely shadowed by the delicate veil of the renascent trees. The nurse had gone.

Automatically Regina went out by the other gate, and paused under the ilices, all sprinkled with the pale gold of their new leaves. It was nearly noon. Was she to go back home? Was not this the just moment, the just occasion for serious flight? She would not re-enter the contaminated house! She would call Antonio to another place and say to him: "Since the fault belongs to us both, let us pardon each other; but in any case let us begin our life over again." Folly! Stuff of romance! In real life such things cannot happen, or do not happen at the just moment. Regina had once childishly run away, leaving her nest merely because it was narrow. Her flight had been a ridiculous caprice, and for that reason she had succeeded in carrying it out. Now, on the other hand, now that her dignity and her honour bade her remove her foot from the house which was soiled by the basest shame, now it was impossible for her to repeat that action!

She hastens her step; her silk flounces rustle. She feels a slight irritation in hearing that sighing of silk which surrounds and follows her. Her thoughts, however, are clearing themselves. As she descends Via Viminale, she seems returning to perfect calm. She must wait, observe, investigate. The world is malicious. People live on calumny, or at least on evil speaking. A man is not to be condemned because a silly school-girl has written down in her note-book a prurient malignity.

It is abject nonsense!

And yet ——

The biggest tree has grown from a tiny seed ——

Though she seems to have recovered her calm, Regina now and then stops as if overcome by physical pain. She cannot go on; something is pulling her back. But presently the fascination, the attraction of home draws her on, forces her to hasten. She walks on and on almost instinctively, like the horse who *feels* the place where rest and fodder are awaiting him.

At the corner where Via Viminale is crossed by Via Principe Amedeo, she stops as usual to look at the hats in the milliner's window. She wants a mid-season hat. There is the very one! Of silvery-green straw, trimmed with delicate pale thistles — a perfect poem of spring! But a dark shadow falls over her eyes the moment she perceives she has stopped. For hats, for silk petticoats, for all such miserable things, splendid and putrescent like the slough of a serpent, for these things he ——

But the thought interrupts itself. No! no! Not a word of it is true! One should have proof before uttering such calumnies! Walk on Regina! Hurry! It is noon. *He* must have come back. Luncheon is ready!

And if none of it is true? Will he not notice her agitation? Can she possibly hide it? And if none of it is true? He will suffer. Again she will make him suffer for no reason. Here she is, pitying him! Guilty or not, he is worthy of pity. Instinctively she pities him, because the guilt has come home to herself.

Via Torino, Via Balbo, crooked, deserted, flecked with shadows from the trees in a little bird-haunted garden; a picture of distant houses against the blue, blue background; a rosy-grey cloud, fragment of mother-o'-pearl, sailing across the height of heaven — how sweet is all that! Regina descends the street swiftly, goes swiftly up the stair, her heart beats, her skirts rustle; but she no longer cares. Antonio has not come in. Baby is asleep. Regina goes to her bedroom, all blue, large and fresh in the penumbra of the closed shutters. She is hot, and as she undresses her heart beats strongly, but no longer with grief. At last she has awaked from a bad dream or she has been suffering some acute bodily pain, which is now over.

There is Antonio's step upon the stair! She hears it as usual with joy. Now the familiar sound of his latch-key! Now the occult breath of life and joy which animates the whole house when he enters it!

"You've come in? What a lovely day! And Caterina?"

"She's asleep."

He takes off his hat and light overcoat, and flings them on the bed. Regina lifts her skirts from the floor, and is hanging them up, when she feels Antonio pass quite close and touch her with that breath of life, of youth and beauty, which he always sheds around him.

"Good God! I have had a hideous dream!" she thinks, bathing her burning face before joining him at the repast.

Antonio went out the moment he had finished lunch. He said he had an appointment at the Exchange. And the moment he had gone Regina went to the window, goaded by an obscure doubt, by a blind and unreasoning instinct. She saw her husband walking with his active step towards Via Depretis. Then she started back sharply, struck not by the absurdity of her doubt, but by the doubt itself.

No; at this hour he would not be going to *that other.* Besides, if he were he would have said so.

But now doubt was running riot in Regina's blood, and she felt her soul crushed by a dark oppression, a thousand times more painful, because more intelligent, than the oppression which she had felt up to an hour ago.

She repented that she had not detained Antonio and told him all.

"But what would have been the good?" she reflected at once. "He would lie. Of course, he wouldn't admit it to me! Oh, God! what must I do? What must I do?"

She sat down on the little arm-chair at the foot of her bed, and tried to think, to calculate coldly.

The cause of her doubt was certainly puerile — the guess of a heartless child. But truth sometimes finds amusement in revealing herself just in that way — by means of a heartless jest. The occult law which guides human destiny has strange and incomprehensible ordinances. At that moment Regina felt no wish to philosophise, but in her own despite she turned over certain questions. Why was all this happening which was happening? Why had she one day rebelled against her good destiny and let herself be carried away by a caprice? And why had this caprice, this feminine lightness, into which she had drifted almost unconsciously, brought about a tragedy? "Because we must have suffering," she answered herself. "Because sorrow is the normal state of man. But I am not resigned to suffering. I wish to rebel. Above all, I wish to overcome this suspicion which is poisoning me. I wish to know the truth. And when I know it — what shall I do?"

She reasoned, and was conscious of reasoning. This comforted her somewhat, or at least made her hope she would not commit further follies. But at moments she asked herself, was not the very suspicion itself a folly?

"We were, we *are*, so happy! But I'm always obliged to torment myself. I imagine I am reasoning, while to have the doubt at all is imbecility!"

But was she not saying this to convince herself there was no truth in it all, while she felt, she *felt*, that it was entirely true? She was afraid of losing her happiness, that's what it was! She wanted to keep her happiness at all costs, even at the cost of a vile selling of her conscience.

Ah! this thought robbed her of her reason! In that case she would be like the most abject of all the women who had ever been in her circumstances! She reasoned no further.

A nervous tremor shook her. Her arm contracted, forcing her to shut her fists.

"Anything! Anything! Misery, grief, scandal! Anything, even the abandonment of Antonio — but not infamy!"

She flung her arms over the bed, hid her face, bit, gnawed the coverlet, and wept.

She wept and she remembered. Once before she had flung herself on her bed and had wept with rage and grief. But Antonio had come, and she had kissed him with treason in her heart. It was she who had made infamous this weak and loving man, the conquest, the prey, of her superior force.

He had degraded himself for her, and now she was lowering him still more, suspecting that he would hesitate a single moment if she were to say to him, "I don't want all this you are giving me! Let us rise up out of the mud; let us re-make our life."

"If he lies, it will be for me, because he will not wish to destroy me. Oh! he is a rotten fruit! But I — *I* am the worm which is consuming him!"

But if, after all, she were deceiving herself? If it were not true? At moments this ray of joy flashed across her mind; then all the former darkness returned.

To know! to know! that was the first thing! Why cause him useless distress? The first thing was to make certain, and then — she would see!

The tears did her good. They were like a summer shower, clearing and refreshing her mind. She got up, washed her eyes, sat down to read the newspaper. She had to do something. But the first words which struck her and claimed her attention were these —

"Arrest of a foreign priest."

She read no further, for the words reminded her of something distant and oppressive, a matter now forgotten, which yet in some way belonged to the drama evolving in her mind.

What was it? When? How?

Here it was. The dream she had had, that night in her old home, after her running away.

Shutting her eyes, she again saw Marianna's little figure running at her side along the foggy river-bank, while she told how Antonio had borrowed money from Madame "to set up a fine apartment."

Profound anguish, rage and shame goaded Regina, forced her to sob, to run, to try and escape somehow from Marianna; but Marianna still ran along by her side, telling of her encounter with the fireman.

"He had become a priest; but coquettish —"

She laughed, not thinking of the priest, thinking of some mysterious, fearful thing.

Regina opened her eyes, passed her hands over her face, still tear-stained, and she felt her mind grow yet darker. At that moment the memory of her dream had for her a solemn signification. From the depths of the unconscious rose up clearly the anguished impression of that distant hour. What had happened then? Under the influence of what pathological phenomenon, presentiment, or suggestion, had she fallen? Perhaps the very hour of her dream had been the hour of the abominable deed.

She remembered to have read instances of that sort of thing — telepathy — clairvoyance ——

Doubtless Antonio had thought of her while he was making love to the rich old woman; his disgust, shame, rancour, had been so violent as to project themselves to her, across space, in the very depths of her subconsciousness. Out of that same depth now rose the memory; and the inductions which accompanied it were some sort of comfort to Regina.

But what miserable comfort! Suppose he had sold himself with disgust, shame, rancour? Still he had sold himself. Suppose it had been for love of herself? Still he had sold himself; he had been capable of that! Regina pitied him, because she saw the pitiable side. But she felt that henceforth in her heart there was room for no other kindly sentiment.

All was ruined; and among the grey vestiges trembled only the yellow flowers of pity — too frail to survive among ruins.

228

But if not a word of it was true? In dark hours the strongest soul becomes the prey of superstition. The dream had been only a dream. In any case, it had knitted itself strangely to reality by the 10,000 *lire*, the beautiful apartment, Marianna's laugh.

Marianna! Ah! She at any rate would *know*! For a space Regina thought of summoning her.

"I will *make* her speak — by violence if necessary! I will send the nurse and the maid out of the house! I'm stronger than Marianna!"

She closed her fist and looked at it to assure herself of her strength.

"If she won't speak, I'll crush her. I'll cry: 'Oh, you who always speak the truth, speak it now!' "

Already she heard her voice, echoing through the warm silence of her drawing-room.

What would Marianna reply? She would probably laugh.

And suppose none of it were true?

Pride pierced Regina's soul and destroyed the half-formed, indecorous, senseless project.

"Neither Marianna nor any one. I will find out myself."

But after a few moments the turmoil in her thoughts recommenced, and she formed other romantic and irrational projects.

She would follow Antonio.

Some fine night he would go out, and, after strolling hither and thither for an hour, he would open the iron gate leading to Madame's garden, the gate of which Massimo had said, "Here is the entrance for her lovers."

Antonio would go in. Regina would wait outside in the deserted street, in the shadow of the corner. Some one would pass and look at her with brutal eyes, imagining her a night wanderer; but she would take no offence. Why should she take offence? Was she not lower than the lowest of night wanderers? Were not her very clothes woven of shame?

Hours of silent torture would pass.

Antonio was in there, in the oppressive heat of that house decked with furs — voluptuous, feline, like the lair of a tigress. It was all so horrible that, even in her insensate dream, Regina could not think of it. Only she saw the Princess dressed in black velvet, her thick neck roped with pearls, her hands small and sparkling. And the small, sparkling hands were caressing Antonio's beautiful head. And he was silent; he had got used to these caresses.

This idea sufficed to produce in Regina an explosion of grief, which quickly brought on reaction. She awoke from her delirium; thought she saw all the folly of her doubt. None of it was true; none! Such things only happened in novels. It was impossible that Antonio should penetrate furtively into the old woman's house; impossible that his wife should wait outside in the shadow of the corner, to make him a comedy-scene when he came out. Ridiculous!

So the slow day wore on in what seemed physical anguish, more or less acute according to moments, which often completely disappeared, but left the memory of pain and the dread of its return.

Outside the feast of the sun continued, of the blue sky, of happy birds. Now and then a passing carriage broke the silence of the street with a torrent of noise. Then all was quiet again, save that in the distance the continuous rumble of the city ebbed and flowed like the swelling of the sea in an immense shell.

About two Caterina woke up and began to cry. Regina heard this tearless, causeless weeping, and went to the nursery. It was papered with white, and, against this shining background, the bronzed and heavy figure of the nurse with the baby, naked and pink in her hands, woke a new feeling in Regina. She seemed looking at a picture which signified something. But now everything had acquired for her a signification of reproach. That figure of a peasant mother, dark, rough, sweet, like a primitive Madonna, reminded her of what she ought to have been herself. She didn't even know how to be a mother like the meanest of peasants! She was nothing. A parasite — nothing but a parasite!

The nurse was dressing the child and talking to her in a "little language." "*Pecché quetto pianto?* (What's all this crying about?) What's the matter? Is little madam cold? Well, we'll put on her lovely little shift, and then her lovely little socks, and then her lovely little *shoosies*. Look! Look! What lovely little *shoosies!* Go in, little foot! What? little foot won't go in? Oho, Mr. Foot, that's all very fine, but in you go!"

Caterina, in her chemise, rosy and fat, with her hair ruffled, cried still; but she looked with interest at her white shoes and stuck out her foot.

"There's one gone in! Now the other. Let's see if this Mr. Foot is as naughty as the other Mr. Foot. Up with him! No, this is good Mr. Foot, and we'll give him a big kiss. Up!"

Caterina laughed. Her eyes, with their bluish whites, her whole face, her whole little figure, seemed illuminated. Regina took her in her arms, danced her up and down, pressed her to her heart, made her play, played and laughed with her. "My little, little one! My scagarottina (the smallest, the last hatched, the favourite of the nestlings)."

"Bah!" said the nurse, very cross. "What's the sense of calling her that? Give her to me. She's cold."

"You had better take her to the Pincio," said Regina, returning the babe to her arms; but Caterina held tight on to her mother, and frowned at the nurse.

"It's too windy on the Pincio," said the peasant, still crosser. "And so, Miss Baby, you don't love me any more, don't you?"

But Regina did not mind the nurse's jealousy. She had so often herself been jealous of the nurse!

When the woman and the baby were gone, Regina wandered a little hither and thither through the silent Apartment. What could she do with herself? What could she do? She did not know what to do. She ought to have gone to visit a lady she had met at Madame Makuline's but the bare idea of dressing herself to go to a drawing-room, where a pack of women would be sitting in a circle, discussing gravely and at length the alarming shape of the sleeves in the latest fashion-book, filled her with melancholy.

What was she to do? What was she to do? Boredom, or at least a feeling which she told herself was boredom, began to oppress her. She could not remember what, up till yesterday, she had been in the habit of doing to exorcise boredom. But she did remember how in the first year of her marriage she used to get bored just like this.

Well, how had she got through that period? What grateful occupation had made her forget the passing of life?

None; she had just been happy.

"What? Am I unhappy now? All because of a piece of nonsense?" she asked herself, sitting down by the window of her bedroom and taking up a little petticoat she was sewing for Baby. "But at that time, too, I was making myself miserable about nothing."

She stitched for five or six minutes. The silence of the room, the quiet, rather melancholy afternoon light, that same distant rumbling of the great shell, which reached her through the warm air, gave her something of the vague and soothing sweetness of dream. The trouble seemed laid.

More minutes passed.

But suddenly the door-bell sounded, and she sprang to her feet, shaken by the electric vibration which infected her nerves.

"Not at home!" she said, running to the maid, who was on her way to open.

Regina returned to her room and shut the door. She didn't even want to know who was seeking her. At that moment, on that day, she hated and despised the whole human kind.

But when the maid told her through the door that the visitor was Signorina Gabrie, Regina rushed to the window and called to the girl, who was just issuing from the house. Gabrie came back. Regina at once repented that she had recalled her. She saw she had been moved to do so by an impulse of despairing curiosity. The student, finding her note-books in disorder, probably suspected Regina had read them; now she had perhaps come in alarm to make excuses for the horrors she had written. A few questions would be enough ——

But Regina quickly recovered her proud dignity. No, never! Neither of Gabrie nor of any one would she ask that which it concerned her to know.

Gabrie came in, colourless in her loose black jacket. She was not well; she coughed. Her eyes, however, had kept their cruel brilliance, sharp and shining like needles.

Regina felt afraid of this terrible girl. The future authoress seemed already mistress of a power of divination superior to every other human faculty. She would read her friend's thoughts through her forehead! But the fear only lasted a moment. Gabrie was nothing! Just a little tattler — despicable!

"I was dressing to go out; that's why I said 'Not at home.' Are you cured? I went to see you this morning."

"I know, thanks. Yes, I am better. Go on dressing. I won't sit down. How's Caterina?"

"She's gone out," said Regina, smoothing her hair at the wardrobe mirror.

"Go on dressing," repeated Gabrie. "I'm sorry to be delaying you."

Regina began to dress. She did not know where she was going, but she would certainly go out just to get rid of Gabrie.

"Shall I help?" asked the girl.

"Yes, please. Hook the collar. Oh, these collars! What a torment they are! One wants a maid just for these precious collars!"

"Haven't you got one?" said Gabrie, dryly, fastening the collar.

"That girl? She's a mere scrub."

"Patience! Hold still a moment! How on earth can you wear such a collar? Well, really, women *are* the victims of fashion!"

Regina felt Gabrie's slim, cold fingers on her neck. The gold-embroidered collar, which reached to her very ears, choked her. She turned round, flushed and angry. Was she angry with Gabrie or with the collar? She did not know, but she flew out at Gabrie.

"*Women!* Aren't you a woman yourself, pray? Be so kind as to drop that tone. I can't endure it!"

"I know you can't," said the other meekly. "But is that my fault?"

Regina looked at her while she held her breath, fastening the overtight bodice. What did Gabrie mean? Had her words some occult signification?"

"How old are you?"

"Why do you ask? I'm twenty. Why?"

"Really?"

"Really. Why should I hide it? As I shan't find a husband —"

"Don't be pathetic. I can't stand that, either."

"I know you can't. Is it my fault?"

"When's your first novel coming out?"

"Sooner than you think," said Gabrie, brightening, but coughing violently.

"Will you put me into it?" said Regina, powdering herself spitefully. The white powder clouded even the looking-glass, and Regina thought —

"Gabrie must find me changed, and she'll be guessing the reason."

She knew she was cross, and felt vexed that she could not command herself. But Gabrie coughed and made no reply. They went out together.

"Where are you going?" asked Regina.

"Home to my studies."

"Come with me. There'll be matter for an authoress's study. Imagine a room, with ten ladies, all mortal enemies, because each one is afraid she isn't so well-dressed as the others!"

"In my books, if ever I write any, there'll be nothing so banal It's useless for you to take me 'in giro' (*Prendere in giro* – 1. to take round with one 2. to make fun of)"

They both laughed at the pun, but Regina felt that the laugh rang false. She could not make out whether Gabrie suspected her of reading the note-book.

"Good-bye," they said, without shaking hands. The girl went off towards Via Torino and Regina turned in the direction of Via Depretis, holding her smart dress very high. In the silence of the deserted pavement her silk petticoat rustled like the dead leaves of autumn. She was thinking of Gabrie, who had flown to her garret like a bee to its hive, and who had an object in this stupid life. She walked on, but did not know whither she was going.

She went a long way, aimlessly; down and up Via Nazionale; then, scarcely noticing it, she found herself in Via Sistina, going towards the Pincio. Her troubled thoughts followed her like the rustle of her skirts.

On the Pincio she found the nurse with Caterina, and they sat together on one of the terrace benches. There was no music, but the fine day had attracted a crowd of foreigners and carriages. From the bench (while the baby bent from the arms of the stooping nurse, picked up stones, examined them gravely, then still more gravely offered them to another baby,) Regina watched the circling carriages. Slowly she passed under something of a spell as she gazed at the too luminous, too tranquil, too beautiful picture — the pearly sky, the flowery trees among the green trees, the charmingly attired idle figures, the faces like paintings upon china.

As in the background of a stage picture, the beautiful shining horses, the carriages full of fair women, passed and re-passed in a kind of rhythmical course, which fascinated with a sleepy fascination like that of running water.

Once Regina's envy of those fine ladies in their carriages had swollen even to sinful hatred. Now, from the depths of the stupor which overwhelmed her, she felt sorry for them, for the tedium of their existence, their uselessness, their rhythmical course — always the same, always equal, as on the park roads, so also in their lives.

"Let us go. It's turning cold," said the nurse.

Regina started. The sun had gone down, clear in a clear sky, scarce tinted by faint green and rose; an ashen light, gently sad-coloured, fell over the picture. Regina rose docilely and followed the big woman whose bronze countenance was framed by the aureole of a wet-nurse's head-dress.

They walked and walked. Caterina slept on the nurse's powerful shoulder, and the ashy-rose twilight threw its haze over Via Sistina. The portly nurse swayed as she moved like a laden bark. Regina, slender and rustling as a young poplar, followed automatically as if towed by the big woman. When the latter stopped — and she stopped before all the shop windows which showed necklaces and rings — Regina also stopped, her looks veiled and vague.

The long torment of excitement had been succeeded by indefinable torpor. She was walking in a dream. Years and years must have rolled by since she had passed along Via San Lorenzo following the bird-seller. Of all her emotions, now only a vague sadness remained. She seemed no longer in doubt, but finally convinced of the monstrous folly of her suspicion. Only she was unable to recover her accustomed serenity.

Three lame musicians, standing before a gloomy house, sobbed out of their old instruments a lament of supreme melancholy. The pavement was crowded with elderly foreign ladies in hats of impossible ugliness. From every cross-street sounded the warnings of motors. Regina, being short-sighted, was always afraid of the motors, especially in the twilight, when the last light of day was confused in perilous dazzle with the uncertain brightness of the lamps. To-night she was more nervous than usual. She felt as if monsters were rampant through the city, howling to announce their passage. Some fine day one of these monsters would overwhelm her and the baby and the portly nurse, grinding them like grains of barley.

In Piazza Barberini, an old gentleman, stooping slightly, and wearing an overcoat of forgotten fashion buttoned up tightly though the evening was almost hot, passed close to Regina. She recognised the Senator, Arduina's relation, and turned to speak to him; but his ironical though kindly eyes were looking straight before him, and he saw no one.

She had met him several times — once he had even come to visit her — and each time he had talked about England and the English laws, and the English women, repeating the refrain of his old song — "Work, work, work! That is the secret of a good life."

Regina had ended by finding him tiresome, like any other old monomaniac. One could get along very well, even without work; of course one could! But to-night she watched the small, bent figure tripping along, melting into the misty distance of the street, and she thought it even more ridiculous than usual. Nevertheless, it seemed to her that this little gnome-like figure had appeared, as in a fable, to point the moral of her unhappy history.

Ah, well! — to talk like the Master — all life, if one considered it, was an unhappy history. Was it not a most discomfortable sign of the times that a girl of twenty, who had left the green river-banks of her birthplace for the first time, should deliberately set down in her note-book the most hideous things of life, which, moreover, were only calumny?

Antonio came home about seven. As on an evening long ago, the laid table awaited him, and the passage was fragrant with the smell of fried artichokes. Regina, not long returned from her walk, was making out the housekeeping list for the morrow.

Caterina was awake, and Antonio took her at once on his arm and sat down by the window. The lamplight always excited Caterina and made her even merrier than usual.

"Like the kittens," said the nurse.

The baby, who appeared to cherish a great admiration for her father, sat staring at him for a long time, then gravely showed him one little foot with its sock on and a new shoe. Antonio understood her.

"Aha! A coquette already! We've got some beautiful shoes, and we want them admired, eh?" he said, nodding his head and taking the little foot in his hand.

But Caterina's face darkened. She frowned horribly, and made a great effort to liberate her foot. She succeeded, but the shoe came off and fell on the floor. Then the young father stooped and, not without difficulty, put the little, hot, pulsing foot back in the shoe, addressing the baby in phrases which, according to Balzac, are ridiculous to read, but in the mouth of a father are sublime.

Caterina replied in her own fashion.

The mother drew nearer, but Antonio and the baby continued their interesting conversation. The young man's eyes were clear and joyous, and once again Regina convinced herself that she had dreamed a hideous dream.

And day after day followed, almost exactly similar to this one.

CHAPTER IV

AN unusually hot April was burning up the city. Towards evening the heavens flamed like incandescent metal. The scent of summer, of dust, of withered grass, made the air almost suffocating.

One evening Regina was visiting the Princess, who two days later was going to Albano.

"Shall you be there long?" asked the pink-china-headed old gentleman, in French, making a great effort to speak.

But, as he did not speak at all loud, Madame's big, yellow face revolved slowly till her good ear was turned in the old gentleman's direction.

"Beg pardon?"

"Will you stay long at Albano?"

"Three weeks."

"Where will you go afterwards?" continued the other, with a seriousness almost tragic.

"To Viareggio, Monsieur. And you?"

"I don't know yet. I am still undecided. Perhaps to Vichy. You will remain in Italy?"

"Probably this year. I am not over well, and I don't wish to do anything fatiguing. How dreadfully hot it is already! One can't sleep. I ought to have got out the hair mattresses."

Madame sighed. Monsieur sighed louder. They both seemed extremely unhappy, she on account of the heat, he because he didn't know what to do with himself for the summer.

"I'm sure there's going to be an earthquake," said Marianna, by way of comfort, as she brought them their tea.

The old gentleman, who for some time had been casting tender looks at Marianna, fixed his little blue eyes on her and said —

"How many cups, Mademoiselle, have you distributed in your life? When I see you without one in your hand your little figure seems to me incomplete."

But Mademoiselle was out of humour, and would neither talk nonsense nor listen to it. Even she was oppressed by the heat. Passing near Regina, she said, in a stage whisper —

"For every cup of tea I have handed he has lost a lock of his hair!"

But Regina also was cross, and did not listen.

The heat made everybody cross and stupid. Regina, moreover, felt at the end of her forces; her pride and her dignity were bending like leaves scorched by the sun. She was anxiously expecting to be joined by Antonio. Perhaps to-day she would really be given a sign; what sort of sign she did not know, but she waited. She waited; ashamed of being in this house, of facing that old woman, who was as impassive as a deaf sphinx; yet ashamed also of being ashamed.

While she waited her memory was busy. The very smallest sign would be sufficient now she had gone over the past, and called up with clearness and intensity each act, each word, which might have an equivocal signification. To-day the bitter-sweet perfume of lilac which pervaded the room reminded her of another occasion two years ago; of words, bitter as the perfume, spoken by herself, and of Marianna's terrible reply.

"To be poor in Rome is to be like a beggar gnawing a bone at the shut door of a palace."

"Just so; and presently the rich man's dog comes by and snatches from the beggar's hand even the bone!"

Ah! Mademoiselle knew the world! While Regina was recalling the distressed and ironical look which the Princess had given her that day, just before her flight, Marianna brought her some tea and began to tell the misdeeds of a very elegant gentleman who frequented Madame's receptions.

"They say he has really lived on the creatures," she said, "and when they can't do any more for him, he flings them away like sucked lemons."

"So much the worse for them," said Regina. "After all, he's the strongest and —"

"Ah! I forgot you were a super-woman!" said Marianna, in a low voice. Then she laughed. "Will you have some more tea?"

Swift and terrible as the thunderbolt came the thought to Regina —

"Marianna knows the secret, and believes that I know it, too, and consent!"

A flame burned her face. Never did she forget the shame which this flush caused her. It lasted a moment. Then she looked contemptuously at Marianna, and remembered that the girl might have spoken without intention; merely one of her usual insolent follies. Still, all her pulses had been set throbbing.

"At all costs I must get rid of this incubus," she thought, not for the first, the second, the hundredth time. To-day she felt that her trouble, real or imaginary, had come to the crisis, and must be resolved, either by deliverance or by death.

The old ladies and gentlemen were all gathered round their hostess, who, whitewashed and wan, seemed in that sparkling circle like a decaying pearl in a broken setting. They were talking of the suicide of a Russian personage, a Mæcenas known to all Europe.

One of the speakers, himself a Russian, told of a dinner he had attended a few days before in Paris, given by artists and noblemen to the rich suicide, and of all the intrigues and evil diplomacy connected with that symposium, and the bonds, more or less shameful, by which its guests were united among themselves.

Regina listened and remembered that she had listened to similar conversations a hundred times. What struck her was the simplicity with which the Russian talked, and the eagerness with which the others listened. No one was abashed; some even gave signs of approbation, and seemed delighted at hearing a scandal, which, for the most part, they already knew. It was the way of the world! And was she to be surprised if one of these wrongs, which, it appeared, were habitual with all the men and women of this earth, had come home to herself? For a moment she asked, was she not a fool to be so disturbed? Then the question horrified her.

She felt herself stifled. The heat of the room, here and there still decked with furs, gave her really a feeling of oppression and suffocation. Surely the feline creatures were becoming alive! Their skins were filling out; they were moving, approaching her! puffing hot breath in her face, musky and voluptuous scent! They fascinated her with their glassy eyes, raised their padded paws, slowly, softly; hugged her, smothered her! Air! air! To free herself, or else to die! Another moment, and she, Regina — erring, perhaps, but not impure, who, on the banks of her native river, had dreamed of all in life which is worthy to support life — another moment, and she would die of asphyxia!

Instinctively she got up and made her way to the marble terrace, whence a stair led to the garden. A man was working at a round plot like a tart, edged with velvet grass and patterned with bedding plants. Everything was soft and artificial in the little green and flowery garden, strewn with wistaria petals. The sunset light flushed the garland of white roses which hung from the laurel above the little gate. At this hour the little gate was shut.

The hot, over-scented air of the garden had not yet brought Regina any relief, when she saw the gate open and admit her husband. A sanguinous veil clouded her eyes. For a moment she could not see the figure advancing towards her. Antonio mounted the stair quite quietly, stopped at her side, and asked —

"What are you doing here?"

He was smart as usual, but not in visiting costume.

"Why are you dressed like this?" said Regina, touching his sleeve. "There is such a crowd of people, and it's so hot. Don't go in! They haven't seen you, and I am just going!"

"Wait one moment," he returned, tranquilly. "Why are you going?"

"At least don't enter this way, Antonio!" she cried, excitedly.

"But why not?" he repeated, opening the glass door.

Regina remained on the terrace, looking at the gardener without seeing him. Her suspicion was monstrous folly! A guilty man would not act as at this moment Antonio had acted. Yet no! Immediately she reflected that if he were guilty be would naturally behave just as he had behaved — pretending not to understand, even if he did understand, what was passing in her soul. But no! Again, no! If he were guilty he would have pretended better. He would not have come in familiarly by the garden gate. He would not have allowed himself the liberty, knowing his wife here, in the *other woman's* house. Yet she was aware that the most astute delinquents pretend sometimes to forget, and commit imprudences just in order to mislead suspicion.

But what startled her at the moment was the perception that now she held Antonio not only guilty, but aware of her suspicion, and resolved to continue the deception.

She went back into the drawing-room, where the discussion of the foreigner's suicide was still going on. It seemed to her tiresome, provincial gossip.

Marianna gave Antonio tea, and while he nibbled a yellow biscuit with teeth even as a child's, he also gave his opinion of the tragedy. Madame bent forward to listen, and fanned herself with a little Japanese fan, which seemed made of polished glass. The rings on her tiny hands sparkled in the light, which grew ever fainter and rosier.

Nothing occurred. There was still no sign, no revelation of the secret. Antonio did not take much notice of Madame, and she, more drooping and impassive than usual, turned her good ear to every one who spoke, now and then replying politely. But in her metallic eyes shone the vague and languid splendour of thoughts far away in matters of her own.

After a while Regina rose. Antonio followed her. They took leave and went away. Marianna ran after them to the ante-room, and kissed Regina on both cheeks.

"Me also?" said Antonio, offering his cheek.

"You to-morrow," she replied, carrying on the jest. Then she said, seriously, " Come about seven, as we've got to go out first. Ah!" she continued, following them to the door, "that man has been back. He offers 300 *lire* or a new fur. But Madame is firm in demanding her own; she says he'll have to be summoned."

"Well, we'll have him summoned," said Antonio. "But was the old fur a good one?"

"Why, it cost 900 *lire*!"

"We'll see about it. *Au revoir!*"

"Good-bye. Are you coming to Albano, Regina?"

"If Madame invites us," said Antonio, and they went out. Regina had said neither yes nor no. They walked as far as Piazza dell' Indipendenza in silence. Then Regina raised her head and asked —

248

"What was that about a fur?"

"Oh, good Lord! don't speak of it! For a whole month I've heard of nothing else. She sent a skin to the furrier to be repaired, and it seems to have got changed or something ——"

"Are you going to Albano?"

"If she invites us — some Sunday."

"I'm not going," said Regina, stoutly.

"Why not?"

"Because — it's too hot," she said, dropping her voice.

"It won't be hot there. She has taken a villa on the edge of the lake. Such roses on the terrace! When they drop they fall straight into the water."

Regina knew all about it, for he had chosen the villa himself, and had described it to his wife a few days ago. They walked on without speaking further. The street lamps burned yellow and dismal in the rosy twilight, and their dull flame increased Regina's melancholy. Her foolish project of spying upon Antonio in the night recurred to her. She saw herself a flitting shadow under that yellow and dismal light, shadowed herself by some night prowler in search of adventure. But suddenly she raised her head proudly, saying to herself —

"No, never again! This is the last time I shall go to that house; and neither shall he go there again. It is time to bring it all to an end!"

When she had reached her room, she took off her silk jacket and flung it on the bed.

"Well! it *is* hot! What a summer we are going to have! Oh, how horrid Rome is in the summer! And *they* are already going away. Quite right, the poor delicate things! But we — yes, gnawing our bones — if they're left to us —"

"What's that you're muttering?" asked Antonio, but went on, without waiting for an answer, "Hasn't Caterina come in yet?"

Regina undressed, flinging down her things and inveighing against the rich, great people, who abandon Rome at its first heat.

Antonio stood looking out of the window. An angry thought flashed through her mind, the worst of the perverse thoughts which had destroyed her peace.

"He's no longer displeased when I am cross. He's afraid of provoking me to a burst of rage. He guesses that I *know*, and believes that I'll bear it — up to a certain point."

"Shut the window!" she said, irritated.

He shut the window, patiently.

"I'm going for the *Avanti* (an evening paper)," he said, moving away; "make haste! it's half-past seven."

Left alone, Regina experienced a sort of crisis, as on the evening two years ago when she had been to the Grand Hotel.

"Ah!" she thought, putting on her home evening dress; "The moment he comes in I'll say to him, 'It's time to end this business! I am moving away — in reality this time! I don't wish you to visit her at Albano. I don't wish you ever again to go to her house. I will never go to it myself. End it, Antonio! End it! end it! Don't you see I am gnawing my heart out? Or is it that you do see and don't care? Why don't you care? At least tell me why! Why do you act like this? I don't know how to bear all these superfluities, these silk petticoats, chiffons, which you have bought me with that money. There! I fling them all from me — all! all! A garret is enough for me, a sack to dress myself in, black bread — but *honour*, Antonio, honour, honour!' Ah, they rob us even of our honour, even of that one gnawed bone! But you'll have to reckon with me, Madame! old viscous moon, blind and asthmatic personification of nocturnal vampires! Wrapped in your furs, isn't it enough that you've had an easy life, a soft life, which has corrupted you, body and soul, but you want pleasure also in your old age? You and your old, rich friends, taking advantage of the poor, of the poor and the young, who have been made tender by tears, by weariness and grief, just as you have been made soft by idleness and satiety!"

"All this rhetoric is very fine," she thought, presently, putting her clothes in order, "but the world belongs to the strong, and I — I am one of the weak. I am weak because I reason too much, while *those* people don't reason at all; they only enjoy. That deaf old witch has never *thought*. She has stolen my Antonio, and I — I have been torturing myself for a whole month thinking whether it is delicate to say to my husband, 'End it! End it!' But I will speak to-night! And he will retort, saying it was all done for me — to give me those things I demanded; and then — then what will happen? No; he won't reproach me at all! He isn't capable of it. We shall forgive each other. And then — what will happen? Is it true we can begin a new life? Yes; even a ruined house can be rebuilt. But it isn't the same house, and one can't live in it without constantly thinking of the horror of the ruin."

Antonio delayed in returning. The nurse also delayed. She was out of temper at present and inclined to take liberties, because she was soon to be dismissed. It was almost night. Regina gazed from the window, vaguely anxious about her child. Twilight still lingered in the lonely street, grass-grown like the streets of a deserted city. The gardens were odoriferous with roses. A few stars twinkled on the still blood-stained veil of the heavens.

And, notwithstanding her proud resolve, Regina was over-come with grief at the thought of abandoning that poetic street, every blade of whose grass had known the illusion of her happiness.

But she kept silence on this evening also. How could she help it? Caterina would not go to bed; she wanted to stay with her papa, whose golden moustache, beautiful eyes, beautiful scented hair, she admired prodigiously. Did Caterina see that her papa was beautiful? That cannot be known. But certainly she looked at his attractive countenance with great pleasure, and seemed to find special delight in touching the shaven face of *Il Papaino* with her little peach-blossom cheek. Antonio sang his favourite rhyme —

> "Mousey doesn't care for cream,
> Mousey wants to marry the Queen;
> If the King won't let her go,
> Mousey'll break his bones, you know."

Each time he repeated those lines Regina remembered, as in a troubled dream, the evening of her arrival in Rome. But to-night Caterina laughed and screamed with mad delight, and admired her papa more than ever; and then they talked together of so many things, of such secret things, comprehensible only to themselves! What could Regina do? Deprive Antonio, who had been working all day, of the pleasure of talking to his baby, wrest the little one from him, and send her away? She was not so cruel. When at last Caterina's big eyes became languid with sleep, and all her little body relaxed and sank, heavy and sweet like a ripe fruit, Antonio said —

"Now I am going out for a little."

What could Regina do? Say to him —

"No; stay. I wish to tell you the horrible things I am thinking of you ———"?

It was impossible. He had every right to go out for a little, at least in the evening, after a whole day of fatigue.

He went out, and Regina sat down and read the terrible column of the *Avanti* called "What goes on in the world."

Madame Makuline left Rome two days later, but Antonio still went daily to the villa to see after the letters and dispatch certain affairs.

On Sunday he showed Regina the key, and told her the old servant left in charge of the house had asked leave of absence.

"At last we are proprietors of a villa," he said, joking. Then Regina was assailed by a temptation. In vain, for some minutes, she tried to put it from her.

"Let us go to the villa," she proposed.

Antonio not only accepted, but seemed delighted. Could he be so cynical?

She put on a soft, white dress, with big, flopping sleeves, in which she looked very young and beautiful with the modern beauty which lies less in line than in expression. The dress was new, and Antonio admired it to her satisfaction. Notwithstanding the internal current of suspicion and resentment which continually fretted her soul, she could not do without pretty frocks. Sometimes she even felt a morbid pleasure in spending *that* money on objects of ornament and superfluity. She had resumed minute care of her complexion, her hair, her nails. She wasted half-hours in rubbing her face with oil of almonds, in dressing her hair to the fashion. What did she mean by it? To please Antonio, or to please others? She did not know, but, perceiving she was no longer angry with herself for her vain refinements, she questioned whether her moral sense were not growing daily weaker and weaker.

Scarcely had they started for the villa when a puff of contemptuous wind ruffled her hair and blew the powder from her face. It was a burning afternoon; the trees trembled at the breath of the hot wind; the Piazza, dazzling in the sunshine, seemed vaster even than usual. A veil of dust obscured the distance of the streets. The east wind was raging, its hot breath pregnant with malign suggestions.

Their heads bent, holding on their hats, Antonio and Regina took their way, and they laughed a little and squabbled a little. Arrived in front of the villa, they looked round like thieves. The street was deserted, swept by the wind; leaves of roses and geraniums fluttered to the pavement; a hot perfume of lilies rose from the garden. They seemed in an enchanted city, new, unknown, not yet inhabited.

When Antonio unlocked the polished door, Regina felt as if entering her own house, long dreamed of, attained by magic. Stepping into the vestibule, cool as the bed of the river, seemed like stepping into a bath. The wolves were covered with cloths, as if they had disguised themselves for fun in their mistress's absence. A small marble head, pallid behind a motionless palm-tree, faced the intruders with smiling lips. Regina walked softly by force of habit, and removed her hat before the veiled mirror. Then she remembered they were alone, and put the hat on the marble head with a laugh.

"Hush!" whispered her husband. "Don't make so much noise."

"Who is there to hear us?"

He opened a door. She followed him. They crossed the saloons and entered the dining-room. Antonio walked on tip-toe with a certain diffidence. He would not let Regina laugh.

"Aren't we here to play at being proprietors?" she asked. "Let's see if we can make some tea!"

"No, no," said Antonio. "I don't want the caretaker to find out we've been here. But stop — there should be some Madeira in the sideboard. Aha!"

They found the bottle and tasted it. Then they put everything back in its place. They were like children. Antonio became merry, and, without making a noise, began also to amuse himself. They returned to the drawing-room, and Regina partly opened the shutters. A green light illuminated one corner. Regina pretended to be holding a reception, mimicked the voice of the pretty blind lady, then lolled on Madame's favourite sofa. It was covered with grey fur, and suggested an immense sleeping cat.

In her soft dress, her hair falling loose on her forehead, her eyes burning, and it seemed artificially darkened, she looked, in the green penumbra, a real, great lady, *blasée*, lost in an unwholesome dream.

Antonio meantime tried to open the door which led to the terrace and the garden.

"Wait a bit," said Regina. "Let's look round up-stairs first. Have you ever been up-stairs?"

"I? Never."

"Well, come now. Leave that door locked. Come here. I want to tell you something!" she said, childishly.

"What is it? I'm looking for the key."

As if guessing her idea, he did not come to the lure.

Then she felt blaze up the wicked doubt which persecuted her. Yes, in this room, perhaps on this very divan, Antonio had stained his lips with hateful kisses!

She bit her lips to repress a shudder, then rose and hastened to the next room.

"Let's go in there. Never mind that door."

He crossed the room and joined her. Cat-like, Regina threw herself on his breast and kissed him. Illusion of the light? It seemed to her that Antonio's face became green, and she believed she had intuition of the drama evolving in his soul. Yes! he must at this moment be remembering something nauseous! an embrace, a kiss, which had stained his soul with infamy! Here, in this place, to kiss the lips of his wife must be castigation for him!

Her delirium was increasing.

"Kiss me!" she imposed upon her husband, fixing on him eyes of tragic flame, and drawing him towards the divan. He certainly resisted; but he kissed her, his lips still scented with the wine. Then Regina, on fire with the madness of her doubt, believed the moment had come for tearing the vile secret from those lips, whose kisses gave her mortal anguish in this place where every object must remind Antonio of his miserable error.

But she was unable to formulate her horrible demand.

Afterwards they penetrated into the study and the library, where Antonio was accustomed to spend what he called his hours of service. It was a real library, with a thousand volumes artistically bound. Madame had shown Regina some ancient books, an illuminated codex, Ariosto's autograph, said to be genuine, some letters from celebrated authors, amongst them three signed George Sand. In spite of her pre-occupation, Regina amused herself looking through the glass of the bookshelves, as the street boys peer into the shop windows. Meantime Antonio glanced at the letters laid on the writing-table at which he was accustomed to dispatch the Princess's correspondence.

Regina presently made her way into the little adjoining room, a boudoir where Madame sometimes dined. Antonio followed. They opened the door and found themselves in a wide ante-chamber, which communicated with the garden. A back staircase led to the first floor. But all doors were locked except that of the bath-room. A little water, blue with soap, had been left is the bath.

Regina was watching Antonio, but he moved with hesitation, and she thought him unfamiliar with the house.

"I want to cross that bridge which connects the two parts of the villa," said Regina, shaking the lobby doors.

But everything was locked, so they descended again and went to the kitchen. Tufts of verdure almost blocked the barred window. Still, the golden afternoon light penetrated at the top. A background of flower-garden was discernible, and rose petals had fallen on the shining pavement. A marble table was splendid in the centre of the kitchen.

"It's like a church!" said Antonio, merry again. "Suppose we dance a little?"

"It's finer than our drawing-room," sighed Regina. "Oh! do be quiet!"

But he whirled her away with him round the table.

A magnificent black cat, asleep on the dresser, raised his great, round head, opened his orange eyes, and looked at the two liberty-taking people without moving. Regina shuddered, however.

"How silly we are!" she said. "Suppose the man were to come in and find us here? I declare I hear steps in the garden! Let us escape!"

But Antonio put on the cook's apron, pretended to cook, and, servant-fashion, spoke against the mistress. He suggested that she was a spy of the Russian Government. Regina listened and laughed, but reflected that in this kitchen was perhaps known and discussed that other secret of which she had not been able to rend the unclean veil.

She resented Antonio's gaiety, and an accident increased her ill-humour. The cat was still watching, now and then giving an ostentatious yawn. She tried to stroke him, stretching her hand over the dresser. But the cat sprang to a ledge higher up, and upset a flask. Big drops of oil, thick and yellow, rained on her white raiment, spotting it irreparably. She nearly cried with annoyance; foolish words came unconsciously from her mouth.

"Even my dress gets stained in this horrible house!"

Antonio listened, but seemed not to understand. He found a bottle of benzine, and helped Regina to clean her dress, then put everything back in its place, threw his arm round her waist, and made her run with him up the stair, careless of her stumbles, deaf to all protests and reproaches.

Thus they entered the garden, and Regina recovered her calm. The sinking sun gilded half the expanse, leaving the rest in deep shadow. The wind passed high up over the tops of the laurels, which were garlanded with white roses. From time to time a rain of rose-leaves, of lime-blossom, of wistaria, circled down through the hot air and fell on the paths. Regina and her husband sat in a green corner close to a hermes, on which was an archaic head. Black, hard, epicene, it had a complacent and sarcastic smile.

"He thinks us a pair of lovers," said Regina, remarking the expression. "No, my dear fellow, I assure you we are enemies!"

"And why?" asked Antonio, coldly.

Then a recollection shot through Regina's mind.

"Do you remember that day in the woods, two years ago, when you — had come for me? There were so many blue butterflies, just like these wistaria blossoms —"

She laughed meaningly. Did he remember? And the remembrance of that hour of pleasure passed in the mystery of the damp, hot woods the day after his coming to Regina's home, after her flight and their reconciliation, seemed to reawaken him to passion.

The childish gaiety which had animated him a few minutes before passed into a nervous tenderness, and this time it was he who sought the lips of his wife in a kiss, which reminded her of his kisses *then*.

And her doubts tormented her more than ever.

At sunset-time they went back into the house, but they did not yet go away. They wandered through the rooms abandoning themselves to childish extravagances. They ran about in the dark, and Regina, wailing over her dress, amused herself spitefully moving the furniture which Antonio put back into order.

Now and then they renewed their lover-like caresses. The warmth of the spring sunset came through the closed shutters and set Antonio's blood on fire. Regina found a perverse pleasure in enjoying the tenderness of her young husband there where she suspected he had stained the purity of his love.

Turbid poison was boiling in her soul. When Antonio kissed her, and trembled under her unaccustomed kisses, she fixed wild eyes on the dark corners, on the opaque brilliance of the veiled mirrors, trying to penetrate into the secrets of their vanished reflections. It seemed to her that the phantasm of "the old moon," of the purchaser of kisses, was there in the depth of some looking-glass, gnawing herself with jealousy and rage at the sight of Antonio giving his wife caresses, a single one of which all her millions was not sufficient to buy.

Thus Regina thought to take her revenge, but a flood of disgust rose more and more bitter from the depths of her heart. Disgust at herself and disgust at Antonio! How cynical must he be if he could thus disport himself in this place which knew his sin! or, if he were innocent, how con-temptible if, with the passivity of a weak man, he could thus violate the house of his benefactress merely to amuse the ill-regulated, hysterical woman, who that day was concealing herself under the white dress and fashionable coiffure of Regina, his wife.

At the bottom of her soul, however, well at the bottom, beyond all consciousness, in its darkest, most mysterious depths, Regina cherished a bitter satisfaction in recognising how utterly this man belonged to herself. Always and everywhere, even in error, it was she who dominated him. And, because of this, notwithstanding all resentment, all disgust, even when she felt she no longer loved her husband, even when she despised herself, thinking her soul stained like her dress, corrupted in the soft air, the half-light, the poisoned fragrance of that house, where, it seemed, "anything might happen," she felt infinite pity for Antonio. And on this pity she lived.

CHAPTER V

AT the end of the week a telegram came from Madame, asking Antonio to go to Albano.

"She can't live without him," thought Regina, assailed by a spasm of real jealousy. "I feel scruples at having merely gone into her house in her absence, but she has no scruples, none! I won't allow him to go!"

She was unreasonable, and she knew it; but the delirium, the quiet madness of doubt, had become habitual with her.

As usual, however, she was unsuccessful in carrying out her proud intention. When Antonio suggested she should accompany him to Albano, she said "Yes."

She said "Yes" up to the last moment, but on Sunday morning changed her mind.

"Don't you go either," she said. "If Madame wants you, why can't she come to Rome? Are you her slave?"

"Regina!" he said, reprovingly.

"I am not Regina, not a queen — not even a princess! I'm sick to death of this life we are leading! All through the week we see each other only for a minute at a time, and now you are going away even on Sunday!"

"Just for once. Why won't you come too?"

"I won't, because I don't want to. *I* am nobody's toady, and it's time you gave up the office yourself! Is there any more necessity for it? If it's true our affairs are so

prosperous," she went on, with open sarcasm, "then why —
—"

"There's no good discussing it with you," he interrupted,
firing up. "You're always unreasonable!"

He set out at noon. In the afternoon Regina went for one
of her rare visits to her mother-in-law. She stayed for dinner,
and once more made part of the picture she had so detested,
but now she had very different feelings from those of old.
Thinking it over, she asked herself why that picture had
appeared to her so vulgar. Merely as types of character the
personages were interesting, or at least seemed so now.

Arduina and Massimo discussed celebrated authors — she
with real animus, he with contempt for her. Gaspare told the
conjugal misfortunes of one of his colleagues. Signor Mario
picked his teeth, and Signora Anna lamented the terrible
conduct of her servant. It was amusing — for once in a way.
The dinner was good; they drank and laughed. Claretta
admired herself in the glass, flirted with Massimo and even
with Gaspare.

In fact, nothing in the environment had changed; yet
Regina was no longer disgusted. Claretta was less elegant
than herself, and Signora Anna took quite maternal
satisfaction in pointing this out. She asked her niece why she
didn't do her hair like Regina's.

"This suits me better," drawled the young lady, putting her
hand to her head and settling the lace butterfly which decked
her locks; "besides, it's the fashion."

"Excuse me," said Massimo, "the women of the
aristocracy do their hair like Regina."

"Madame Makuline, perhaps?" said Claretta, ironically.

Regina glanced at her. Did she mean anything, the pretty cousin? Did she know anything?

When the others sat down to cards Regina went into the bedroom which once had seemed to her a haunt of incubi. It was open to the balcony, and the moon illuminated the curtains, projecting a silver dazzle across the interior. The great bed was a white square in the centre of the room, corners of chairs and tables caught the light, a scent of pinks perfumed the silence and the peace of that great matrimonial chamber, nest of humdrum *bourgeois* felicity. Regina thought if Antonio had brought her to Rome on a night like this, and had introduced her into that room shining thus, wrapped in the dreams of mid-May, nothing would have happened that had happened.

She leaned from the balcony; pinks were at her feet; over a sweet heaven of velvety blue passed the moon distant and melancholy, distant and pure, like a sail lost in the immensity of the ocean of dream.

Naturally Regina's thoughts flew to the terrace on the shore of the Albano lake, where rose-leaves fell like butterflies on the iridescent mother-o'-pearl of the moonlit water.

What was Antonio doing? Was it possible that the monstrous dream which crushed her could have any reality? Under the infinite purity of the heavens could such wickedness be wrought on earth?

But when she had returned home, the incubus settled down on her again, victor once more in that strife which too often proved her the weaker.

She expected Antonio by the last train. He did not come, neither did he send an explanatory telegram. Regina waited till midnight, then went to bed, but passed an agitated night, perhaps because for the first time she was alone.

Very early she had Caterina brought to her. The baby, in her little nightdress, sat on the pillow and seemed uneasy at her father's absence.

"Papa?" she asked.

"Papa isn't here. He'll come very soon, very soon, very soon! Go to sleep. Lie down. Give me little foot — my little foot. That other one is Papa's? Very well, you can give it to him when he comes," said Regina, drawing the baby down. Caterina was in the habit of giving one foot to Mamma and the other to Papa. Regina took both the little feet, but Caterina wished to keep Papa's free. Then she touched the lace on Regina's nightdress with her rosy finger.

"*Ti è to?*" she asked.

"*Questo è tuo?* — Is this yours?" translated Regina. "Yes, it's mine. And little Caterina, whose is she? Mine, isn't she? all mine! And a little bit Papa's; but very, very little, because Papa is naughty, and doesn't come home, and leaves poor little Mamma all alone!"

She relieved her mind thus, talking in baby language to the rosy little creature; and while she made Caterina give her wee, wee, wee, dear, dear little kisses, and felt there could be no greater pleasure, she still thought of the monstrous visions

266

which had agitated her all night. Doubtless Antonio had slept at the villa on the shore of the lake, in a room of which the window was a wondrous picture of the landscape and the sky. And in the silence of the night, while outside the woods, the waters, the heaven, were a poem of beauty and purity, an odious idyl was taking place within.

"My little, little Caterina, my pet, put your arms round me! Let us sleep together," said Regina, laying the baby's hand on her face, and closing her eyes, as if to exclude the evil sights. "There! shut the little peepers! that's the way!"

The child obeyed for a moment, but suddenly became cross, struggled, and with her little open hand gave her mother a slap on the face.

"Oh, how naughty!" said Regina. "I'll tell Papa, you know! You are not to hit your Mamma! Ask my forgiveness at once; love me at once, like this! Say, 'Dear, dear Mamma, forgive Baby! Baby will never do it again.' "

But Caterina struck her a second time, and Regina became really angry.

"You are very, very naughty," she exclaimed, taking the little hand and administering pandies. "Go away; I don't want Baby any more. Baby isn't my little, little one any more. I don't love her. She also has grown wicked!"

Caterina began to cry — real tears, and this consciousness of grief, so rare in a child, struck the young mother profoundly.

"No, no! My baby at least shall not suffer! It is too soon!" she thought, and again gathered the little one in her arms, smoothed her hair, and kissed her little trembling head.

"Come here, then! Hush! hush! hush! She won't be naughty any more. Hush! Mamma does love her! That's my own pet! There, there! Listen! Here comes Papa!"

At this suggestion Caterina calmed herself by magic. Then to Regina a thing she had already suspected was clearly revealed, and she marvelled that she had ever doubted it. Caterina loved her father more than she loved her mother! With that wondrous instinct of a babe, Caterina felt that he was the kinder, the weaker, the more affectionate of the two; that he loved her more blindly, more passionately, than her mother loved her. Consequently, she preferred him.

Regina was not jealous, nor did she question if this proved her too much or too little a mother. But that morning, in the whirl of sad and ugly things which veiled her soul, she felt an unexpected light, she felt that supreme sentiment of pity, which in the dissolving of all her dreams sustained her like a powerful wing, spread, not over herself, not over Antonio, but over their child. They two were already dead to life, corrupted by their own errors; but Caterina was the future, the living seed which had had its birth among withered leaves. The soil around it must be cleared. And for the first time she thought that, not for herself in a last vanity of sacrifice, not for him whose soul was eternally stained, but for the child, she must draw Antonio out of the mire.

He came back by the 7.20 train, and had scarcely time to dress, swallow his coffee, and run to the office.

At the midday meal he told of the wonders of Albano, of the villa, of the night on the lake.

"Such flowers! such roses! Marvellous! I lost the last train because I had meant to take it at Castel Gandolfo, and Madame and Marianna insisted on leaving the carriage and walking part of the way. You can't imagine the splendour — the moonlight. I was thinking of you the whole time! I didn't wire, because it was too late."

"Is any one blaming you?" asked Regina, absently.

"You were angry, Regina?"

"I? Why?"

Antonio must have seen that some distress was clouding her spirit, for he began to talk volubly, trying to distract her. He complained of the Princess.

"What a nuisance she is! She made me take this journey all for the sake of that old fur. 'Beg pardon?' " he went on, mimicking her. " 'It's not for its money value, but because it's a precious remembrance ———' Perhaps George Sand gave it to her! She talked of nothing else. Even Marianna couldn't stand it, and proposed to skin the furrier if he didn't send it back at once."

"Did you sleep at the villa?" asked Regina, who was not listening.

"Well, she couldn't well send me anywhere else!"

"Oh, of course not!" said Regina, with evident sarcasm. And, without raising her eyes from her plate, she went on, "Is Madame a Russian?"

"Why, yes — didn't you know it?" answered Antonio, quickly.

He said no more, but his voice had shaken with a scarce perceptible vibration, which Regina did not fail to observe.

Without a look, without a sign, at that moment they understood each other, and each knew it. Regina thought Antonio's face darkened, but she did not dare to look at him. She went on eating, and only after a minute raised her head and laughed. Why at that moment she laughed she never knew.

"I was awake all night," she said; "I felt just like a widow."

"Well, wouldn't you like to be a widow? I know quite well you don't love me any longer," he answered, half fun, whole earnest.

"Oh, *zielo!*" said Regina, light and cruel, imitating the cry of heartless jest which she had heard from a spectator at a popular theatre, "what a tragedy of a honeymoon gone wrong!" Then changing her voice, but still satirical, "On the contrary, my dear, it's you who want to be a widower."

"I don't see it."

"It's true."

"How do you make it out?"

"Why, what would happen if you were a widower? You'd marry again at once. You're one of the men who can't enjoy life alone — who are no good living alone. I'm sorry for those men."

"You are sorry for me?"

"I pity you heartily."

"Why? Because I am your husband?"

"Yes, because you're my husband. Take away!" said Regina to the maid, pushing her plate aside contemptuously. When they were again alone, she added, "Next time don't be so stupid as to marry a *poor* woman."

270

He looked at her, and she thought his eyes were illuminated by a flash of anger, cold, metallic, such as she had never seen in him.

"*I* shouldn't know what to do with riches," he answered quietly.

The servant reappeared at the door, and Regina was silent, struck with a sense of chill. It appeared to her that Antonio's words had an intention of dogged defence, a sharp and crushing reproach like a blow. She felt herself mortally wounded.

The strife was beginning then? For to-day they said no more. On the contrary, after their meal they went together to their room and took their siesta in company, and before going out Antonio kissed his wife with his accustomed slightly languid but affectionate tenderness.

But from henceforth Regina fancied he would be on guard ready to defend himself at all points.

After this they bickered continually. She found annoyance in nothings, criticising all his little defects, and accusing him veiledly in a manner that he ought to understand if he were guilty. Antonio defended himself, but without too much heat, too much offence. She could not avoid the thought that he feared to drive her to extremities, and great sadness overwhelmed her. Why were they each so cowardly? Why did she not dare to confront him openly, though all within her, all her thoughts, recollections, instincts, rose up against him and accused him? Well, at last she confessed it to herself. She was afraid; afraid of the truth. Above all, she was afraid of herself. She believed that nothing kept her generous, enabled her to contemplate pardon, but the hope she was deceived. If it were certainly true, would she pardon? Sometimes she feared she would not.

Most of all her own weaknesses saddened her — the contradictions and phantasms of her sick spirit. Day by day her soul was revealed to her. She had thought herself superior, delicate, understanding; instead, she found she was cowardly and weak. She was like a tree never brought under cultivation, which might have borne good fruit, but, with its tangle of barren branches, only succeeded in throwing a pestiferous shadow. Was it her own fault?

However, in measure as she learned to know herself, she tried to improve. Instinct, too, would not suffer her to persevere in a small strife, in vulgar and inconclusive affronts. The bickering ceased and a truce followed, the result of anguished incertitude and vain hope.

She compared herself to a sick person, who ought to submit to a dangerous operation, and has decided to do so, in hope of regaining health, but who for the present prefers to suffer, and postpones the fateful moment.

Meanwhile the outward existence of this pair followed its equable course, apparently tranquil, all compounded of sweet and monotonous habits. May died, having again become pure, blue, chilly. The sky, after a few days' rain, had taken an almost autumnal tint, beautiful and suggestive.

Like a vein of milk in a poisoned flood, nostalgia for her distant home mingled with Regina's sorrow. Memory absorbed her, penetrated to her blood with the scent of the new leaves which perfumed the shining evenings in Via

Balbo. During some walk to Ponte Nomentano or in Trastevere, it sufficed for the splendour of silvery green on the Aniene, or the yellow vision of the Tiber, in the depths of the green, velvety, monotonous Campagna — like the harmonies of a primitive music — to give her attacks of almost tragic homesickness. But now-a-days she knew the nature of this malady — it was the vain longing for a land of dreams lost to her for ever.

She liked these little expeditions, which once she had despised, calling them the silly pleasures of little *bourgeois* resigned to their gilded mediocrity.

Sometimes Antonio proposed a walk beyond the Trastevere Station for the long, luminous afternoon; and she would meet him at the Exchange. More often they went to Ponte Nomentano, taking the baby with them, carried on the servant's arm. Antonio would amuse himself pretending to pursue Caterina; the maid would run and the baby contort herself with joy, screaming like the swifts, pink with the fearful delight of being hunted and not caught. Then Regina would linger behind, looking at the vermilion sky, the rosy lawns, the tranquil distance, all that grand country of aspect monotonous and solemn; like the life of a poet who has sung immortal songs without ever having had an adventure or committed a crime.

And, watching Antonio running after his child, quivering himself with innocent joy, she once again believed herself deluded in her mistrust of him.

CHAPTER VI

ONE evening, however, they were walking alone together towards Acqua Acetosa. Making a short cut to the Viale della Regina, they crossed certain narrow lanes beyond Porta Salaria, and Regina suddenly stopped before an *osteria* (tavern).

A bright interior was visible through an open doorway. At the far end of the room was a glass window coloured by the declining sun, and against this luminous background passed and re-passed, light-footed and black, a couple of dancers, dancing to the strains of a husky concertina. A girl, pale and thin, but bright-eyed, was seated by the door, her arm on the corner of a table, her fair hair mixing in with the shining background. She was something like Gabrie, and dressed like her in a pink blouse. For a moment Regina thought it was she.

"Why, look! there's Gabrie!"

"So it is," replied Antonio.

They drew nearer. The girl got up, thinking them customers. She was half-a-foot taller than Gabrie. The couple went on dancing, black and light against the orange brilliance of the window, and Regina and Antonio passed on. They were speaking of Gabrie. From that instant Regina felt a vague perturbation; but she had no idea of beginning a hateful discussion. She said, almost involuntarily —

"One of these days I mean to bring that poor girl with us. I hardly ever see her, but I do so pity her. She coughs incessantly."

"She is a poor thing; consumptive, I fancy," said Antonio. "You shouldn't let her kiss Caterina. But why is it you don't see her?"

"Because she's ill-natured. She does nothing but observe people and take away their characters."

By force of old habit, Antonio held Regina's hand in his as they walked. Before them spread the *Viale*. Visions of depths of the Campagna, vivid in its pure spring green, appeared in the distance to right and left through the motionless plane-trees, against a pearl-grey sky shot with colours from the sinking sun. The gardens were overrun with roses and lilies, whose fragrance mingled with the scent of herbs and of strawberries. Now and then a carriage went by and vanished into the distance of the deserted *Viale*.

"Who was it told me the same thing of Gabrie?" asked Antonio.

"Marianna, perhaps?" suggested Regina, sharply.

"I believe it was."

"She's just the same herself. One's no better than the other; that's what makes them friends."

"Oh, there's no one like Marianna," said Antonio, and looked away into the distance.

Then, in one second, flashing and following each other like lightning, a succession of ideas started up in Regina's mind.

She would have snatched her hand from Antonio, but fancied he might guess her thoughts from the action, and she stiffened herself to endure the contact. She stiffened in appearance, but her heart was beating violently, two, three, ten, many strokes; — the hour had come

It seemed to her that some one, some mysterious being, black in the sunset brilliance, had passed by smiting her heart with a hammer. And her heart awaked from the evil stupor of the long oppression. Now she could arise, shake herself, walk; walk, breathe, cry aloud; live, and make a supreme effort to rid herself of the shadow, of the weight of the incubus — or else she must fall again under that weight, under that black shadow, and must die.

From day to day Regina had expected this hour of conflict, yet from day to day she had put it from her like a bitter cup.

Now it had come, and she felt a mysterious fear. Again she would have wished to put it off; but a strange impulse, what seemed an instinct of self-preservation superior to her will, clutched her and forced her to speak.

She remembered none of the words prepared, for weeks and months; only Antonio's sentence about Marianna gave her a thread to which she clung desperately, as to a thread which would guide her out of the dark labyrinth.

She had turned and turned in the maze of the evil dream, but she had come back to the precise point where she had stood on the day of the catastrophe.

"No," she began, in a toneless voice; "you cannot guess how malignant Gabrie is. Oh, much more than Marianna! Marianna sees, and sometimes at least says nothing. But

Gabrie —— If you can bear it, I will tell you something, Antonio."

He turned round and looked at her. She looked at him. It seemed as if for that moment they understood each other without more words. However, she went on.

"You will be patient?"

He looked straight before him, indifferent, too indifferent.

"Go on."

"Gabrie says you are Madame Makuline's lover."

He reddened. Anger deformed his face. He dropped Regina's hand and flung it from him, opening his lips with gestures of astonishment and wrath.

"She said that to you?" he cried.

His voice resounded in the silence of the road.

"She told me, yes."

He stood still. Regina stood still. Her heart beat. His hands, hanging down, groped as if trying to lay hold of something. The gesture is customary with actors at the dramatic moments of their part. Regina feared that Antonio acted his part too well. Then she thought, forcing herself to be just —

"If he is innocent, it's natural he should be upset."

"And you, you ——" he burst out, "did not strike her? You actually thought of bringing her with us to-day?"

"Antonio," exclaimed Regina, looking at him with feigned surprise, "you promised to be patient!"

"But it's abominable!" he said, lifting his hands. "How do you suppose I can be patient? If you are joking let me tell you it's a hideous joke. If what you tell me is serious, I am astounded at your calm."

His face paled rapidly as it had flushed, but it paled too much; it became almost grey.

Regina did not move an eyelash, so narrowly was she watching him. She saw that his agitation was real, but she did not know, could not find out, its precise cause. For some moments, however, the strong desire that Antonio should not belie his indignation induced in her a wave of joy. She abandoned herself to it. It was not mere desire, it was certainty of having been deceived! Yet — an inexplicable thing happened; the hope of having been deceived did not restore her kindness. She became cynical — cruel.

"Come!" she said, with bitter gaiety, "why should I be angry? why should I strike Gabrie? Suppose she had told me the truth? Let's walk on," she added, trying to take his arm again.

But he repulsed her, and remained standing.

"Let me alone! What do you mean by the truth?"

"The fact that every one believes it, without daring to tell me, as she dared ——"

"Every one believes it? But — Regina, do you believe it?"

"I also!"

"Listen to me," he said, indignant again, but with an indignation different from the first — deeper, more scornful — "listen to me! Are you not ashamed of yourself?"

"Walk on," she said, moving but not trying to take his arm this time; "don't let us make a scene in the middle of the street."

And she walked on, blind, all involved again in the fearful shadow from which she had thought herself freed. The momentary hope was over. Why? She did not know. Can one know why the sky becomes suddenly covered with cloud?

Antonio's attitude was that of a man who is offended. He followed her scarcely a step behind, and repeated, mechanically —

"You ought to be ashamed —"

She was no longer able to abandon herself to her ardent desire of believing him innocent. She could not! — could not!

"Every one believes it?" repeated Antonio, walking by her side, but not touching her. "And you tell me in this way, in the street, suddenly, as if it were a joke! And you, you believe it yourself! And you speak of it like this!"

"How would you have me speak of it?"

"At least you should have spoken sooner."

"Perhaps I heard it to-day, a little while ago, for the first time."

"That's impossible You were too calm a little while ago!"

"One can pretend," she said, with a forced smile, which furrowed her cheek like a sign of pain.

"A little while ago?" he repeated, closing his hand and shaking it on a level with her face. "Then why do you say every one believes it? Have you just learned that too? Did you hear it from that — that — I don't know what to call her — there is no word — And you — you aren't ashamed to demean yourself to such scandal-mongering with a creature like that, a degenerate — You ——" he continued, forcing himself to scorn, "you, the superior woman, the

exceptional fastidious woman, the great lady — the great
lady!" he repeated, raising and coarsening his voice.

Then Regina fired up. Sombre redness made her face from
forehead to chin a circle of fire; in their turn her hands were
agitated in tragic gesticulation.

"Antonio, hush!" she said, not looking at him. "What do
you expect? Life is like that — stupid and vulgar. The most
horrible things are revealed by the gossip of silly women, and
whole dramas are played on the high road in the course of
an evening walk. It wouldn't do if that happened in a novel!
The author would be accused of vulgarity, if not of
nonsense. In real life, on the contrary, see what happens. The
grand lady goes to a garret in Via San Lorenzo to discover
the cause of her unhappiness; the superior woman comes
out into the street to ——"

"Regina, have done! have done!" cried Antonio. "You
reason too much and too coldly for you to believe what you
are saying. No, it is not true! You do not believe it! Tell me
you don't believe it!"

And he tried to take her arm, but this time it was she who
repulsed him.

"Let me alone! That is what you men are! If I had been
another woman, another sort of wife, I should have lain in
wait for you at home, like a tigress in her lair. I should have
made a scene, one of those scenes called strong, which are
so pleasing at the theatre or in a novel. Whereas, I have
spoken to you quite quietly. I repeat a thing which every one
is saying, and I ask nothing better than that we should laugh
at it together. But you — you begin with noisy words, *'aren't*

you ashamed,' and *'scandal-mongering,'* and *'the great lady.'* Yes, certainly, I am a lady; more of a lady than those other women. It is just that I don't value conventionalities; that is the calamity."

"Then would you prefer me to be silent? Is that it? Don't torment me like this, Regina! In my opinion it would have been better to have this scene at home. Well, your jealousy is the last straw ——"

Regina laughed. Her laugh was genuine but strident, hoarse, as if proceeding out of rusty iron.

"My dear, you are raving! Jealousy! Come, not that!"

"Why did you say you believed it?"

"Did I say so? Surely not."

"I tell you, you did say it."

"I said I believed people believed it."

"I don't think so," he protested. "Well, 'people' are always malicious."

"That, at any rate, is true. People are malicious. You see, our position has changed; we are living comfortably in spite of our slender income, so at once people hatch a scandal. The very excuse you make that you have become a speculator just now, when you might have been one all along ——"

"That is absurd!" interrupted Antonio. "I was a bachelor before, and had more money than I knew what to do with. Besides, you are supposed to have money of your own. No one knows that I began speculating by a mere chance ——"

"What has all this to do with it? The world has no need to know our affairs. Chance!" she repeated, her face darkening as she remembered the *"chance"* in which she had so childishly believed, while instinct had warned her of fiction, fiction clever but thin, like the invention in a novelette.

"What do you mean?" she went on, reassailed by a stifling wave of rage and suspicion. "The world is malicious just because every day, every hour, these strange chances are happening. You know the background of life better than I do. Shame upon shame! How often have you not yourself pointed out to me smart young men who are living on their mistresses?"

Antonio made no answer, and she continued —

"So I said to myself, 'The appearance itself that we are not living merely on our fixed income, the excuse that you play, and have capital at your disposal in result of a game where, as at every game, one sometimes wins but sometimes loses, or the excuse that you are *that woman's* agent — confidential servant — all that has given rise to suspicion.' What do you expect?" she repeated for the third time. "The world is malicious. We — you — are seen for ever going to that house. Everything is seen, commented on, suspected. Your own relations — do you think your own relations have no doubts, make no allusions? Why, a few days ago Claretta -"

Having reached this point Regina became alarmed and silent. She felt herself saying things untrue, giving form to the phantasms of her suspicions. She had no wish to deceive. She wanted the truth. Was she to seek it with lies?; the truth must be sought with truth. This was her desire: but she was unequal to achieving it. As during their nocturnal walk along the Po, that evening of Antonio's arrival, so now she felt a veil suspended between them. They saw, but could not touch each other — so near were they, yet so far, separated by the black veil of lies. Why continue this conversation woven of deceits Words, words! Cold, vain, vulgar words! The truth was in silence, or at least in those words which the lying lips were unable to shape. Regina reflected —

"If *I* dare not speak my real thought, I who have nothing shameful to conceal, how can he speak his? It is useless to insist. He will not confess. None the less, we may come to an understanding. I will say to him, 'Let us go back to living modestly as we did at first. Let us break off all relation with *that woman*, and it will shut people's mouths.' He will understand. He will return to me purified by my silent pardon, by my delicacy. And it will be all over. How is it I never had this happy thought before?"

But she had no sooner formulated the "happy thought" than it seemed to her just one of her usual romantic ideas — a phantasy on a pleasant walk at sundown, along the paths of a spring landscape. Life was a different matter! Reality, naked and ugly, but at least sincere, was a different matter! — like an ugly woman who makes no effort to deceive any one. Away, away with every veil! away with each stained garment! They must listen to each other; they must rend every disguise, even if it were generous and of the ideal.

While she was hurriedly weighing these thoughts in her mind, Antonio interrupted —

"And you knew all this and said nothing? Why did you say nothing? I can't make it out. Certain things have become clear — your ill-humour, your hints and insinuations, your obstinacy in not coming to Albano. But I cannot comprehend your silence. Ah! how hideous all this is! Hideous! Hideous! Certainly the world is malicious; its malice would be monstrous if it weren't ridiculous! We needn't pay attention to it! You are right; in a city like Rome, where anything seems possible, and nobody believes what is said ——"

"No, we must pay attention to it," said Regina; "just because in a city like Rome anything seems possible. It mayn't matter so much to me, but suppose the calumny should reach the ears of my mother, down there in that corner of a province, where the smallest things seem gigantic! My mother has had great sorrows, but none of them could equal this."

"And do you suppose *my* mother wouldn't care just as much?" interrupted Antonio, piqued.

"No doubt she would. But it's for you to consider your mother, I mine! However, it shows you that even at Rome one must heed the clatter of tongues. If it were only you and I in face of that clawing animal, the world, I'd laugh at it. But, my dear, we aren't alone! Caterina will grow up. And if she were to know ——"

At this he gave a cry almost wild.

"If she were to know! But has it been *my* fault?"

Again Regina felt as if a stone had struck her full in the face. Yes; if there was fault, it came home to herself! *She* was the mother of the evil which was stifling them. Antonio's cry was one not of defence, but of accusation.

She rebelled against it.

"I admit," she said, "the fault is not entirely yours. But neither is it all mine."

"Who's saying the fault is yours?"

"I have said it to myself a thousand times. Antonio, there is no reproach that I have not made to myself. How often have I not groaned, 'If I had not been guilty of that lightness of which I was guilty, Antonio would not have forced himself to change our position. He would not have become that woman's servant, not ——' "

"You said it to yourself a thousand times?" he interrupted. "Do you mean you have been thinking of this for a long while? Why did you not first speak to me? Why? Why? That's what I require to know!"

"Oh, don't get angry again!" prayed Regina. "Why didn't I tell you? Because I didn't believe it."

"Do you mean you do believe it now? And that you waited to tell me till exactly now, to-day, at this moment?"

"I waited for an opportunity ——"

"Nonsense! There was no lack of opportunities — worse ones even than this!"

"I repeat I don't study conventionality. Another woman would have made a scene, conjured you sentimentally to swear the truth on the head of our child. I don't do such things. Once only I was betrayed into a piece of dramatic nonsense. Once was enough!"

"What has this to do with it?" he said, angrily. "You could have spoken just as you are speaking now. Well, speak on. Say again what you said a minute ago. You said that you reproached yourself a thousand times as having been the cause of this — calumny. What did you mean?"

"You aren't listening. I reproached myself for having involuntarily given birth to this calumny, by constraining you to become that woman's slave. It was natural people should be suspicious. They are suspicious also of men much richer and much less attractive than you. Madame got rid of the others, Cavaliere R—— and Signor S ——, to make a place for you. Naturally, those men spoke ill of you. Probably they started it. However," she continued, returning to her first point, "remember, Antonio, that I repented of my caprice. Remember well. I gave up all my pretensions and follies and came home to you because I had at last understood that your love was all I required for happiness."

"You said so, I know. But I didn't believe you. You said it because you pitied me. I didn't want your pity, Regina!" he went on, drawing a deep breath, as if struggling with a sob. "Now it is I who am playing the sentimental part, saying that you had humiliated me overmuch because I — had not tried to content you. Shall I follow your lead and say I am not like other men? Better or worse — who knows? I don't set up to be *superior*, as you do" (his voice shook with angry grief). "I'll call myself inferior, yes — a little *bourgeois!* How often have you not thrown that in my teeth! But for that very reason — What was I saying?"

Regina, overwhelmed herself by a strange mingling of grief and contempt, replied ironically —

"You were saying that we are two beings unlike the rest of the world, a hero and heroine of romance, in fact. Perhaps some day Gabrie will pick us up, as one picks mushrooms!"

"At this moment, with your scornful superiority, you are a poisonous mushroom!"

Regina had been staring straight before her, with eyes lost in the luminous distance. Now she turned to look at him, ready to make a bitter reply. But she saw his face so grey and miserable she did not venture to speak. What, moreover, could she say? Why continue vainly to beat about the bush, talking of the edifice of their error, without daring to penetrate within it?

Antonio went on —

"Yes, you had humiliated me overmuch! I must say it to you once straight out. After reading your letter I would have committed any crime only to free myself from the insulting weight of your reproaches. It was driving me mad. It was a degrading accusation which you had brought against me! And I wanted to get you back — as much out of pride as passion! To get you back, not by force, not by love, but by money. That was my obsession. Money — money at all costs! So I went and gambled. And I took the post which I did not particularly admire. I offered myself to Madame. That was my crime, because now I recognise that Cavaliere R—— was only doing precisely what I did myself a little later."

Regina listened and was silent, but she shook her head. He was lying, still lying. He was accusing himself of venial errors to make her believe him innocent of his real sin. Lies — always lies; and yet ——

"I thought you had perhaps repented and would come home; but by this time I knew you! Your letter, your manner, had revealed your character. You would come home to live with me, perhaps resigned, perhaps not, but certainly unhappy. And I was ready to give my blood to prevent that! I wanted you happy. I loved you, Regina, just for your pretensions, which proved you the delicate, fastidious creature, above me by birth and by breeding. Who, you say, can know the dark secrets of his own heart? In a few days I had become another man. I dared to improve my position. I succeeded. And now you blame me for what I have done for you — only for you!"

Regina made no answer. He also kept silence, perhaps thinking her convinced. They went on a little way. A light-haired man, dressed like a Protestant minister, had come up with them, and walked by their side. Carts, laden with bottles, passed, and carriages going to Acqua Acetosa.

Regina thought —

"He doesn't want my pity. He was driven mad by humiliation! I see. Perhaps he thought I should come home only to torment him, and that presently I should desert him again. And I am still trying to persuade myself he is innocent, while he doesn't even know how to keep up the lie! Yet he has been lying for two years, every day, every hour, every minute. How, how has he been able to do it? Well, and wasn't I brooding over my project of flight secretly for days and for months? Was not that also treason? And are we not both lying now? Why all these vain words, these *sous-entendus*, if we are not each in turn trying to deceive the other? What is he thinking at this moment? What do I know of his soul, or he of mine? We have always mistaken each other, and we mistake more than ever at this moment. No, we do not know each other. We are more of strangers to one another than to that man passing along at our side. We have shared our bed and our board, we have a child, part of ourselves, and yet we are strangers! We are enemies — we offend each other; each in our turn, we hide that we may wound deeper!"

"Shall we go back by Ponte Molle, or by the way we went the last day?" asked Antonio.

"There might be a carriage down there, perhaps?" said Regina.

"To go back!" she thought, in profound desolation. "To take up our life of deception and shame! No, I will not! I will not! It must not go on!"

And at last she felt the courage to bring in the end that very day.

Her resolution calmed her. She seemed to lift her head, to open her eyes, to see again round her the beauties of Nature, the purifier. Just here the road broadened out. Never had she seen the Campagna so beautiful, so splendidly and magically coloured. It seemed a picture by a luminist painter — a green landscape with detached pines waving against the dazzling background of crimson and gold, an exaggeration of light, in whose intensity the figures of the passers-by, the half-naked vendors of the spa water, the mounted soldiers, the beggars lying in wait at the cross roads, stood out like bronze statues.

Regina had taken her resolution, but at the cross roads it sufficed her to note the angry movement with which Antonio flung a coin to the beggars to understand that her husband was still offended, and to revive her forlorn hope of his innocence.

They took the short cut. Up and down, up and down by a little path, dark, fragrant, part warm grass, part sand. The Protestant pastor, who seemed uncertain of the way, followed them.

The sun was sinking, silver on the gold horizon; over the flushed grass, the shadows of the pines grew long; the eastern sky took opaque tones — the ashy violet of a pastel. For a moment Regina could have believed herself in the mountains. She could see no more than the path mounting through grass to the low summit, all green against the luminous void. Up and up! The free breath of spring restored the natural colour to Antonio's face. Spring is intolerant of ugly people. The countenance of the fair young minister became like a pink peony, scarcely opened.

But here they were at the low summit, and from it appeared the azure vision of the real mountains.

That day the picture of the Acqua Acetosa had a character almost biblical. Men were sleeping on the grass beside their carts, in which the load of flasks sparkled in the sun; women, children, many dogs, a little black donkey, were all so still as to seem painted on the green background of the Tiber; a line of scarce distinguishable sheep were coming down to the

290

river to drink; boats rocked softly among the bushes of the bank. A soft breeze diffused the perfume of the flowering elders.

While Antonio and Regina were descending the steps cut out on the hillside, a carriage arrived laden with five foreign ladies wearing the usual impossible little hats made of one ear of corn, a poppy, and a bunch of gauze. The lady who got out last began a dispute with the driver.

"Everywhere these horrible foreigners!" said Regina, nervously, and let Antonio go down to the fountain by himself.

She made her way to the river-bank, far up beyond the excise official's hut. He was walking about before the tavern, and the point to which Regina advanced remained completely solitary. Low noises reached her, overpowered by the song of the larks and the music of a streamlet gurgling at the bottom of a cleft near by. In the hedge leaves rustled like the *frou-frou* of silk, and the elder-flowers, already over-blown but still sweet and rosy in the sun, leaned forward as if to listen to the gurgle of the water. Beyond the cleft a mass of greyish flowers covered the declivity; below the Tiber rolled on, clear, calm, imperial. The reflection of the setting sun crossed an angle of the river, making an enormous, trembling, fiery serpent across the water, which seemed brought to a halt on its incandescent back. Sparkles of gold caught fire, went out, and lighted up again, swiftly, irrepressibly, where the reflection of the sun terminated. Everything suggested the illusion of a fight between the water and the raging fire in the river's depths. Far off, where the sky grew pale, the water had conquered and was already spreading the solemn sadness of its ashy calm.

Of course Regina thought of her own distant river. She sat on the rough grass of the declivity and waited.

Never had she felt quieter and stronger than at that hour. As over the river so over her soul, ashy calm was advancing, subduing the vain fire of passion. An old thought started afresh into her mind.

"Every hour will come. This one has come, and others, and others are on their way, and at last the hour of death. Why do we torment ourselves? My life and Antonio's from henceforth will be like a faded garment; yes, like this —!" she said, drawing round her feet the edge of her white but soiled dress. "Well? that means that we shall wear it more contemptuously, but also more comfortably, without considering it so much — thus!" she cried aloud, casting her skirt's hem away from her, over the rough, sand-covered grass.

She looked if Antonio were coming. For some moments he had been speaking with the owners of the five little hats. Then Regina saw him take them down, down, as far as to one of the boats moored at the bank. The boatman ran up, spoke with Antonio, and presently the boat laden with the five little hats was on her way to Ponte Molle.

Then Antonio looked round for his wife and came to her with his swift., light step.

"I put them in the boat partly that we might get their carriage," he said, throwing himself on the grass at her side.

"I hope I haven't made you jealous, Regina, now you've begun at it!"

His voice was gay; too gay.

"On the contrary, I hope I have done with it," she said coldly. "If you have no objection, we will speak further and end the matter."

"Oh, I knew we'd have to go on! Well, speak!" he said, kicking at a branch of elder. "To begin with, tell me what were the allusions, the insinuations made by my cousin — by my relations — by every one, in fact — as a treat —"

Regina watched the nervous movement of Antonio's hand. Her eyes had again become sweet, soft, child-like, but with the sweetness of childish eyes when they are sad.

"Listen, dear," she began, and her voice also was sweet but sad; "don't let *us* fall into scandal-mongering. If the thing isn't true, what does it matter? If it is true ———"

"If it were true —" he interrupted, raising his head, while his hand still shook. Regina was silent, not looking up. "What would you do? Would you leave me again?"

She shrugged her shoulders disdainfully.

"*If it is true*. Then you are still supposing it! Ah, that's what I cannot endure, Regina! It means you don't believe me. It means the malicious words of some stranger have more value for you than mine!"

She was tempted to reply, "And are not you a stranger to me?" but dared not yet.

"Yes, yes I see that's what it is!" he went on, despairingly. "Now this suspicion has got into your head, now, now you believe me no longer! But I hope to cure you, see! I *hope*.

Begin by telling me everything. You ought to tell me, you ought, do you hear? It concerns your honour — everybody's honour. Tell me! tell me!"

She shook her head.

"What is the use?"

"Tell me all," he commanded. "There's a limit to my patience also!"

"Don't raise your voice, Antonio! The excise officer is there. Don't be so *small!*"

"Have done with your own smallness! I am small yes, I'm small, and that's just the reason why I want to know! You see, you are driving me mad! Tell me! I insist."

Regina turned and looked at him. Her eyes, large and melancholy, sparkled in the reflection of the sunset. Never had Antonio seen them more beautiful, sweeter, deeper. At that moment he was overpowered by some sort of fascination and could not turn away from those eyes, burning and sad like the dying sun. Regina said —

"And when I shall have told you everything you want to know, what will you do? How will you know, how do I know, if the things I have heard are or are not real illusions, evil surmises? or whether the doubt has not come of my own instinct?"

"But a few minutes ago you said you didn't believe it! I don't understand you, Regina!"

"And I, do I understand you? Can we understand each other? Think, Antonio, think. Have we ever understood each other? How do I know you speak the truth? How do you know I speak the truth? Look," she said, stretching her hand towards the Tiber; "we seem near to each other, while, on the contrary, we are distant as the banks of this river, which for ever gaze at each other, but will never come into touch!"

"For pity's sake, finish it!" he said, bitterly, but supplicatingly and humbly. "Be merciful, my dear, and don't torment me. Don't say these horrible things. It's very possible I don't understand you, but you, you *ought* to understand me. Let us discuss, let us see together what is to be done. I — I will do whatever you wish. Haven't I always done so? Am I not good to you? Do you say I am not good to you? Tell me what I am to do, but don't doubt me! It's the last straw. If we lose our peace, our concord, what is there left for us?"

He spoke softly, humbly, almost sweetly, but with that sweetness one employs towards a sick and fractious child. He took her hand and laid it on his knee, and on it he laid his own. Regina felt his hand pulsing and vibrating, but its fondness no longer had power to stir her blood.

Yes, it was undeniable. He had always done her will. He was the weak one, and this was at once his crime and his defence. Yes, he was kind, too kind. He had given her in sacrifice not his spirit only, but his body; this miserable mortal flesh he had sold for her. He had given her all; he would still give her all. In a moment, if she demanded it of him, he would confess his shame. How could she have doubted it? Then she told him the whole story.

"Listen. One day I went to see Gabrie, who had been ill ——"

CHAPTER VII

SHE told him all with brief, quiet words. She spoke softly, her eyes, her fingers, resting on the embroidery of her dress. She seemed the guilty one, but dignified in her error, ready to be punished. She told of her doubts, how they had swelled and flamed. She repeated the reproaches she had made to herself, described her visions, her delirious cruelty, her suspicions, the dream, the presentiment, her intention of pardon.

Meanwhile the sun went down. The golden serpent withdrew to the shore, following the sparkling veil of victorious water. The river was divided into two zones — one of tender violet under the pale heaven of the east, the other blood-stained beneath the burning west.

But in water and sky the conflict was ended between the colours and the lights. All was unified and confounded into one supreme harmony of peace. The light bad re-entered into the shadow; the shadow still sought the light. The pale water floated into the luminous zone, and the glowing waves retreated slowly towards a mysterious distance, beyond the horizon, whither the human gaze could not follow.

The crowd of grey flowers slept on, motionless on the declivity. The leaves were silent; everything had become drowsy, lulled by the simple song of the trickle in the depth of the miniature abyss.

And in all this harmonious silence, Regina, as she ended her tale, *felt* the solemn indifference of nature for man and for his paltry fortunes.

"We are alone," she concluded, taking suggestion from this impression of solitude and abandonment; "alone in the world of our sins, if there is really such a thing as sin. Let us pity, each in our turn, and renew our existence. If we are at war, who will help us? Our relations, our friends, might die for us without their death bringing our suffering one moment of relief. I once read of a husband who wished to kill his wife. At the moment he tried to wound her she — bewildered — flung herself on his breast, instinctively seeking his protection against the murderer. How often have not I, in those days of doubt, while — to my shame — I was spying upon you, while I was wrestling with the idea of turning to strangers that I might know — *know* — how often have I not felt the impulse to come to you, to pray you to speak, to save, to protect me! See! Nature herself is indifferent to us at this moment, while, perhaps, our whole future is being decided. Every atom, every sparkle, every wave, runs to its own destiny without attending to us. We are alone; alone and lost. If we separate, where shall we go? and, moreover, if we did wrong, was it not precisely that we might not be separated?"

"But," said Antonio, with one last attempt at defence, "you once wished ——"

And Regina felt a final touch of impatience. She was speaking as he ought to have spoken, and was he still resisting? What did he want?

"There's no good in beginning all over again!" she cried. "This is enough. It seems to me that already I am reasoning too much for you to understand that between you and me there is no longer room for reproaches."

"Yes, Regina," he sighed; "you reason too much, and that is what terrifies me!"

His eyes sank. He looked at his hand, raised it, and let it fall heavily on Regina's, which he had retained all this while on his knee.

"Why do I reason too much? Why are you terrified?"

"Because if you really believed in my guilt you would not speak as you are speaking. You speak like this because you do not believe it — yet ——"

She felt her heart beat. He was right! But she summoned her forces and overcame herself.

"Look at me!" she commanded.

Antonio looked at her. His eyes were veiled in tears.

*　　*　　*　　*　　*　　*　　*

Then it was true.

Regina had never seen her husband weep, nor had she ever imagined he could weep.

At that moment, when everything darkened within her, not in swift passing eclipse, but in unending twilight, a confused recollection came to her of something far off — so far off that for years and years it had not returned to her mind. She saw again a man seated before a burning hearth. This man crouched, his elbows on his knees, his face on his hands, and he wept; while a woman bent over him, her hand laid on his bald head.

The man was her father, the spendthrift; the woman her patient mother.

Was it a dream? or a reality of her unconscious infancy, far away, forgotten? She did not know; but at that moment in the shadow of her soul a light appeared, rose-red like the reflection of the burning hearth in that distant picture of human error and of human pity.

She did not think of laying her hand on her husband's head as her mother had laid hers on the head of that father who, perhaps, had been more guilty than Antonio; but she remembered the serene and beautiful life of that woman who had fulfilled her cycle as all good women must fulfil theirs, mid the love of her children and for their sake. Never had the widow made those sad memories to weigh upon her children. If they suffered, as by law of nature all born of woman must suffer, the memory of her did not add to their grief, but softened it.

"And I, too," thought Regina, "must fulfil my cycle. Our child must never know that we have suffered and have erred."

So she must pardon; more than ever she must pardon! Like the waters of the river, she must pass silently towards the light of an horizon beyond the earth, towards the sea of infinite charity, where the greatest of human errors is no more than the remembrance of an extinguished spark.

*   *   *   *   *   *   *

They came home in the carriage left by the five foreigners. A tender and transparent twilight had fallen around and within them. Resigned to the Nostalgia of a light lost for ever, not joyous nor very sad, like husband and wife re-united after a long separation, they clasped each other by the hand, silently promising to help each other as one helps the blind.

Thus they returned into the circle of the city and of the past.

It seemed to Regina that a long time, a whole period of life, had passed since she and her husband had stopped before the wayside tavern. But, returning, as their driver pulled up at the same place to light his lamps, she saw the girl in the pink blouse still sitting by the inside door, and the couple, light-footed and black against the background of golden glass, were at their dancing still.

THE END